The
GUESTHOUSE
at LOBSTER
BAY

ALSO BY ANNIE ROBERTSON

My Mamma Mia Summer
My Mamma Mia Christmas
If Harry Met Sally Again
Four Weddings and a Festival

Annie Robertson

The
GUESTHOUSE
at LOBSTER
BAY

W

WELBECK

Published in 2021 by Welbeck Fiction Limited, part of Welbeck Publishing Group
20 Mortimer Street London W1T 3JW

Paperback ISBN: 978-1-78739-620-3
E-book ISBN: 978-1-78739-621-0

Printed and bound by CPI Group (UK) Ltd., Croydon, CR0 4YY

10 9 8 7 6 5 4 3 2 1

This is for my little boy,
who shared his home and toys.

Prologue

'Merry Christmas,' said Emma, waving to her colleagues who were still at their desks, finishing up for the holidays.

'Merry Christmas,' some of them mumbled back but nobody looked up from their screen.

Emma skipped down the three flights of steps to the ground floor, glad to be out of the office, and flung open the door. The crisp, late-afternoon air rushed into her lungs and she drank it in, tightened her scarf against the cold, and put in her AirPods to call her sister.

'Hold on,' Jane answered.

'Okay,' replied Emma, heading along Carnaby Street, admiring the colourful Christmas lights that hung over-head, which never failed to make her smile after a long day. Through her earphones she heard Jane tell the kids to 'stop drawing on the kitchen table', to 'pick up the Lego' and to 'sit down and watch telly' so that she could 'talk to Auntie Emma and make the dinner in peace'.

'What's up?' said Jane abruptly, still in handling-the-kids mode.

'Any idea what I should buy Chris for his Christmas?' she asked her sister, who was like the Nigella of gift-giving, she never failed to come up with a perfect little something, whoever it was for.

'Emma, it's four o'clock on Christmas Eve, why have you left it so late?'

'It's been crazy busy at work,' she replied, which was the truth but not the whole truth; she hadn't bought Chris a gift because she couldn't think of anything, which, given they'd been together for six years, wasn't ideal.

'You do too much for that company for not enough money,' said Jane, which was about as close to big-sisterly concern as Jane got.

'You're probably right,' said Emma, who'd had similar thoughts herself but didn't know how to change things. She'd been with the company for 10 years, working her way up from general dogsbody to design assistant to interior designer and then design consultant, which basically meant a lot more responsibility and many more hours for very little extra pay.

'There's no "maybe" about it, Emma. New Year, new job. You've got to sort it out.'

'I will,' said Emma, pretty certain she wouldn't, because what were the options? The same job in a different

2

consultancy made no sense, even if it might be nice to work with people who enjoyed each other's company, and a boss who didn't frighten everyone half to death. And she wasn't in a position to set up on her own, not while living in the shoebox of a flat she'd shared with Chris for the last five years. The way she saw it, it made more sense to stay put, even if it did sometimes feel like working in a funeral parlour. 'More pressingly, what should I get Chris?'

'Budget?'

'About a hundred.'

'Options are: music, movie, book, grooming, food, clothes, gadget or experience-voucher,' said Jane, firing off the list without having to think.

'He's got all the music he wants, seen everything he wants to see, his grooming consists of shower gel and shaving foam, we haven't space for extra stuff, and he's not really an "off-roading, gun-toting, jump-out-of-a-plane" kind of a guy,' said Emma, wishing Chris had a bit more vim about him – not too much, just enough to ignite a spark between them again, and to prove he did have some testosterone, that it hadn't all been lost by sitting at his computer eight hours a day in the council planning office.

'So then a book, something yummy and a nice winter jumper.'

'You don't think that's a bit yawn?' Emma pushed away a thought that 'yawn' summed up their relationship these days. It'd been ages since they'd done anything fun together. They used to go to gigs, and plays and stand-up shows, but now 'fun' seemed to consist of a takeaway in front of the telly followed by an early night, and not the kind of 'early nights' they used to enjoy. Not that it was just Chris's fault, Emma knew she was to blame too; she hated not having the courage to let him go.

'You could always add in a cock ring to spice things up,' said Jane, as if she'd read Emma's mind.

'We'll be opening our presents at his mum's,' said Emma, as if this were the only thing holding her back from such a present.

'Mummy, what's a cock ring?' Emma heard Lily ask.

Emma chuckled as she listened to Jane explaining to her five-year-old daughter that she'd said 'clock ding, to fix Uncle Chris's grandfather clock'.

'I swear, they miss nothing,' whispered Jane after Lily had been sent back to the telly with a bowl of crisps to keep her occupied.

Emma laughed, glad that the interruption had distracted from talk of her sex life and the state of her relationship. 'Thanks for the suggestions,' she said, having arrived at

4

the entrance to Liberty. 'I'd better get on. Merry Christmas! See you at New Year.'

'Merry Christmas, Em. Hope it's a good one.'

The streets were quieter by the time Emma left the department store with a bag of perfectly pleasant but uninspired gifts for Chris. As she strolled onto Regent Street, she soaked up the last-minute bustle of shoppers and the relaxed Christmas cheer of office workers heading home with boxes of chocolates poking out of their bags and Christmas flowers under their arms. Overhead the lights twinkled elegantly, and Christmas music seeped from the stores, giving Emma a warm glow. Wanting to prolong the feeling, Emma made an unusual snap decision not to wait at her usual bus stop and instead to grab a drink and walk some of the way home.

Having bought a hot chocolate, Emma continued down Regent Street, watching her bus whizz by, glad of her decision to take her time. She stopped to gaze at Hamleys's winter wonderland window display, where she caught sight of her reflection. The Santa hat she'd been wearing most of the day in the office was positioned jauntily on the top of her dark wavy bob, and her bright-green scarf jutted out from her coat like a jolly snowman's. She laughed at herself then continued south, drinking the warm peppermint chocolate and smiling at a couple with their cherry noses pressed against the window of the diamond jewellers, their arms wrapped round each other's backs. She was trying to figure out which Christmas scent was coming from the soap shop – cinnamon, ginger, orange, cranberry? – when a blinding white flash and deafening, violent blast threw Emma off her feet, blowing her hot chocolate and gift bag out of her hands.

Moments later, Emma resisted opening her eyes. The alarms and screams that replaced the Christmas carols, and smoke that wiped out the smell of the soap shop engulfed her lungs and stung her nostrils, telling her all she needed to know. And when she did at last open them she discovered a horror scene. Everything was mixed up. There was glass everywhere. People were covered in blood and dust. And all the lights had gone out, in the shops and overhead. People lay scattered on the ground and, not far from where she was, a lower half of a leg sat next to a tattered Christmas present.

'Help!' she heard someone cry, a gut-wrenching cry that forced Emma into action.

A short distance away she met the eyes of a woman a little older than herself, her eyes filled with terror, her skin pale. Without thinking, Emma scrambled to her feet and stumbled to her, pulling off her scarf and tying it as tight as she could above the woman's knee to try and stem the bleeding of her severed leg. But as hard as Emma tried, the blood continued to flow, forming a stream that ran off the pavement and into the gutter.

'I'll get help,' said Emma, staring into the woman's eyes, which were dark against the paleness of her skin.

But as Emma waited to get through to emergency services she saw the woman's breathing become shallower and shallower, until she was barely moving at all. By the time someone picked up and told her help was already on its way, Emma could see no movement at all.

'Just hold on, help's coming,' she said, trying to sound reassuring, taking the woman's hand in hers and gently pushing back her hair that had fallen over her eye. 'They're on their way.'

She searched the woman's eyes, watching for a glimmer of light, then held her breath as the woman exhaled for the final time.

'No . . .' said Emma, bringing her cheek close to the lady's mouth, but there was nothing to feel, and Emma knew, from the first aid course she'd taken years earlier, that she'd lost too much blood for chest compressions to help.

She closed the lady's eyes, tucked her hair behind her ears and was about to button up her coat to protect her from the cold, when she noticed she was wearing a name-necklace, which read Dawn.

'Sleep in peace, Dawn,' she said, reaching once more for her hand, which was already losing heat. An unbearable sensation of numbness filled Emma's body, as if she wasn't really there at all.

Emma had no sense of how long she'd been with Dawn, but when she looked up she was hit by just how surreal it all was. Everywhere people were fleeing in panic and fright, the walking wounded staggered past. It was impossible to count how many emergency vehicles had arrived, the blue and red strobes replacing the elegant Christmas twinkle. It was chaos, motion and noise everywhere and yet, to Emma, it was also a frozen, silent tableau.

Just then a phone vibrated in Dawn's pocket. Emma reached for it and found a message shining out against a backdrop of two beautiful, smiling children. It read: *Mum, it's almost Santa time!!! Hurry up and come home! Love you. Miss you. xxx*

'Shit,' she muttered, staring at their angelic, beaming faces, her numbness rapidly turning to anger.

After that everything blurred into one, only the odd detail remained clear: handing Dawn's phone to a policeman and knowing the awfulness of the call he'd have to make; a sheet being placed over Dawn; a fireman asking if she was injured; phones ringing relentlessly, and the crinkle of someone wrapping a gold foil blanket around her shoulders.

She sat on the pavement next to Dawn's lifeless body, staring blankly at the unfathomable scene in front of her as if watching a horror movie. Even if she had had the faculty to reason what to do next, there was no way she would have moved; shock rooted her to the ground.

At some point, Emma's own phone rang. She didn't look at it or answer – she hadn't the capacity to speak and, even if she did, what would she say? How could she ever explain any of it to anyone?

Eventually someone took her by the arm, pulled her to her feet and directed her to follow a gaggle of others, all draped in gold.

'I need to wait with Dawn,' she stammered.

'Who?' asked the voice.

'Dawn,' she indicated, but when she turned she discovered Dawn's body had been removed, only the dark stain of blood remained where she had lain.

It was then that Emma realised she was shaking uncontrollably and freezing cold, despite the blanket.

'Follow the others, someone will take care of you,' said the voice.

Emma did as instructed, picking her way through the aftermath towards Piccadilly Circus, but rather than get on the bus that was being used as a makeshift shelter, she kept walking, down Haymarket, her feet carrying her without any conscious thought. Just before Trafalgar Square,

Emma caught sight of her reflection again in a window, which stopped her dead in her tracks. She was still wearing her Santa hat, her skin was white as snow, and the gold of the emergency blanket gave her the appearance of an enormous Christmas cracker.

'Bastards,' she said, knowing that for many, including Dawn's daughters, the innocence of Christmas had just been shattered for ever.

Chapter 1

'Auntie Emma, what are you looking at?'

'Huh?' replied Emma, emerging from a trance she hadn't realised she'd been in. Her five-year-old niece, Lily, pushed her way onto Emma's lap, a Barbie doll in one hand, a toy comb in the other.

'You've been staring at that computer for ages, love,' said Emma's Mum, Liz.

'Have I?' Emma shook away her daze, rejoining the hub-bub of activity in Jane's kitchen: their mum was preparing sandwiches at the island, a frilly apron tied around her small, curvy figure; Jane was hanging laundry on the dryer, and Emma's seven-year-old nephew, Jake, was rolling around next to the bifold doors with their new puppy, Bear.

'It's a house – bo-ring,' said Lily, peering at the screen and pushing away the laptop to make room for her doll on the kitchen table instead. Emma noticed that Lily's silvery blonde hair was not dissimilar from her doll's.

'You're not looking at that guesthouse in Scotland again, are you?' asked Jane, unable to hide the note of disdain in her voice. Jane couldn't understand why anyone would want to live anywhere other than Hertfordshire, even if it did mean living in a tiny box of a house that cost a small fortune. And she certainly couldn't understand why anyone would want to run a guesthouse.

'I can't help it, there's just something about it,' replied Emma, shifting Lily further along the bench then flicking through photographs of the impressive, sandstone townhouse at Lobster Bay with its high ceilings, magnificent-sized rooms, and stunning sea views. She'd been looking at the property for a couple of months, since New Year's Eve, trying to imagine herself living out her dream of owning a bespoke guesthouse and being part of a Scottish village community, but she hadn't quite mustered the confidence to arrange a visit. Unlike her sister, Emma found the idea of living on a windswept Scottish peninsula far more appealing than living within shouting distance of London – she'd take sand over concrete any day of the week.

'The only good thing about it is the price tag,' said Jane, tightening her blonde pigtail and hoisting up her skinny jeans. Emma often wondered if the two of them really were biological sisters – they couldn't be more contrasting in their appearance. Jane had inherited the tall, thin, straight-blonde genes from their father, Emma the shorter, curvier, wavy-brown ones from their mother. And the differences didn't stop at the physical: Jane had always been outgoing and impulsive, unlike Emma who verged on cautious and unspontaneous.

'It is outrageously cheap,' mumbled Emma, still trying to figure out why it was so inexpensive; had she missed something? She couldn't find anything on the photos that rang alarm bells, and certainly not anything that a lick of paint wouldn't fix, which she was more than capable of doing herself. At the price the agent was asking for, Emma could barely have bought a two-bedroom flat in her sister's town, let alone a seven-bedroom semi-detached house. As far as she could tell, it was a steal.

'It would take years to do it up, is that really what you want?'

Emma knew in her heart of hearts that it was, but she knew Jane wouldn't understand. Jane had always been happy living in soulless new-builds on estates where the most people knew of each other was what type of car was parked in their driveway. But Emma had always craved community and a home that was welcoming and full of soul that she could share with family, friends and neighbours, and she'd harboured a dream of a guesthouse ever since she could remember. When her friends were fantasising about becoming pop stars and actors, Emma was poring over glossy magazines of beautiful bedrooms and bathrobes. Over the last decade she'd lost sight of her dream, but all of that had changed after the events of Christmas Eve.

Within a week Emma had quit her job, left Chris, moved back in with her mum, and found her dream guesthouse – the fresh start she craved. She hadn't told her mum or sister about what she'd witnessed, she knew they could never understand, but she was certain they knew something was amiss – after all, it was so unlike Emma to do so much on impulse. And now here she was considering buying a guesthouse in Scotland!

All that mattered to Emma now was to find a community that she could be part of and a home she could share with others. And there was something about this house that called loudly to her, something that told her this could be the home, business and community she longed for, that all the hard work required to make it perfect would be worth it. If only she could find the courage to buy it and live out her dream.

'It wouldn't take her that long to do up,' said Liz, bringing the sandwiches to the table and shooing her grandchildren towards the sink to wash their hands. 'All that experience as an interior designer, you'd have the place done up in no time.'

Emma twisted her lips, contemplating just how much work needed to be done. The bedrooms needed painting and the dining room too, but those wouldn't take that long – she could manage a room every couple of days if she knuckled down to it. Maybe an initial couple of weeks' work, a month tops. The more she thought about it the more it seemed like a viable option.

'I've never understood your fascination with guest-houses,' said Jane, stepping over the bench to sit down for lunch. 'I think you're insane to even consider it.'

'I love the idea,' said Emma, who'd planned to study hospitality at university and gain the necessary experience of running a small hotel for a few years after graduating, but her father had died suddenly of a heart attack in her last year of school and, with Jane already at university, her mother had needed Emma's support. In the end it had been easier to study interior design part-time at the local college than head off to uni, but now, finally, over ten years later, there was an opportunity to do just what she wanted. 'I think it sounds fun, having the world come to you, never quite knowing who the wind might blow in.' Emma had always been a bit of a home bird. Unlike many of her peers she never caught the backpacking bug. She much preferred the idea of the world coming to her.

'Right,' said Jane scathingly. 'Like drunk wedding guests who vomit all over your bathrooms, small children who soak the mattresses with pee and small dogs who poop on the carpets.'

'Sounds a lot like your life,' said Emma, gesturing to Bear, his back arched and bum curled towards the floor, about to make a deposit on Jane's pristine limestone.

Quick as a flash Jane was up and onto him, arms outstretched in front of her, releasing him into her pocket-sized garden then rapidly sliding the doors closed behind her.

'That's one thing for certain,' said Emma, watching her sister scrub her hands. 'If I do buy this house, it will have a strict "no dogs" policy.'

'Why don't you like dogs, Auntie Emma?' asked Jake, his mouth full of egg sandwich, his elbows on the table.

Emma wrinkled her nose. 'It's not that I don't like them exactly, I just don't like the smell, the hair, the slobber.' She widened her eyes at Jake. 'And I really, *really* don't like picking up their poo!'

'That I don't blame you for,' said Jane, clocking the small parcel on the lawn that Bear was now sniffing as Jake laughed his head off. 'But seriously, doesn't it concern you just a little, the idea of running a big house like that on your own with any old stranger walking through your door?'

'I guess whoever ran it before must have done the same,' said Emma, skipping through the photos once more. From the abundance of net curtains, lace tablecloths and chintz curtains, Emma surmised that it was more than likely an elderly lady who was selling the house; there was next to no evidence of anything masculine in the pictures at all.

'It was probably a couple,' said Jane, knowingly. 'You know, someone to do the handiwork, someone else to do the housework. Can you really manage all that on your own? You might have a flair for design but housekeeping and DIY? Really? I'm not sure, Em. And don't forget the breakfasts; you haven't really progressed beyond the pancakes and scrambled eggs you used to make for Mum and Dad when you were little – and even then you used salt in the pancakes and sugar in the eggs!'

'So?' said Emma, feeling herself on the defensive as if she were 14 again and Jane was jibing her about a boy she liked, pointing out every reason under the sun why Emma wouldn't be right for him. Part of her felt like buying the place just to prove Jane wrong. 'There are ways around these things – a housekeeper, a handyman.'

'Those all cost money.'

'And I could offer continental breakfast,' went on Emma, refusing to let her sister diminish her excitement. 'Or bacon butties and scrambled eggs – I'm pretty sure even I could manage those.'

'Even when you've been up at five thirty every morning for the past six months? Because that's what it will take, and that's fine if you've got someone doing it with you, but it sounds like a hell of a lot for anyone to take on by themselves.'

Emma bit into her tuna sandwich far harder than necessary. The truth was that she knew her sister had a point, she wasn't the best cook on the planet, nor was she even that good in the morning, and there was no denying that she was by herself. The first decision she had made after Christmas Eve was to break things off with Chris. To Chris it had come out of nowhere; he said it was a kneejerk reaction to the trauma, but for Emma, nothing had ever been clearer. She'd been thinking about it for over a year – ever since Chris's brother's wedding – but kept hoping things would improve. Then, on Christmas morning, she finally decided to leave him. She left the same day, convinced her decision was right but nervous about how her future would look alone; Chris had been a good friend to Emma over the years, even though he'd never been 'the one'.

'I'm not saying you shouldn't do it,' Jane went on. 'I'm just saying be realistic about what it entails.'

'It *would* be a lot of work,' said Liz, looking over Emma's shoulder at the photos. 'But it's something Emma's talked about since she was young. So long as she's doing it for the right reasons and not running away, she'll make a success of it.'

'I'm not running away,' said Emma, surprised by her mother's comment.

'Not even from Chris?' asked Jane, exchanging a knowing look with Liz.

'No,' Emma said tetchily. She could tell her mum and sister had been talking about her behind her back.

'Alright, no need to bite my head off, you know I want you to be happy. But you can't deny you do have a tendency to compartmentalise things then throw away the key.'

'I do not!'

'Whatever, Em,' said Jane, rolling her eyes. 'Just make sure it's the right decision, not a snap one, that's all I'm saying.'

'Fine,' said Emma, bruised by the exchange.

'I suppose it would kill two birds with one stone – an income and a house,' said Jane, her tone a little kinder, sensing she'd wounded Emma. 'It's not as if you can keep crashing on mum's couch.'

Emma knew her sister had a point. Her mother had a life of her own, a new partner, Gary, and it wasn't easy to conduct the relationship with her adult daughter snoring on the sofa. It was time for Emma to stop imagining her dream and start living it, to prove to herself, and her sister, that she could make this happen. And there was definitely something about the house that called to her, beckoned her in.

'You know what your father used to say?' said Liz, out of the blue.

'What?' asked Emma, always keen to hear a memory of her late father, whom she'd been so close to.

'Sometimes you just have to jump and see where you land.'

On hearing her father's words, Emma felt a sudden surge of spontaneity course through her body, and a conviction that The Guesthouse at Lobster Bay was meant for her. Then and there she decided that straight after lunch she would contact the estate agent to arrange a viewing.

'That's all well in principle,' said Jane, totally unaware of her sister's revelation, 'just so long as she doesn't find herself in the North Sea without a life jacket.'

Christmas Eve

"Emma?"

Emma heard Chris call for her before her key was even out of the lock, his voice sounded unusually panicked.

'Jesus,' he said, standing in the hallway. His small mouth fell open, his soft eyes scanned her from top to toe. Emma noticed that his usually neat, fair hair was dishevelled, his collar undone.

Behind him, in the hall mirror, Emma saw what he saw. She was filthy from dust, blood stained her clothes and smeared her face, and her hands were scratched and grazed.

'I've been trying to call,' he said, helping her take off her jacket and tidying her hair. An image of her doing the same for Dawn flashed into her mind.

She took out her phone.

9.05 p.m. 173 missed calls. Emma blinked in confusion, unclear how she hadn't heard it ring.

'Are you hurt? What happened?' he asked, following her into the lounge, where she sat down on her couch. She clutched the ash armrest and stared at Chris's abandoned gift wrapping. 'It's all over the news. A suicide bomber. People are dead. Injured. What happened? I've been trying to call.'

'You said,' said Emma, her voice soft and distant, feeling as if it belonged to someone else.

'Emma?'

Chris stared down at her expectantly. Emma looked up blankly.

She wanted to explain but even if she could, what would be the point? What sense would it make? She could tell him everything and still not be understood.

This must be how it feels to come back from the moon, she thought.

She got up, her gaze in the middle distance. 'I don't think I feel up to Christmas at your mum's. Let her know?'

'Of course,' he said, reaching a hand out to her which he withdrew when she flinched.

'I think I'll take a shower. Go to bed. It's been a long day,' she said, trying to offset the flinch with a half-smile.

'But Emma—' he said, his eyes brimming with tears. She wondered how it was that he was able to cry when she could not.

'We'll talk in the morning,' she said, touching him lightly on the arm, though her instinct told her they wouldn't.

Chapter 2

Emma pulled on the handbrake of her ageing Volvo estate and hoped that it would be secure enough to prevent the car, and her, from rolling down the steep incline into the small harbour at Lobster Bay that lay in front of her.

'Stunning,' she whispered to herself once the car had definitely stopped moving and creaking, and she was able to relax and take in the view. It had been an extremely long journey, split over two days, but all 450 miles of it, even the part in the pouring rain, now seemed worth it.

Sitting back, Emma drank in the warm, early summer sun and watched the sea sparkle, two eider ducks bobbing happily on its surface. It didn't seem possible that this was now home, that soon she would come to know every weathered stone in the harbour wall, the pantile roofs on the old fishermen's cottages and the rhythm of the sea that lapped the small crescent beach.

She reached behind her to rummage amongst her belongings for her beloved old camera, which she held to her eye. She focused in on a guy around her age, ruggedly good-looking with choppy blond hair, who was working on a boat at the side of the harbour. As Emma focused in on him, he seemed to become aware of being watched. Glancing around, he suddenly looked up and through her viewfinder Emma saw his unshaven face stare straight down the barrel of her lens.

'Sorry,' she said, even though she knew he couldn't hear her, and brought the camera down. She cringed and offered a cheerful, if somewhat embarrassed wave that went unreturned. Instead he turned his broad back on her and continued about his labour.

'Oops,' said Emma, returning her camera to its bag in the back of the car, where her life's possessions lay neatly packed. Jane thought it was appalling that Emma had so little to show for her 31 years, but Emma wore her lack of possessions as a badge of honour. As an interior designer it wasn't easy to have few possessions, every job offered up clients' cast-offs, usually furniture that was neither old nor tired. By now Emma could have had a warehouse full of discarded items, but since leaving college she'd lived by the rule, 'only own something if it's beautiful *and* functional'. It never failed to amaze her how so few things met the criteria, and besides, she'd never had the space for things anyway.

Emma raked through her small holdall on the passenger seat for her lip gloss, the bag bringing back a memory of the first place she'd lived after finishing college and leaving home at 21. Emma had gone to London and moved into a furnished flat with an old school friend. She remembered, as if it were yesterday, placing the holdall on her new bed and unpacking. There was something in the act that made Emma, for the first time in her life, feel as if she'd grown up, that life was finally her own. Four years later Emma packed the same holdall and moved in with Chris, into a tiny one-bed apartment where there was room for little more than the bare essentials, and many of those had been left behind when she called the relationship off.

And now here she was, the same holdall by her side, gazing out over the beautiful harbour. Emma could hardly believe the previous 10 years belonged to the same life. She watched two tourists in matching anoraks saunter down to the beach with an ice cream, and a guy wearing a headband paddle his surfboard out onto the water, his little dog perched on the back. She pinched herself. London felt otherworldly, as if the last decade and the events of Christmas Eve had happened to someone else. It wouldn't have surprised Emma at all if she suddenly awoke to discover it as all an elaborate, if somewhat cruel, dream.

Relaxing further into her seat, Emma watched the guy at the boat complete his job, jump into his van, which read *A Wilson: Boatbuilder,* and roar off up the steep, winding road and out of sight. She was contemplating a stretch of her legs and an ice cream of her own when her phone rang.

'Hello,' she answered.

'Emma, it's Pamela.' Emma's heart skipped a nervous beat at the sound of her solicitor's educated Edinburgh voice. 'The monies have been received by the vendor. Congratulations, The Guesthouse at Lobster Bay is all yours.'

'Thank you!' said Emma, doing a tiny chair dance, relief and excitement fizzing out of her pores.

'As arranged, the keys have been left in the ceramic hedgehog under the front hedge.'

'Brilliant!' laughed Emma, unsurprised that the previous owner, Hilda, would have an ornamental hedgehog as her safe place. From the photos it was evident that Hilda was particularly keen on knick-knacks and that clearly extended to the garden too.

'Well, good luck!'

Emma thanked Pamela for all her hard work and hung up, in disbelief that the house was hers and still incredulous that she'd had the spontaneity to buy a house she'd only viewed online.

As she drove up the narrow road away from the harbour to the centre of the village, she thought back over the last few months and how she, sensible old Emma Jenkins, had come to buy a house she'd never actually seen in person.

*

'I'm calling about The Guesthouse at Lobster Bay,' Emma had said tentatively to the estate agent who'd answered the phone. She suspected everyone else enquiring about the house would be older than her, more than likely someone looking for a retirement project. She had worried that the estate agent wouldn't take her seriously: guesthouses are, after all, she'd thought, traditionally the domain of the retiree, not designers who've worked on homes for Russian oligarchs, pop stars and minor royalty. But, despite her concerns about how her enquiry would be received, Emma had made the call, reassuring herself that she'd worked on similar projects for clients. She knew she could make the house into a stunning destination retreat for those in search of escape, rather than just your average coastal B & B that an older retiree might run.

'Oh yes,' answered the cheery estate agent in a lilting Scottish accent. To Emma's relief she sounded far more receptive than Emma had imagined she would; in her experience estate agents had a propensity to be guarded and unfriendly. 'It's a real cracker that one. Shall I book you in for a viewing?'

'I'd like that but I'm in the south of England and I'm not sure when I can get up – maybe in a couple of weeks?' Emma said, thinking she might get a more reasonable train fare if she waited until then.

'I wouldn't advise waiting that long, my dear, there's been a lot of interest all of a sudden, what with it being the start of spring. The house has already got four notes of interest and another second viewing tomorrow. Closing date is set for Friday.'

Emma felt her heart sink and, at the same time, a steeliness rise up in her – knowing she had competition made her want the house even more.

'If I were you, I'd just go ahead and make an offer – you can't lose on this one.'

'I haven't organised a mortgage yet,' said Emma, her sensible streak battling her newfound spontaneity. She knew that despite her lack of job, with the projected income of the guesthouse and the small amount of money her father had left her, she'd be able to secure a mortgage, but only if time didn't stand in her way, and that looked like a distinct possibility.

'Ach, don't worry. So long as the vendor knows your position it's fine. We've a few cash buyers interested but you never know, sometimes a wee personal note to the owner about your intentions for the place can make a smaller, less certain offer seem a bit more enticing.'

Emma found her spirits rising once more and before she knew it the estate agent, Doreen, had given her the details of the vendor's solicitor, Pamela Brydon. Half an hour later Emma had given herself a mind-numbing crash course in Scottish property law and found herself composing an email to Pamela to instruct an offer, complete with a scanned copy of a handwritten letter to the current owner, which she posted later.

To Whom It May Concern,

I hope you won't mind me writing to you in person. I wanted you to know how much I've fallen for your beautiful home, and how I truly believe I'm destined to become its new owner even though I haven't been able to view it in person. I hope you won't think me foolish, I've never done something as impulsive as this before. You can ask anyone who knows me, they'll tell you I'm terribly sensible by nature and rarely do anything spontaneously. But your home has me captivated and I would love to live there and look after the place for as long as I am

*able - my forever home - as I can tell you
have done.*

*I realise I'm not in the strongest position -
I'm unable to offer much over the asking price
and I haven't yet secured a mortgage but I
assure you, should you accept my offer, your
home couldn't find itself in better hands.*

Sincerely,

Emma Jenkins

It had been a nail-biting few days but, less than a week later, Emma picked up a phone call from Pamela to tell her that her offer had been accepted. Her mother and Jane almost fell to the floor when she told them but despite their concerns about Emma moving so far away on her own, Emma's conviction remained. The only condition of the sale was that Emma had to have a mortgage in place within two weeks, which she managed by the skin of her teeth. And now here she was, another four weeks later, the monies transferred, the sale complete.

Who thought one phone call could lead to this, thought Emma, as she opened the wrought-iron front gate of the property and glanced to her right, looking under the privet hedge for the ornamental hedgehog, which she found nestled in the farthest corner. Crouching down, she lifted the top off the hedgehog to reveal three keys on a keyring with a picture of an ageing dog.

'That'll be the first thing to go,' she said, looking at the picture of the slobbery dog then replacing the lid.

Emma unlocked the bottom lock and then, as she turned the Yale, took a deep breath in anticipation. The heavy wooden door needed a shove of her shoulder and was met by the resistance of a pile of post lying on the Victorian-tiled vestibule floor but, unfazed by a creaky old door, Emma put the key into the lock of the inner glass door – admiring the beautiful antique glass, etched with tiny birds and ivy – and opened it.

She gasped as the enormity of what she'd taken on hit her. The place was vast, with ceilings that even the longest feather duster would find hard to reach. The woodchip-lined walls were coated in a peachy colour that, despite her training, Emma found hard to put a name to.

'What is that smell?' Emma had expected a scent of bacon and lavender polish, maybe even a slight staleness to the place, but this smell was nothing like that – it was more a cross between wet dog, old Weetabix and sulphur.

Pulling the cuff of her top down around her hand, she placed it over her nose and reached for a note with her name on it, propped up against an old bonbon jar on the brown wood sideboard.

Dear Miss Jenkins,

I trust you will find the house in order. Should you require any advice please contact Rhona, her number is in the top drawer of the desk.

Most importantly, please ensure Wilbur is fed twice a day.

Sincerely,

Hilda Wyatt (former owner)

'Who's Wilbur?' asked Emma, placing the curt note back on the sideboard. She had no intention of feeding the neighbourhood cat, if that's who Wilbur was. Cats were almost as much as a mystery to Emma as dogs. 'And more to the point, who's Rhona?'

Her questions unanswered, Emma ascended the grand staircase. It didn't take too much to imagine away the patterned burgundy carpet and appalling red-and-peach-striped wallpaper, which wound its way up the bottom section of the walls with a scrolled border above it. As Emma rounded the curve in the stairs she imagined Hilda Wyatt, 30 years earlier, picking out the decor in the belief that she was choosing an elegant classic, little realising that 30 years on it would be the epitome of dated.

Desperate to explore all of the house, Emma climbed the first and second staircases to the very top. On reaching the spacious, cobweb-strewn landing, lactic acid tingling her thighs from the climb, Emma went directly to the largest room at the back and stood beside the two large sash and case windows that looked directly out to sea.

Despite the peeling paintwork, and the more alarming rotting woodwork of the window that crumbled as she ran her finger along it, Emma gazed out, blown away by the beauty of the view. The sea shone a brilliant silver and an island in the distance was the shape and colour of a sperm whale. Above that the clouds shifted quickly in the wind, great cottony clouds, white and light grey, broken by fragments of blue. It was as near to a perfect view as Emma could imagine.

'Home,' she said, her heart rate lowering, a calmness spreading over her, which told her everything was going to work out, despite the huge amount of work to be done that the estate agent's photos had failed to show.

Glancing around, Emma applied her 'is it beautiful *and* functional' mantra to everything in the large room. On inspection she realised that the only thing she had any intention of keeping was the magnificent four poster bed, currently clad in hideous chintz curtains, and perhaps two antique scroll chairs positioned in the window, the rest – a cornucopia of unrefined, dark wood furniture clad in embroidered linens and lace – would have to go.

Emma's phone rang as she was moving into the smaller back bedroom at the top of the house, its bijou bathroom complete with peach suite, floral wallpaper and knitted loo roll cover.

'How's it going, love?' asked Liz.

'I'm in,' said Emma, careful not to convey her sense of horror at the condition of the decor, and grateful that her mum hadn't figured out how to use video calling.

'Is it everything you imagined it to be?'

Not wanting to give her mother any reason to worry, Emma told her, 'You won't believe the views, they're absolutely beautiful.'

As they continued to chat, Emma nosed around the top floor. Two further bedrooms and a bathroom looked out over the higgledy-piggledy rooftops and chimney pots of the village beyond, which Emma knew she could look at every day for the next 10 years and still see something new each time.

Back on the landing Emma climbed the shaky Ramsay Ladder that had been left down and stuck her head up into the loft, which was full of Hilda's discarded possessions.

'Is the house as stunning as it looked online?'

'It needs a bit more work than I thought but all cosmetic,' said Emma, purposefully ignoring the worrying signs of loose brickwork in one corner of the attic, daylight seeping through. *Today is not the day for unearthing structural problems*, Emma told herself. *Today is only about the things I can fix myself.*

'Thank goodness for that,' said Liz, with a sigh. 'I was worried you'd open the front door to discover damp and rot and all sorts.'

'Not found any so far,' said Emma, pushing the loft hatch closed and shoving aside any worries about what the condition of the roof might be.

'And there's plenty of room for you to spread out and still accommodate guests?'

'Absolutely.'

Emma wandered down to the middle floor to investigate a further three generously sized bedrooms, all in need of drastic makeovers but two with incredible sea views and all majestic in their own right. 'I think I might make the top floor my apartment and use the rest of the house for the guests.' Emma had spent weeks putting financial projections together for the bank, which had included everything from set-up costs to cleaner's wages, so she was confident three rooms would provide adequate income to pay the mortgage and bills each month, and leave a little extra for herself.

'I can't wait to visit,' said Liz, as Emma descended the staircase to the ground floor.

'Nor me, Mum,' she said, determined to have as much work done as possible before her mother's visit. 'Come soon.'

Emma clicked off her phone and went to the dining room at the front of the house. She pushed back a heavy, dusty old curtain and rolled up the nets, allowing light to flood in. The light caught the dust which danced all around the fusty room, over the heavy tables, the sombre fireplace and gothic dresser. Heaving a window open and drinking in the fresh salty air, Emma watched an elderly lady walk gingerly by, pulling her shopping trolley behind her, no doubt on her way to the plethora of shops Emma had spotted as she drove through the village earlier. A young mum dashed past chasing her toddler who was perilously close to the kerbside, and a middle-aged man, walking his dog, stopped to read the notice board across the road outside the little library. It was a far cry from the pace of London and, despite all the work that was required, the prospect of living in such a beautiful village thrilled Emma to her core.

Full of gladness and excitement, Emma moved from the dining room to the sitting room that overlooked the generous garden leading down to the sea at the back of the house; all the chintz, knick-knacks and antimacassars in the world couldn't hide the beauty of this magnificent room with its large open fireplace, Edinburgh press and large bay window with French doors at its centre; it had a warmth to it that none of the other rooms had. She couldn't wait to make it into a welcoming retreat for her guests.

'I need to figure out the basics – cooker, water, gas and fuse box,' Emma said to herself, standing at the living-room windows, distracted by a wren flitting under the lavender plants, a robin fighting off a sparrow at one of the feeders, and great tits vying for space in the climbing roses. She pulled herself away and made her way through to the kitchen at the back.

'Oh my God!' she said, immediately putting her arm over her nose as she entered the dated pine kitchen. 'Where the hell is that smell coming from?'

The smell that she'd first noticed in the hallway was 10 times worse in the kitchen. Gingerly she sniffed the sink, suspecting the drains, but it wasn't that. She opened the fridge in search of something covered in mould but again, nothing. Opening the door to the original Victorian larder, tentatively looking for a dead mouse or rat, Emma realised rapidly that this was not the source of the smell either.

'Which only leaves the laundry room,' she said, reaching out hesitantly for the handle, horrified at the prospect of what she might find decaying inside. When she did at last grasp the handle and edge the door open, Emma was confronted by something big and black and stinking. Before she could stop herself she let out a scream and quickly slammed the door behind her.

Chapter 3

'Oh my God!' said Emma, her heart racing, keeping her hand firmly on the handle of the door in case the-beast-in-the-laundry-room should manage to open it. Stretching for a chair at the kitchen table, she pulled it towards her and angled it beneath the knob, praying it would do the trick while she figured out what to do.

'Rhona,' she said, going straight to the sideboard in the hall to pick up the note from Hilda. 'The note said to call Rhona if I needed advice.' Not that she was clear if advice really stretched to dealing with unrecognisable animals in the laundry room. She wondered if she should call the RSPCA instead.

'Her number is in the top drawer of the desk,' read Emma from the note, going immediately to the living room and the solid, leather-topped desk, which had an old, black analogue phone on it. As instructed, there in a clear plastic wallet, in shaky handwriting, was the number for Rhona, which Emma dialled immediately.

The phone seemed to ring for an eternity but then, eventually, just as Emma was about to give up, it was answered.

'Hello?'

'Rhona?' she asked, aware that she sounded not only out of breath but also slightly panicked – not a great first impression.

'Yes.'

Emma's shoulders dropped marginally. 'I'm sorry to disturb you,' she said, moving through to the entrance of the kitchen where she could keep an eye on the laundry room door at a safe distance. If the thing broke loose she could shut the kitchen door and leg it outside. 'My name is Emma, I'm the new owner of the Lobster Bay Guesthouse—'

'Oh hi,' said Rhona, sounding as if she'd been expecting Emma's call. 'I've been wondering who'd be crazy enough to take on the old place!'

'Right, that would be me,' said Emma with a tight laugh, trying to figure out what Rhona meant by the remark but knowing now was not the time to ask. 'Ms Wyatt left me a note to say I should contact you for advice and, well, I hope you don't mind, and I hope I don't sound completely mad, but there's something in the laundry room and I've no idea what it is.'

Rhona released a great snort of laughter. 'You've found Wilbur then,' she said, in between laughs. 'Wait right there, I'll be straight over.'

Not wanting to take any chances, Emma sat on the front step while waiting for Rhona to arrive. It was less than five minutes before a battered Fiat Panda careered into view and a tall, sinewy woman with wide eyes and an even wider smile parked up in front of the house and jumped out.

'You must be Emma,' she said, striding past Emma, giving her a reassuring pat on the shoulder before shoving a large bunch of keys into her back pocket and entering the house before Emma was even on her feet.

'Correct,' said Emma, following the woman inside, still wondering who she was and why she had keys to Emma's house.

'I'm Rhona, the cleaner,' she said as if she'd read Emma's mind.

Of course, thought Emma. *Ms R. McGregor, the housekeeper I agreed to employ as part of the sale.*

'Wilbur sure can give people a fright. But he's a big softy once he gets to know you.' She talked at breakneck speed, disappearing across the hall and into the kitchen.

In the kitchen Rhona was about to open the laundry room door when Emma shouted, 'Stop!'

'You alright?' asked Rhona, stopping as instructed.

Emma took a deep breath and released it slowly. 'What *is* Wilbur, *exactly?*'

Rhona's forehead crumpled in puzzlement. 'He's a Newfoundland,' she said, as if everybody under the sun knew what a Newfoundland might be.

'A what now?'

'A Newfoundland,' she repeated. 'You know, a Canadian rescue dog. They're amazing. People call them "nanny dogs" because they're so gentle and tolerant of children.'

Emma's brow furrowed. 'There's *no way* that whatever's in there is gentle. It's enormous.'

'Gentle giants,' said Rhona casually, oblivious to Emma's racing heart. 'You ready?'

'Not in the slightest.' Emma crept behind the kitchen table.

'Well, you'd better gird your loins because he's coming . . .' and with that Rhona opened the laundry room door and the most enormous dog Emma had ever seen in her life, black, hairy and slobbering, with a head the size of a basketball, came lumbering out.

'Oh my God,' she squealed, her whole body tensing as the dog came towards her.

'Relax,' said Rhona. 'Trust me, this dog wouldn't harm a fly, plus he's ancient, you can easily outrun him.'

Emma looked down at the huge animal whose head came up to her waist; he eyeballed her, his lower eyelids drooping, exposing the reds of his eyes. He looked more like a hungry bear to Emma than a gentle dog.

'Why's he drooling like that?' asked Emma, keeping her distance so that the slobber that looked like tennis shoe-laces dangling from the dog's mouth wouldn't come near her.

'Probably because he's excited, or hungry, or both. He always does it. You'll get used to it.'

'What do you mean,' "I'll get used to it"?' Emma sidled away. Mercifully the dog quickly lost interest and started sniffing the edges of the skirting instead.

'Over the next few days and weeks,' said Rhona, fetching a large water bowl from the laundry room and filling it at the sink. 'Before you know it he'll be your best friend.'

'I'm sorry, I still don't understand – who does the dog belong to?'

'Well you, of course!' said Rhona with a laugh, as though Emma was being intentionally ridiculous.

Emma felt suddenly exhausted from the journey and the emotion of the day began to bubble to the surface; she composed herself with a long exhale.

'Didn't your solicitor discuss it with you?'

'Discuss what?' asked Emma, though she knew the answer before it was given. At no point had Pamela mentioned anything about a dog.

43

'That Wilbur was included in the sale.'

'I don't understand,' said Emma, her head light. She reached for the back of a chair to steady herself.

'Why don't I make you a cup of tea? You look like you could do with one. Grab a seat in the living room and I'll bring it in.'

Before Emma could say that her box of food, including the teabags, was still in the car with the rest of her belongings, Rhona had already got mugs from the cupboard and tea from the larder. It was only then that Emma really registered she'd bought not just a home but a business which included: a furnished house and fully equipped kitchen, a housekeeper and, it seemed, a dog, too.

'Go! Sit down before you fall down,' said Rhona, shooing her away with a teaspoon.

Emma took a seat in the living room on an ugly but surprisingly comfortable floral sofa that was positioned in such a way that she could see the birds flitting about on the feeders, the garden behind, and a vast expanse of sea beyond. Watching the birds busying about the place took her mind off things for a moment, and she wondered how many previous owners of the house had enjoyed watching the birds and sea from the window. The history of houses was something that always interested Emma, she liked nothing better than to find old photographs of when they were first built and trace them through the years. Her favourite design jobs were those where the client wanted to incorporate the building's history into the design scheme. It occurred to her that once she was settled she should visit the village museum to see if they knew anything of the guesthouse's history.

'Here you go. I even found a biscuit,' said Rhona, coming in and handing Emma her tea. Wilbur skulked in behind and lay down by the fireplace, keeping a comfortable distance but still within sight of Emma, who had an idea she was being watched.

'Thank you,' said Emma, receiving both gratefully and watching Rhona take a seat on the fireside fender; Emma gathered from Rhona's physique and her choice of uncomfortable perch that she rarely sat still for long. 'So, what were you saying about the dog?'

'The care home where Hilda moved last month has a strict no-dog policy,' said Rhona, as if this explained everything.

'So why didn't she rehome it?'

'She tried but nobody would take him,' replied Rhona, scrunching the dog's ears.

Emma's mouth turned down in disgust as she watched the dog lick his groin with his long, thick tongue. 'I'm not surprised.'

'Not because he's difficult but because he won't settle anywhere else,' said Rhona, coming quickly to the dog's defence. 'A friend of Hilda's took him for a while, but he kept wandering home and sitting on the front step, waiting for Hilda to come back.'

Emma wasn't so opposed to dogs that she couldn't see the tenderness in the story, and there was something slightly cute about his doleful expression, but still, there was no way she was going to take him on.

'Who's been looking after him?'

'I have,' said Rhona, fussing the dog some more, who sat up and positioned his jowls on her thigh leaving a wet patch of drool. 'I've been nipping back and forth each day to feed and walk him.'

'Won't he settle at yours?'

Rhona glanced into her teacup. 'I have four kids, so I haven't time for a dog, otherwise I'd have him in a heartbeat.'

'Wow, you do have your hands full,' said Emma, impressed that someone so young and slender could have so many children.

'When Hilda realised there was nowhere else for him to go she decided he should stay here and that whoever bought the property would look after him. As far as I understand, it was a condition of the sale.'

'It's the first I've heard of it,' said Emma, wondering if, in the hurry to complete the sale, she had missed a crucial document. 'I'll call my solicitor, and a dog home.'

Rhona paused and cocked her head to one side in a way that was not dissimilar to Wilbur, whose ears seem to raise up an inch or two at Emma's mention of a dog home.

'Why don't you stop in and speak to Hilda before you do anything? She might have thought of someone else who could take him on, you never know. And I'm sure she'd like to meet you – everyone's been dying to find out who bought the place.'

Emma rolled her eyes and let out a light laugh. 'Does *everyone* think I'm crazy?'

'Crazy or a grafter,' said Rhona, with a wink.

'If I'd known just how much work the place needed I might not have been so keen.'

Rhona wrapped her hands around her mug, her large rings chinking against the porcelain, and Emma noticed she wasn't wearing one on her left ring finger. 'Didn't you see the house before buying it?'

Emma shook her head, despairing of what Rhona must think of her. 'The estate agent told me the closing date was set, if I didn't make an offer that day I'd more than likely miss out. And I *really* wanted it.'

'Huh,' said Rhona, draining her cup of tea. 'I guess the reduction in price brought in a few more potential buyers then.'

'Had the house been sitting on the market for a while?' asked Emma, who hadn't noticed a price reduction in the few months she'd been looking at it online.

'A couple of years,' said Rhona, with a rising inflection.

'A couple of *years*?'

'Maybe three . . . or a little more.'

'How come?' said Emma, who felt a bit winded at the discovery. She pushed away a seed of doubt that crept into her mind.

Rhona paused before saying, 'Maybe because Hilda didn't really want to sell.'

'Then why did she?'

'Her daughter, Judy, has power of attorney and she insisted. Hilda couldn't manage any longer and she couldn't depend on me or Judy to be able to help as often as she needed. The truth is it grew too much for her a long time ago. But she persevered, and people kept coming.'

'When did she stop taking guests?'

'She didn't, she's still got bookings,' said Rhona, putting down her mug and getting up to fetch something from the desk. 'Take a look.' She handed Emma a leather-bound diary.

Emma flicked through the pages of what turned out to be a bookings diary. It was mostly empty until she reached roughly halfway through the year when it suddenly became full of Hilda's writing. In her elderly scrawl she'd written the names and phone numbers of guests, where they were travelling from, and the number of nights they'd be staying. Emma couldn't believe how many bookings there already were for a house that was in such a poor state of repair.

'But this is for June,' she said, doing a rapid calculation in her head. 'That's only a month away.'

'Right,' said Rhona, nodding her head pragmatically. 'Looks like someone's got their work cut out!'

Chapter 4

Rhona coaxed Wilbur back to the laundry room and reassured Emma that she'd be back tomorrow, when her kids were at school, to help however she could.

'I've left a note with Wilbur's feed times on it, and don't worry about walking him. I've already been out with him this morning. He's old, one walk a day is fine.'

'Good to know,' said Emma, trying to conceal her fear of walking a dog the size of a small horse.

'You'll be fine! Why not nip out for a short walk on your own, get some supplies in?' called Rhona, heading outside and unlocking her car door. 'You'll feel better for it and ready to tackle anything with something in your belly.'

'Good idea,' said Emma, checking her pocket for her bank card and grabbing her house keys before pulling the front door shut.

'No need to lock the door – you're in Lobster Bay now!' called Rhona, and with that she folded herself into her car and was off at a pace.

'So – I – am,' said Emma to herself, looking down the elegant road on which the house was located. The cherry trees that lined the street were still bursting with soft pink blossom which contrasted perfectly with the powder-blue sky. Overhead, gulls circled the pantile rooftops, calling to one another in flight, and the warmth of the spring sun beat off the pinks and orange of the ancient stone.

Walking the short distance up the narrow road towards the shops in the centre of the village, Emma passed an old cinema now being used as an art venue, and a small pub with an A-frame outside, which advertised rooms.

Arriving at the main street, Emma was drawn into the greengrocer on the corner by the display of fresh spring pro-duce outside. On entering the shop a bell chimed above her. She couldn't remember the last time she'd heard a shop bell; when she'd lived in London she'd shopped at the local Tesco Metro, and for the last few months, living at her mother's, they'd had the groceries delivered. There was something about a shop bell that made Emma feel as if she'd stepped back in time, and that, in her book, was no bad thing.

'Hello,' said Emma, to the young woman sitting behind the counter. Emma guessed she was in her early to mid-twenties; her pretty face was hidden behind big plastic glasses and her thick hair, dipped blue at the ends, was largely concealed by what looked like a large, home-made bobble hat.

'Hi,' said the woman, barely looking up from her phone.

'I just moved into the village. I bought the guesthouse one street down.' Emma indicated vaguely in the direction of the house, not entirely certain of her bearings. She surprised herself with her own chattiness, marvelling that village life was already having an effect.

'Huh,' said the woman, chewing her gum a little more intensely. Emma felt the woman's dark eyes follow her as she studied the jars of home-made preserves.

'I might try a couple of these – guess I'll be needing some for guests' breakfasts,' she said, placing some jars of jam on the counter. 'And some Jersey Royals and asparagus for my dinner.'

'Sure thing,' muttered the woman, grudgingly putting down her phone. She weighed and bagged the vegetables without chat. '£7.29.'

Emma held her card to the machine and avoided further small talk with the reticent young woman, who bagged Emma's items in silence.

'Would you like your receipt?' she asked, pushing the items towards Emma.

'No, thank you,' said Emma, taking the bag. 'See you soon.'

'Guess so,' mumbled the woman, returning to her phone.

Putting the grumpy greengrocer behind her, Emma continued along the street. She wandered past a funky little yarn shop, its window full of brightly coloured wools, baskets and throws. Emma made a note to stop in when it was open to see if there was anything suitable for the house. She'd decided on the long drive up that she would fill her home with as much local design as she could, anything from bedspreads to lampshades, and do her best to use reclaimed and sustainable furniture. This little gem looked exactly like the sort of thing she was after.

Further on, past a deli full of calorie-loaded treats and a tiny estate agent, its window full of quaint little houses for sale, Emma found the butcher. She felt on entering as if she'd stepped back in time again. The walls were lined with images of men in long white aprons, stern in appearance, wielding cleavers, and there were photographs of prize-winning cattle and rosettes and trophies everywhere. There was even a blackboard that listed the farms from where the day's meat had come. And, most impressively to Emma, there was barely a trace of the smell of meat.

'How can I help today?' asked a guy around Emma's age who hurried out from the back with a smile. He wore baggy cargo pants under his apron and a pair of Vans, and his dark hair sprouted from beneath a headband in curls.

She wondered if it was the same guy she'd seen on the beach earlier in the day with his surf board.

'I'm looking for a nice bit of lamb,' said Emma.

'Ah-hah – for how many?' His lilting Scottish accent sounded wholesome and friendly and Emma took an instant liking to him.

'Just for me. Anything that's quick to cook.'

'A steak or a chop will grill quickly.'

'A steak would be great then.'

'Very good,' he said, selecting a piece from the display unit and wrapping it for Emma. 'Anything else for you?'

'Actually, yes,' said Emma, adopting her business hat. 'I've just taken over the guesthouse here in the village – I don't suppose you do trade accounts?'

'So, you're the new owner!' he said, breaking into an even bigger smile and coming out to greet her. He extended his arm, his wrist covered in bracelets of leather, beads and twine. 'Phil Hughes. Pleased to meet you.'

'Emma,' she said, shaking Phil's hand, which was strong and warm.

'You'll have your hands full with that place!' he said, rubbing a hand on his scruffy facial hair.

'That's what I keep hearing!' laughed Emma.

'My family's dealt with the previous owner for decades.'

'Hilda?'

54

'She's quite the character.'

'I heard that too!'

'She used to buy rump steak for her dog and our cheapest sausages for her guests.' Phil's eyes, conker brown, sparkled at the memory.

'Why doesn't that surprise me!' said Emma, who had momentarily managed to forget about Wilbur. He could be certain he was never going to receive the same treatment from her.

'Personally, I keep the steak for me and the cheap sausages for my dog,' said Phil.

'Good plan,' said Emma, who was now almost certain that it was Phil she'd seen that morning with his dog perched on the back of his surf board. She marvelled at the fact she was living in a community where it was possible to surf with your dog in the morning and be at work in the afternoon, and quietly congratulated herself for making the best and biggest decision of her life.

'We can definitely set you up with a trade account. Let me get you a price list,' he said, nipping behind the counter and grabbing one for her, along with a business card.

'Thanks,' said Emma, taking it from him. 'And how much for the lamb?'

'Consider it a welcome gift,' he said, with a broad, open smile.

'That's really kind, thank you,' said Emma, grateful to Phil for making her feel so welcome; it was the boost she'd needed after the reception she'd had at the greengrocers.

'See you around,' he called after her.

'Absolutely!' She waved, noticing as she passed the window that Phil's eyes seemed to follow her as she left.

One last stop and then back to the house, thought Emma, not quite ready to call the old place home. She crossed to the other side of the road to another cluster of shops where the mini-market was, opposite the road to the guesthouse.

Emma took time to wander round the market making a mental note of their ample stock. Between the independent shops and this place, she figured she'd rarely have to leave the village. It really was like living in the 1950s, exactly how she'd dreamt it would be.

After a good look round, Emma took a jar of mint sauce, a scented candle and some lemon sorbet to the counter.

'So, what have you got?' asked the cashier who had a hint of Ann Widdecombe about her – thick, unruly hair, a turned-down mouth and rotund figure. Emma suspected from the woman's heavy accent, gravelly voice and pallor that she smoked at least 40 a day. Her name badge read *Sheena*.

'Just the three items, thanks,' said Emma, never more aware of her English accent.

'Haven't seen you in here before,' said Sheena, not unfriendly in her manner but with a directness that took

Emma aback. People barely looked at her in London. She'd used her local Tesco for two years before anyone acknowledged her, and even then it was little more than a grunt.

'I just moved into the guesthouse.'

'Hilda's auld place?'

'Exactly,' said Emma, liking the fact that everyone seemed to know Hilda. She wondered how long it would take before everyone came to know her too.

'Where have you come from?'

'London, well, via Northampton.'

'Oh aye.' Sheena gave her the once-over; Emma didn't mind, she'd expected people to be a little suspicious of her coming from the south. 'What's your connection with here?'

'Nothing at all.' She stopped herself from telling Sheena that it had been a long-held dream of hers to run a village guesthouse and that she wanted a fresh start. She had a feeling that if she told her, Sheena would have the story of Christmas Eve out of her within minutes, and Emma wasn't ready yet; she wasn't sure she'd ever be ready for that.

Sheena's eyes pressed Emma for more information.

'I'm an interior designer and the house is a great project,' she said, being careful to avoid anything too specific. 'Plus, you know, you don't get much better than Lobster Bay.'

'Aye, that you'd be right about',' said Sheena, scanning Emma's items.

A small queue had formed behind Emma, meaning Sheena had no choice but to process her payment and let Emma go without further interrogation.

Jeez, what a bunch! thought Emma, exiting the shop, amused by the eccentric collection of locals and loving the fact she already knew two of them by name.

Emma was about to head back to the house when she noticed a young woman with a pixie haircut and an apron dress position a sign outside the door of the little museum across the road from the greengrocer. Crossing the street, Emma smiled and asked if they were open.

'We are,' she said merrily. 'Come on in.'

'This is lovely,' said Emma to the woman as she entered the tiny shop at the entrance to the museum. The shelves were adorned with all sorts of lobster and puffin-themed gifts: plates, cups, teapots, and the floor-stands were full of cards depicting the local villages, beaches and skies.

'Are you visiting the area?' asked the lady, busying her-self behind the counter.

'Actually, I've just moved in, one street down.'

'To the guesthouse?'

'Yes,' said Emma, amazed that it took so little informa-tion for people to make correct deductions around here.

'One of my cousins is the housekeeper there.'

'Rhona?'

'You've met already?'

'She came to my rescue just an hour ago.'

'Let me guess,' said the lady, her eyes twinkling delightedly, 'Wilbur!'

'You know him?'

'*Everyone* knows Wilbur, he's a bit like our village mascot!'

Emma offered a tight smile, the idea that she'd been left not only someone's beloved pet but also the village mascot made the burden all the greater.

'You can't walk five paces with Wilbur without someone stopping to chat.'

'He certainly looks like a character,' said Emma.

'He fits in around here.'

'I'm beginning to see that,' said Emma, with a laugh.

'I'm Jennifer, by the way.'

'Emma.' She shook Jennifer's hand, spotting the henna tattoos on her hands, and the multiple ear piercings, and a tiny stud in her nose too.

'Lovely to meet you.'

'Do you happen to know anything about the guesthouse? I thought it might be nice to discover a little of its history, maybe incorporate some of it into my design scheme.'

'That's a great idea,' said Jennifer, enthusiastically. 'I don't have anything on display but maybe you could leave it with me and I can have a look through our archives?'

'That would be amazing! Thank you. Are you sure it's not too much trouble?'

'Trouble?' said Jennifer with a laugh. 'Trawling the archives is my *raison d'etre*, nothing makes me happier.'

'Then I'll look forward to seeing what you come up with,' said Emma, taking a lobster tea towel from a display case and placing it on the counter.

'I'll give you a call at the house when I've something to show you.'

'Thank you,' said Emma, paying for the tea towel.

'No problem.'

Emma left the museum and was about to turn down the road to the house when a van came roaring past, causing her to jump back.

'Hey!' she called, throwing up her hand in annoyance. She caught just a glimpse of the driver, who looked like the rugged guy she'd seen earlier at the harbour.

'Arsehole' she muttered, irritated by his recklessness, before ambling back down the road towards the house, where she found someone standing at the front door.

'Hello,' she called, offering a wave to a woman in her fifties with a sharp grey bob.

'You must be Emma,' she said, extending her fine hand.

'Yes.' Emma shook her hand firmly before realising that the woman's grip was far weaker than hers and adjusted hers accordingly.

'I'm Judy, Hilda's daughter.'

'Oh hi,' said Emma, slightly taken aback. There was something about Judy, knee-length tweed skirt and a starchy white shirt with the collar popped up, that seemed a little stuffy for the village. It was hard to imagine that she'd grown up here; she had more of a county-town vibe about her. 'Would you like to come in?'

'No, no,' replied Judy, holding tight to the strap of her leather handbag. 'I'm sure you're very busy. I simply wanted to stop by to welcome you and check everything is in order.'

'It is, thank you,' said Emma, putting her shopping down in the vestibule. She thought to mention Wilbur, but Judy looked even less like the sort of woman who could handle a 10-stone dog than Emma did, so she left the subject alone. 'I love the house.'

'I'm sure it will take a while for you to make it how you want it, my mother rather let it go towards the end.'

'Not at all,' said Emma, who sensed the woman was rather embarrassed by the state of the place. 'I can tell it's been a much-loved home.'

'I appreciate you saying so. Most of the potential buyers were more interested in the business; in the end I was glad it went to someone who wanted it as their home, as well as a business. I felt it would make the transition easier for my mother.'

Emma could tell from Judy's tone that it hadn't made the transition easier, but there was something about her, a tension, an unease, that prevented Emma from enquiring further.

'I'm just glad you accepted my offer. I know it couldn't have been the strongest one you had.'

Judy's forehead creased for a fraction of a second before replying, 'You took time to write, though sadly I misplaced the note and my mother refuses to believe it exists.'

'That's a shame. I wanted your mother to know I fully intend on taking good care of it.'

'Not to worry,' said Judy, a distant expression in her eye. She appeared to shake off an unhelpful thought. 'Everything will be fine in the end.'

'It's a big change for everyone,' said Emma, pondering what Judy had meant.

'Isn't it,' she said primly. 'Well, I'd better leave you to get on. Best of luck.'

*

Emma crept into the kitchen being careful not to disturb Wilbur, who she hoped would be sleeping in the laundry room. She left her groceries on the work surface, placed the lamb in the fridge and the sorbet in the freezer, before sneaking out front to start unloading the car. She knew she couldn't ignore the dog forever, she'd need to deal with him on her own at some point, but he could wait until the car was empty at least.

Over the next hour Emma diligently took box after box up the two flights of stairs to the top floor. She decided on the large room at the back as her private sitting room and the smaller room next to that as her bedroom. The rooms at the front of the house she would use as further guest rooms, but only once the rooms on the first floor were up and running.

'There, job done,' said Emma, placing the last of her clothes in the small Edwardian wardrobe, which she'd scrubbed meticulously clean. She closed the mirrored door and caught sight of her reflection. Her hair, scraped back off her face with a hairband, was damp at the front from all her labours, and her plump cheeks were pink. Satisfied with her efforts she took a well-earned rest on the little chair by the window and surveyed the room. Her little en-suite bathroom, free of knitted loo-roll holders and embroidered towels, looked more like home now that her toiletries lined the shelves. The pine bedstead was much more inviting with Emma's crisp, white bedding, the antique dressing table felt more familiar with her brush and hairdryer laid out, and a couple of books and a reading lamp by the bedside made the room feel homely.

'I could sit here all day, but I can't,' said Emma to herself, now staring out of the window to sea, watching the billowy clouds pass by, revelling in her new home. If it weren't for the behemoth task of decorating that lay ahead of her, and the fact that there was an ancient, drooling dog in the laundry room, Emma might have thought she was dreaming. But there was no avoiding the dog, which Emma had no choice but to head downstairs and tackle. Part of her wanted to call Rhona, or even Phil the butcher to help, but, driven by a determination to prove to herself, and her sister, that she could manage this new life on her own, she decided to go it alone.

In the kitchen, Emma picked up the note Rhona had left for her outlining Wilbur's routine, noting he was due his second feed of the day.

'First things first,' she said, eyeing the laundry room door. 'Where is the dog food kept?'

Emma opened every kitchen cupboard, checked under the stairs and rifled through the larder but found nothing.

Tell me the dog doesn't just eat raw steak, thought Emma, remembering what Phil had told her.

With no other option but to look in the laundry room, Emma very carefully, trying desperately not to disturb the dog, edged the door open. In the dim light of the room she could just make out Wilbur, nestled in his bed in the corner.

'Good boy,' she whispered, noting a slight tremble in her voice that surprised her. Emma had never been afraid of dogs, grossed out by them, yes, but there was something about this situation, her entering his territory, the sheer size of him, that put her on edge.

'Nice and easy,' said Emma when she saw his eyes open and fix on her. 'No need to get up.'

And with that, as if he had understood Emma and chosen to defy her, Wilbur stretched out his front paws, opened his jaws wide in a yawn, exposing a very large set of yellowing teeth, and got slowly to his feet.

'Steady now,' she said as he sniffed her feet suspiciously. 'Let's get you outside.'

Emma opened a door which led into the back passage then threw open the door to the garden, releasing Wilbur into the area which was overlooked by the large windows of the living room and the kitchen. Slowly he climbed down a small flight of steps, which led to the grassy section of the garden where he cocked his leg against a small flowering shrub.

'Delightful,' said Emma, her voice no longer trembling as she followed Wilbur down the garden and explored the flower beds, bird feeders and winding path that led to a small vegetable section and shed, and beyond that a second garden of steep meadow that led down to the sea.

Looking back towards the house, Emma surveyed the property and pinched herself in disbelief.

I made this happen, she thought, admiring the handsome stonework of the house, her eye wandering up to where the roof joined the next-door property. Emma was no expert but even to her untrained eye she could tell the roof was in need of repair – nothing urgent, she thought, but something that shouldn't be left unattended for long.

Watching Wilbur sniff round the lawn, Emma thought about how far she'd come in such a short space of time. Was it really possible that less than five months ago she was still with Chris, living in a tiny apartment and working in London? Standing amongst the soft landscaping of the garden and breathing the fresh salt air, it hardly felt possible.

Right, back to business, she thought, galvanising herself, Wilbur now content sniffing the edges of the shed.

Venturing down the back passage she found some shelves full of DIY supplies and an entire floor-to-ceiling cupboard lined with tins of dog food, bowls, bones, leads, grooming brushes and poop bags – it was better stocked than some pet shops she'd seen.

Guess I've found Wilbur's cupboard then, she thought, emptying a large tin of revolting-smelling dog food into a bowl and placing it outside. As far as Emma was concerned, dogs ate outside. She had no intention of letting it eat in the kitchen and, if she had her way, he'd learn to sleep in the back corridor rather than the laundry room.

'Come on then,' she called out, standing just inside the back door.

Within seconds Wilbur was up the steps and straight to his bowl.

Yuck, yuck, yuck, she thought, turning up her nose as she watched Wilbur greedily snaffle up the contents.

Emma was about to head in when a loud bang caused her to start, and her heart to race. She steadied herself, the way she'd learned to, with a deep breath, and looked out over the high garden wall to the neighbouring property. The wall was around six foot high, tall enough to obscure most things but low enough for Emma to see the top of her neighbour's back door being opened and then banged shut again, followed by the unmistakeable sound of raised voices from within.

Christmas Day

'Merry Christmas,' Chris said tentatively, handing Emma a cup of tea as she woke. 'How did you sleep?'

'Really well, I think,' said Emma, sitting up, surprised that she'd managed to fall into such a deep sleep. She felt as if she'd slept a lifetime in one night. She repositioned her crinkled linen bedspread. 'Did yesterday really—?'

Chris nodded the answer. 'How are you feeling?'

Emma took a moment to consider her response. 'Mostly it feels like a horrible dream,' she said, sipping her hot tea, wondering what she should be feeling. Could it be right to feel almost no connection to what happened at all?

Chris placed his hand on Emma's and rubbed his thumb slowly over a nasty scratch. She pulled it away, unable to recall how the scratch got there, and cupped her fingers round her warm mug.

'Did you finish wrapping your mum's presents?' she asked, finding comfort in the banal, and then she remembered – the *white flash, the deafening noise, Chris's presents blowing out of her hand. 'Shit.'*

'What?'

Emma shook her head sharply, trying to eradicate the memory. 'Your presents, I had them with me when—'

She couldn't bring herself to finish the sentence.

'Please don't worry about it,' said Chris in a voice that Emma found smothering. Was this how it was going to be, she wondered, everyone treating her like a porcelain doll?

'But now you won't have anything to open,' she said, struggling to understand why she felt more upset about that than what had happened.

'Emma,' he said, rubbing her knee. 'All I ever want for Christmas is you, and this year, well ... I very nearly didn't.'

'Chris, come on,' she said, raising an eyebrow at his histrionics.

'I'm serious, Emma, you could have died.'

'But I didn't,' she said, taken aback by the anger in her voice, and the sudden hatred she felt towards the bomber who was responsible. The image of Dawn's daughters on her phone flashed in front of her, and she found herself questioning: why her, a mother, and not me? 'Two little girls woke up without their mum this morning, on Christmas Day, for Christ's sake, and God knows how many others lost loved ones. Don't feel sorry for me, Chris. I'm here. Feel sorry for them.'

'I didn't mean to upset you,' he said, his eyes full of remorse and confusion.

Emma sat back, feeling guilty for being so harsh. 'It's not your fault,' she said, softening her tone. She reached for his hand, held it tight, and looked him straight in the eye. 'There's no reason why you should know how to deal with this.'

'But I want to help.'

'I know,' she said, casting her gaze towards their clasped hands, a sudden realisation hitting her. 'But you're always going to want to protect me, to understand something I may never make sense of, or have any desire to share; it's an impossible situation.'

'We have to give it time, Em.'

Emma shook her head, loosened her grip and slipped her hand away. Neither one of them said anything but both of them knew their relationship was over.

Chapter 5

'I can't believe that a lick of paint on a front door can make such a difference,' said Rhona, her paint-splattered hands on her slender hips, shirt sleeves rolled up, admiring her handiwork. Over the course of the morning, she and Emma had transformed the front garden and entrance. Emma had clipped the hedge with an old pair of shears she'd found in the shed, removed a bin liner of weeds, had a clearance of garden ornaments and had even been out first thing in the Volvo to the DIY store on the outskirts of the village to pick up some fresh gravel and paint.

'Whenever I looked at the house online I knew the first job I'd do, if I got it, would be to change the front door from dismal brown to a deep Scots pine green,' said Emma, who was pleased with the transformation. The colour had a majesty about it which suited the house, but also a warmth.

'It completely changes the feel of the place. It really does,' said Rhona, dabbing a rag on the brass letterbox which she'd accidently caught with paint.

'It's a good start.'

'But only the beginning, right?' said Rhona, who had phoned first thing and offered to come in to work.

'A drop in the ocean,' said Emma, who was pleased that Rhona came with the house. Even after less than 24 hours, Emma could see that she was invaluable.

Emma had gone to bed the night before fretting about all she needed to do to the dilapidated decor before she could open to guests in a month's time. Exhausted from the move, she slept solidly for eight hours and woke with clarity on exactly what needed to be done. Her plan was to work solely on the guest areas – entrance, hallway, sitting room, dining room and three bedrooms – before tackling her apartment on the top floor, the last two bedrooms, and the kitchen in the autumn when she should be less busy.

'So, what's next?' asked Rhona.

'Let's prep the vestibule.' Emma moved inside, careful not to rub against the wet paint on the door. She grabbed some soapy water from the kitchen, rags, an industrial-sized pot of primer, brushes and the stepladder, and the two of them set to work covering the Victorian tiles with old sheets, dusting the highest corners, and washing down the mouldings.

'How long were you working for Hilda before she went into the home?' Emma asked, looking down from the stepladder to Rhona who was sitting cross-legged on the floor doing a final clean of the skirting.

'A few years – four, I suppose, since my youngest, Ella, started nursery.'

'She's seven?'

'Yup, if that's possible. It seems like only yesterday that she was a baby.'

'And the others?'

'14, 11 and nine,' said Rhona, broddling a cotton bud into the join of the skirting to rid it of a stubborn piece of dirt.

'Have you family around to help out?' asked Emma, curious to know what had happened to the kids' dad but feeling unable to ask.

'My mum and my dad help loads, plus I'm fourth generation Lobster – I can't walk five yards without bumping into a relative!'

'Oh, that's right. I met your cousin, Jennifer, at the museum yesterday.'

'Jennifer's one of many!'

'Sounds amazing,' said Emma, drying down the walls. 'It must be nice to be rooted in a community.'

'It has its upsides but trust me when I tell you it also has its downsides. There's a lot to be said for living in a city.'

'Maybe . . .' said Emma, and then, without warning, Dawn's face, her stare full of fear, suddenly burned in Emma's memory.

'You don't sound convinced,' said Rhona.

Emma had to fight to concentrate on Rhona's words, which sounded far away compared to the clarity of Dawn's face, which looked as real now as it had on the day itself. And then Emma remembered seeing the victims' faces on the front pages of the newspapers, and of how she'd searched for Dawn amongst them and not recognised the ruddy-cheeked woman smiling out at her. It was then that she made the decision not to find out more about her; she couldn't face the pain of knowing how much hurt Dawn's loss had caused.

'Had you family in the city?'

Dawn's face began to fade, and Emma managed to pick up the thread of the conversation.

'My mum's in Northampton and my sister in Hertfordshire so I had family nearby but not in the city,' said Emma, who couldn't remember mentioning London to Rhona but then yesterday had been such a whirlwind of activity and she'd been so tired by the end of it, she figured she must have forgotten.

'What about your dad?'

'Dad died when I was 17,' said Emma, though she could hardly believe it had been so long. It felt like yesterday that they were holding his hand in the hospital and saying their goodbyes. 'After that Mum decided to sell the family home. She bought something manageable and tiny, so I've been a bit rootless since then.'

'Sounds tough.' Rhona looked up from where she was sitting.

'Yeah, it was,' said Emma, scrunching her nose, remembering how hard it had been to put herself through college and take care of her mother at the same time.

'Have you any siblings?'

'A big sister. She has two kids. My nephew, who's seven like your youngest, and my niece who's five. She's busy with her family and my mum has a new fella so, you know—'

'You're pretty much on your own?'

'I was with someone for a few years,' said Emma, thinking of Chris.

'But not any more?'

'He wasn't the one,' said Emma, who still felt a bit uneasy about how the relationship had ended. It wasn't because she felt calling it off was the wrong thing to do – she knew that it was right for them both in the long term – but because she knew she should have done it sooner; if she had, Chris might not be hurting so badly now.

'In the end, I had to be cruel to be kind,' said Emma, beginning the sanding of the woodwork.

'Were you the one to call if off?'

'Yup,' said Emma, though she wasn't certain if walking out could really be classed as calling it off. If there was one thing she could change about the break-up, it would be how she handled it. Under different circumstances she would have been kinder.

'And then you moved here?' asked Rhona. Emma detected a hint of intrigue in her voice.

'I saw an opportunity to live out my dream, or what I imagined was my dream, to have a fresh start,' she said, feeling a little bad for not telling Rhona the full story, but how could she when she hadn't fully come to accept it as her own? In many ways it still felt to Emma like a very vivid nightmare, one she couldn't shake from her mind, and that also had a horrible way of creeping up on her when she least expected it, no matter how hard she tried to ignore it.

The rough scratching of sandpaper on paint momentarily took the place of their chatter, leaving Emma with the impression that Rhona had sensed something of her past had been left unsaid.

'How about a tea break before we start painting?' suggested Emma, wanting to divert Rhona's curiosity and keep the mood light. She put down her sandpaper block and wiped her dusty hands on her jeans.

'Let me go,' said Rhona, getting up. 'You get some fresh air.'

With Rhona in the kitchen, Emma stepped out of the vestibule and into the warm, bright morning, stretching her arms above her head and rolling her head from side to side. She'd been in Lobster Bay for less than 24 hours, and already she could feel the sea air ridding her lungs of city grime and the slower pace of life calming her busy mind.

Just as she was about to take a seat on the little bench Hilda had left in the front garden, she heard a shout from the kitchen. Before she could go to investigate, Wilbur bundled through the hall, into the vestibule and out the front door, leaving a streak of black hair stuck to the tacky green paint.

'So sorry,' yelled Rhona, rushing out behind him. 'I forgot to shut the kitchen door.'

'I'd have done the same,' said Emma, the pair of them dashing out to the pavement and after him.

'Wilbur!' yelled Rhona, who'd had the foresight to grab his lead on the way out.

'Wilbur!' Emma yelled too, even though she knew it wouldn't make a blind bit of difference.

On the other side of the street a small dog started yapping and straining on its lead, causing Wilbur to turn 360 degrees and run straight back towards Rhona and Emma. Rhona flung out an arm to stop Emma moving any further then dropped to her haunches.

'Come boy,' she said, whistling him in, then she whispered to Emma, 'Crouch down beside me.'

Emma did as she was asked, not understanding why, and for a moment it looked as if Wilbur was going to come, his large shoulders and head drooped in submission, but no sooner than he'd taken a few steps towards them, a door banged, causing Emma to start and Wilbur to take off once more.

'Wilbur!' exclaimed Rhona, getting to her feet, throwing her arms up in frustration.

The two women watched as Wilbur bounded at full tilt towards the source of the noise – the scruffy house adjoining Emma's, and the moody-looking guy from the harbour, who had slammed his front door shut.

Before either woman could do anything to stop him, Wilbur had jumped up on the guy, his front paws on the man's chest, and was licking his face.

'Oh, God,' said Emma, not sure what she found more mortifying – the dog licking the man's face or the realisation that the guy who'd caught her photographing him at the harbour should turn out to be her neighbour.

'Down,' said the guy firmly, and to Emma's astonishment Wilbur promptly sat, looking eager to please the man who now had him held tightly by the collar, his muscles flexing beneath his grubby, washed-out T-shirt.

'Sorry, Aidan,' said Rhona, hurrying over.

'No bother, Rhona.' He gave the dog an affectionate tussle before releasing him to her. 'How are the kids?'

'All fine, thanks,' she said, attaching the lead to Wilbur's collar as Emma joined them.

'Sorry,' said Emma, feeling flustered and a little out of breath. 'It's my fault, I should have locked him out back. I had no idea old dogs could move so quickly.'

'Figures,' said Aidan. 'Why would a city girl know how to handle a dog like this?'

Emma recoiled at the remark. It was such an odd thing to say to a complete stranger. First of all, she hadn't chosen to take on the dog, so it was hardly her fault that she was left with a disobedient mutt. And second, how the hell did he know she was from the city?

'Have you guys met?' asked Rhona, holding Wilbur close on a short leash.

Emma shook her head, still indignant about the comment. The guy held her gaze, his lapis-blue eyes shining in the sunlight.

'Aidan, Emma.'

'Hi,' said Emma, grudgingly reaching out her hand. Aidan shook it, his grip remarkably strong.

'Where's your camera?' he asked, his full lips forming into a smirk.

Emma floundered and looked away, her cheeks flushing red, but she could still feel Aidan's eyes on her.

'Maybe we should get Wilbur back inside,' suggested Rhona, glancing between the pair of them.

'Good idea,' said Emma, moving away.

'If you need any help with him just ask,' called Aidan, patronisingly.

Not bloody likely, thought Emma, opening the garden gate, Rhona and Wilbur close on her heels.

'What was that about?' asked Rhona, as soon as they were safely back indoors.

'Yesterday, at the harbour, he saw me photographing him. I've obviously pissed him off.'

'I shouldn't worry about that,' said Rhona, shooing Wilbur into his bed, which Emma had repositioned in the back corridor the previous evening after letting Wilbur out before bed. 'Tourists take pictures of him repairing the boats all the time. He's like the unofficial poster boy of Lobster Bay.'

'How do you know him?' asked Emma, trying not to show that she could see why he held such a position. There was something annoyingly handsome about him, from his thick, choppy hair, to his unshaven jawline – he wouldn't have looked out of place in a Gillette ad.

'We went to school together.'

'You're friends?'

Rhona scoffed. 'I wouldn't go that far. When you've lived in a small place all your life you develop something that's more akin to distant family than friendship. There's an unspoken camaraderie or shared bond. I don't know what, exactly.'

Emma didn't know either, but she wished that she did. 'I guess I won't be depending on him to nip to the shops for me if ever I'm sick.'

'I don't think anyone depends on Aidan for anything. My advice would be, be polite but keep your distance – he comes with a whole lot of baggage.'

'Sounds like good advice to me,' said Emma, wondering why she felt the tiniest bit disappointed.

'And what are you going to do about Wilbur?'

'I can't keep him,' said Emma, though a small part of her wanted to give it a go if only to stick two fingers up at Aidan. 'I guess it's time I contacted my solicitor, and I think it's also time I went to see Hilda.'

Chapter 6

Having emailed Pamela about the dog, Emma set off with instructions from Rhona on how to find the coastal path which led to the next village along and Hilda's care home. She walked via the main road with its whitewashed cottages and sandstone villas until the houses stopped and the sea came into view.

'This must be the one,' said Emma, following a small brown sign with a symbol of a backpacker on it.

Making her way down a narrow road that meandered its way along the side of the cliffs, Emma marvelled at the beauty of the place. Down to her left lay the picturesque harbour and the golden beach beside it. Small boats trundled in and out, the putt-putt of their engines carrying up to where she stood. Houses clung like limpets to the steep banks, their roofs a brilliant orange in the sunshine, and gulls circled overhead.

She took out her phone, snapped a photo then pinged it to her mum who called immediately.

'Now I really can't wait to come visit,' said Liz. 'It's too beautiful for words.'

'I feel so lucky,' said Emma, tearing herself away from the view and carrying on to where the road stopped, and the footpath began.

'What have you been up to today?'

As Emma negotiated the first section of the path, steep and muddy from the spring rain, she thought about where to begin . . . Wilbur, the locals? Certainly not Aidan.

'I met the housekeeper. She's incredible – tons of energy, knows the house inside out, and she helped me this morning to make a start on the vestibule.'

'That's great, love. I was worried you'd struggle to meet people, what with you having to spend so much time in the house.'

'I've already met some locals and my next-door neighbour too,' she said. *Though the less said about him the better.*

'Well done, Emma. I told Jane you'd make a go of things.'

'Thanks, Mum,' said Emma, though she was never keen to hear that her mother and sister had been talking.

She was always left with the feeling that her mother only ever reported back the good, when she knew full well the two of them would be unpicking every aspect of her life, including the bad.

'And everything else is okay?'

'Everything's fine, Mum,' she replied, keeping the state of the house and the unfriendlier locals to herself. Since her father died, Emma had purposefully held back on how much she told her mother about her life, not because she didn't want her to know what was happening but because she didn't want her to worry. Since her husband's death, Liz struggled with bouts of anxiety and depression, so Emma tried hard not to tell her anything that might cause it to flare up. Her anxiety was part of the reason Emma hadn't told her about the blast, and while Emma knew her mother sensed something had happened, and she felt guilty for not telling her, her desire to protect her always prevented her from doing so.

'Have you been in touch with Chris?'

Emma let out a despairing laugh. 'Mum, Chris and I are finished, there's no reason for me to contact him.'

'I know, but your sister and I were talking and—'

'Mum, enough,' said Emma, recalling the exchange in Jane's kitchen. 'I know you guys think I'm running from Chris but I'm not. I promise.'

'If you say so, it's just—'

'I do say so,' she said, modifying her tone and thinking about how to redirect the conversation. 'Can you believe I've got my first guests in a month?'

'That's exciting.'

Or terrifying when you know just how much work's to be done.

'You need to practise cooking breakfast.'

'I'll add it to my list,' said Emma, deliberating avoiding telling her mother how much she already had to do, and hearing a shout from the background.

'I'd better get on, Em. Gary's calling for his lunch. You know how it is.'

'Sure, Mum,' she said, wishing that her mother had found someone a little more able. For all she liked Gary, she couldn't help feeling he was more of a hindrance than a help. Her mother seemed to spend all her time running after him. After all that she'd been through, Emma wished her mum had found someone who could take better care of her rather than the other way around. 'I've got another call coming through anyway,' said Emma, holding her phone away from her ear to see who was calling. Pamela Brydon flashed on the screen. 'I'll call soon.'

'Hi, Emma,' said Pamela, once Emma had switched calls. 'How are you?'

'Good, bar the dog. You got my email?'

'I did.'

'I went through the missives and didn't see anything. Am I tied to this animal?'

'It wasn't in the missives, Emma, but I'm afraid it was in the list of fixtures and fittings you agreed with the previous owner.'

Emma racked her brain and recalled the document that listed all of the business paraphernalia, but there was no mention of a dog.

'I have the document in front of me,' said Pamela, who was never short of brilliantly efficient. 'Newfoundland dog is listed right at the bottom, just under the collection of ornaments.'

Emma let out a snort. She remembered now, she'd thought it was probably a porcelain dog – it never occurred to her that it might be a real one. 'But that can't be legally binding. I bought the furniture, it's mine to do with what I want, I can get rid of it if I want, surely the same applies to the dog?'

Pamela hummed tightly, a tic Emma had come to realise was Pamela's way of forewarning Emma she was wrong about something. 'Unfortunately, you signed a document stating that you would, and I quote, "care and be responsible for the dog for the rest of its natural life".'

Emma stopped in her tracks. 'How is that possible? There's no way I would have signed that.'

'You signed it electronically, alongside the indemnity insurance. I suspect you scanned through them in a hurry and signed the dog one without realising.'

Emma released a long, despairing sigh and continued towards the care home which she could now see in the distance. 'Is there anything we can do?'

'It's not my area of expertise but I can talk to a colleague. "Care" of an animal could entail rehoming it, if that was in its best interest. I'm not sure if that would still make you "responsible" for it though.'

'Can you ask your colleague what they think? I genuinely can't take care of this animal.'

'Leave it with me, I'll see what I can do.'

'Thanks, Pamela,' said Emma, clicking off her phone and continuing her walk towards Hilda.

*

'Good afternoon,' said Emma, approaching the reception of Seaview.

'Hello, I'm Wendy,' said the welcoming, plump woman in an ill-fitting pink blouse, behind the desk. 'How can I help?'

The blandness of these places never failed to amaze Emma. The home her grandmother had been in was almost an exact replica of this one – blue carpets, beech wood, and pastel patterned fabrics – the only thing that gave this one any identity of its own was a small pinboard behind the desk with photos of a residents' party, complete with paper hats, noise makers and balloons, and a small handmade poster advertising a summer fete.

'I've come to visit Hilda Wyatt.'

'Certainly,' said Wendy. 'Please can you sign in?'

Emma filled in her details on the sheet of paper in the red binder – name, time, person visiting. Scanning the rows above she noticed that Hilda had had one other visitor that day, but Emma couldn't make out the scrawled name.

'I'll take you through.'

Wendy escorted Emma into a large common room which had a scattering of wipeable armchairs and occasional tables. Several residents were sitting snoozing, a group sat round a large television at one end which was blaring out an afternoon antiques programme, while a few read by the large windows that looked out to sea.

'Great view,' said Emma, trying to focus on that rather than the overwhelming smell of ammonia and floor cleaner.

'Hilda is particularly fond of it. She says that even after a lifetime of looking at the sea, each day it looks and feels entirely different.'

'I can believe it,' said Emma, who felt certain she would never tire of looking at it either.

'While you're here,' whispered Wendy conspiratorially, 'could I ask you to twist Hilda's arm into making some of her famous shortbread for the Summer Fete?'

'Hilda,' said Wendy, not giving Emma a chance to say that she probably wasn't the best person to coax Hilda into anything. She placed a hand gently on the rounded shoulder of an elderly woman, her grey hair cropped short.

'What!' started Hilda, who'd clearly been off in a world of her own.

'You've a visitor—'

'Emma Jenkins,' said Emma, when Wendy looked for her name and failed. Emma was going to say she was the new owner of the Lobster Bay Guesthouse but stopped herself, not wanting to make Hilda's home sound like a business acquisition or remind the elderly woman that her home of several decades was no longer her own.

'Oh, you,' said Hilda, as her small eyes, which gleamed a beautiful jade despite the cloudy cataracts, roamed over Emma. She waved Wendy away with her stick. 'I've been expecting you.'

'Have you?'

'Well of course,' barked the woman, her voice surprisingly powerful for someone so small. 'You'd better sit down.'

Emma sat opposite Hilda with a nervousness that took her back to her school days and being dragged up in front of the headmistress. Discreetly, Emma observed Hilda, from the slight dampness around her mouth to her sagging bosom, thin ankles and brand-new purple slippers, which didn't quite match the rest of her muted attire.

'It's the most beautiful view,' said Emma, telling herself not to babble. Instinct told her Hilda wouldn't tolerate a babbler.

'Is it? I hadn't noticed.' Hilda removed a tissue from under the cuff of her aquamarine wool cardigan and blew her nose with a tremendous trumpeting.

Oh really? Emma remembered what Wendy had just told her, and wondered what game Hilda was playing with her and why. *A game of keep Emma on her toes,* she thought.

'Your home is beautiful,' said Emma.

'It's your home, not mine. This is my home now.' Hilda's eyes settled on her small hands clasped on her soft trousers as if the prospect of looking around her new surroundings was too painful.

'I think it will be your home for quite a while before it becomes mine, even if you're not there,' Emma said with a smile.

'Meaning?'

'Meaning your life is everywhere in that house, not just your things but your spirit, too. I really do want to take good care of it, so that it might be my forever home—'

'I never wanted to sell it in the first place.'

Respectfully, Emma refrained from telling Hilda that she knew, that Rhona had told her. Instead she gave her a moment to reflect.

'But I don't suppose that's your fault.'

Again, Emma said nothing.

'I have my daughter to blame for that.' Hilda met Emma's eye, her pain evident to see. 'Despite my best efforts, she still managed to sell it.'

'I really will do my best to look after the place for you,' said Emma, feeling rather sorry for the old woman, and thinking about what her 'best efforts' had entailed.

Hilda let out a derisory puff, giving Emma the distinct impression that she didn't believe her. She thought better of mentioning the note. 'The only thing that matters to me now is that Wilbur is given the best life possible.'

'About Wilbur,' said Emma, twisting her lips as she searched for how best to tell Hilda that one, she had no idea she'd signed up to keeping the dog, and two, she really couldn't care for him.

'Yes?' Hilda's eyes narrowed. 'I trust you're getting on well?'

'Absolutely, no problems whatsoever,' said Emma, astonished by the fear Hilda instilled in her, and her own capacity to lie.

A raised eyebrow from Hilda caused Emma's mouth to turn dry.

Does she know Wilbur escaped? thought Emma.

'We had one little incident but he's fine. He's in good hands,' she confessed, deciding for now to stick with the smaller issues. The bigger issue of what to do with him was a matter for another day, and only when she'd heard back from her solicitor.

'I'm pleased to hear it, because if anything ever happens to him . . .'

Hilda didn't need to finish her sentence; from the steely look she gave Emma there could be no doubt in Emma's mind that the consequences would be dire.

*

In all the months that Emma had been thinking about the house and running the business it had never occurred to her that she would run into hurdles that felt personal. Yes, she had realised that it wouldn't be easy working long days on her own and she knew there would be times when she might feel lonely or homesick, but she hadn't for a moment contemplated conflict with the locals. After her run-in with Aidan and now with Hilda, Emma decided to investigate the loft, where neither neighbour nor former owner could get to her.

'Crikey,' said Emma, her eyes adjusting to the dim light. She pulled herself into a standing position in the centre of the attic, its substantial wooden beams just skimming her head. Above her something scraped and bumped, and her heart beat a little faster at the prospect of rodents, but when she heard the cry of the seagulls she realised it was them scrabbling about on the slates.

Turning slowly, pulling her cardigan closer to stave off a draft, Emma took in the contents of the vast space. Years' worth of discarded furniture was piled along one side. On another side, endless mirrors, paintings and prints. The next wall had a surplus of old duvets, cushions and throws, all neatly packed away in plastic vacuum bags, propped up with rolled carpets and rugs. Emma had a notion that there might be some vintage treasures to be found amongst the junk.

'And what's in these?' she asked herself, going over to the last wall which had countless packing and filing boxes stacked neatly on top of one another.

Her fingers tickled the tops of the lids, creating a trail of prints which stopped when she came to one lying partially open.

'Wow,' she whispered as she removed the top to discover a collection of old pictures.

She picked up the photo on the top of the pile, a four-by-six colour print of a family outside the front of the house. Looking more closely Emma recognised something in the eyes of the mother, which made her certain it was Hilda. She stood in a flouncy floral dress with her arm linked through the arm of a tall man with iron-straight posture who smoked a cigarette. On either side of them stood two teenagers, a girl of around 16 in a batwing sweater and a boy a few years younger in a bright tracksuit, squinting at the sun.

'This must be her family,' muttered Emma, wondering what had become of the menfolk in Hilda's life; there was no trace of them in the rest of the house nor mention of them either. She placed the photo to one side and lifted another smaller one in faded colour of a soldier in uniform and a smiling young woman in a short tunic dress and a Twiggy haircut with two small children at their feet.

Uncertain if this was Hilda and her young family, she picked up another, which was instantly recognisable, of Hilda and Wilbur sitting in the garden of the house. Hilda was positioned on one of the Victorian cast-iron chairs that were still out back, her hand placed on the back of the dog's head. Wilbur appeared to be gazing at her adoringly with an expression which Hilda seemed to return.

Looking at the picture Emma was struck with a huge feeling of guilt. Since Hilda moved out last month the dog had been left alone, only seeing Rhona twice a day for food, exercise and affection. It was clear from his expression in the picture that no one could replace his mistress.

It's not fair for me to keep him, even if that is what Hilda wants, thought Emma, placing the photo in her pocket. *There's no way I can give him the attention he needs.*

Despite herself, Emma felt she should try to extend a little kindness towards the dog, even if it was only until the lawyers got back to her and she found him a new forever home.

Chapter 7

Emma woke purposely early the next morning to take Wilbur for a walk before anyone else would be up and at it. The fewer people out and about, the fewer doggy distractions, she reasoned.

'How does this work?' she asked Wilbur, reaching for his harness, which hung in the cupboard in the back passage.

Wilbur spun in circles as Emma tried to figure out what went where.

'Hold still,' she said, trying to slip the U-shaped portion of the contraption over his head, eventually managing to lasso him.

'And I guess this goes under here . . .' she said, grimacing as she reached under the dog, his wagging tail causing his entire body to move.

'No pulling, okay?' said Emma, trying to assert herself, as she secured the harness with a click and then clipped the lead onto the hoop of the back plate. 'Any pulling and we come straight back, understood?' She raised her eyebrows and fixed her eyes on him. Wilbur looked away. 'Fine. Let's go.'

Emma stepped out into the morning sunlight and let out a contented sigh. A good night's sleep had put an end to her concerns about Hilda and Aidan, today was a new day and she intended to make the most of it.

'Which way?' she asked, and Wilbur led her down the wide road, strolling easily at her side, only stopping occasionally to sniff the base of a tree.

'Well, this is nice,' said Emma, feeling a little silly for having been anxious about taking him out. *Maybe he is the gentle giant Rhona said he was.*

But just as Emma was thinking how they might end up getting along after all, Wilbur dug his paws into the ground and starting barking. It was the loudest bark Emma had ever heard.

'Stop it!' She looked around fully expecting people to pull back their curtains, open their windows and shout at her to silence her dog.

Wilbur kept barking.

'Wilbur, enough!' she said, yanking his lead to see if a short, sharp jolt might quiet him. It had the opposite effect.

Without warning, Wilbur pulled with all his might and he, with Emma after him, bolted down the pavement towards a large crow. Coming within a few feet of it, Wilbur lowered his head and began barking faster and louder.

Emma pulled and pulled but the dog would not budge.

'Wilbur!' she shouted, but it was no use: until the crow flew off she knew there was nothing she could do.

In the distance Emma noticed a woman in a grey skirt suit round the corner on the same side of the road.

'Wilbur, please,' she pleaded, hoping he would give up before the woman reached them. He didn't.

The woman crossed the road to the other side. Emma offered a friendly 'Morning' and an apologetic look, both of which were ignored by the woman who continued quickly, turning up the street towards the shops.

'I don't blame her,' said Emma, feeling her cheeks begin to flush. 'I'd have crossed the road to avoid us too.'

The crow suddenly took flight and Wilbur, with the agility of a much younger dog, bounded after it, taking Emma with him. Eventually the bird flew out of sight and Wilbur settled, but not before Emma had lost her patience and her confidence.

'Home,' she ordered, changing direction and walking back towards the house.

The two of them were nearing home when a car pulled in and Emma spotted Jennifer getting out.

'You start early,' said Emma, keeping Wilbur a safe distance away. The last thing she wanted was Wilbur to jump up on Jennifer and cover her smart dress in gigantic paw prints.

'I could say the same of you,' said Jennifer, coming over to stroke Wilbur's head.

'Careful. Slobber.'

Jennifer bent down and tussled Wilbur's jowls. 'A little slobber never killed anyone.'

'Are you sure?' said Emma, with a dubious laugh.

'You'll get used to it.'

Emma wasn't so sure.

'How was your first night?' asked Jennifer.

'Good, thanks. I found lots of old treasures in the loft, including some pictures of Hilda and her family.'

'Oh, that reminds me, I found some documents in the archives, some photos and floor plans of the house. It's not much but you never know, something else might turn up in time. I'll drop them in later if you like.'

'I'd love that, thanks, Jennifer.'

Having said goodbye, Emma and Wilbur had just reached the house when Wilbur started pulling towards Aidan's place. As Wilbur pulled, Emma observed the state of his house. The black front door was peeling, the paint on the windows was almost bare, the hedge was overgrown, and the gravel was littered with bits of machinery.

'We're not going in there if that's what you're hoping,' said Emma, who could think of nothing worse than having to be polite to Aidan first thing in the morning – until she noticed what Wilbur was doing.

'You're kidding me,' she said, clocking the dog positioning himself in a way that only meant one thing. That's when Emma realised not only would she have to pick up the poo but that she'd come out without a poo bag.

'Bloody brilliant,' she muttered, trying not to be unnerved by the dog, who fixed his eyes on Emma as he went about his business. 'Are you done?'

Wilbur stood up and was rounding back on himself to inspect his poop when Aidan's front door opened.

'Crap,' said Emma. She attempted to pull Wilbur away before Aidan spotted them but, as she tried, Wilbur clocked Aidan and yanked the lead out of Emma's hand, bounding straight towards him. Emma closed her eyes and exhaled slowly. 'Not again.'

'Hiya, big guy,' said Aidan, immediately fussing Wilbur. 'What you doing out here?'

'We were out for a walk,' said Emma with a terse smile.

'Oh yeah,' said Aidan, patronisingly. 'Who was walking who?'

Emma smirked in contempt, wanting to tell him to *blow it out his arse* but instead she bit her tongue.

Aidan crouched down to fuss Wilbur some more, whose tail beat against Aidan's leg, which, Emma noticed, looked particularly muscular in the work trousers he was wearing.

'You're a good boy. A good, good boy,' he said, before turning his attention to Emma who quickly removed her gaze from his thighs.

'Looks like you've got a lot of shit to shovel,' he said, glancing at the poo as he handed Wilbur's lead to her.

Emma narrowed her eyes and ground her teeth. She had a good mind to scoop it up and throw it into his garden. *Not that he'd likely notice, the dirty fecker,* she thought.

'Have a good day!' he called, getting into his van before racing off with a spin of his wheels.

*

'There, not bad, if I do say so myself' said Emma to herself, standing back to admire her handiwork. She'd spent the last hour plucking all of Wilbur's hair that had stuck to the tacky paint of the front door, and freshened it up with another coat.

'Good to know I'm not the only one who talks to myself,' said a voice.

Emma turned with a jump to see Judy standing at the garden gate.

'Hello,' said Emma, trying to brush a hair off her face while avoiding splattering herself with paint from the brush she still held in her hand.

'Lovely to see you've got rid of the brown. My kids used to refer to it as "jobby brown" when they were little!'

Emma let out a laugh, not so much at the kids' accurate name for the colour, more at hearing Judy, so proper, using the word 'jobby'!

'It was definitely in need of an update,' said Emma.

'Much like the rest of the house.'

'It certainly has a lot of character,' Emma said, hoping to be diplomatic.

'Much like the previous owner.'

'That I can't argue with.' Emma put down her brush on an old rag and joined Judy at the gate.

'You've met her then?'

'I popped over yesterday.'

'How did you get on?'

Emma bobbed her head from side to side thinking of how best to describe the encounter. 'I can't pretend it was easy.'

'Let me guess, she was belligerent, scornful and intimidating.'

'Well,' said Emma with a small laugh, amazed by Judy's accurate appraisal of their meeting, 'I might not put it quite like that—'

'Because you're far too polite and good-natured but I assure you, after a lifetime with my mother, I know *exactly* how she behaves.'

'No harm done. I'm sure it wasn't easy for her meeting me, I *have* taken over her home,' said Emma, but at the back of her mind was still the issue of Wilbur, especially after this morning's antics, and how she would ever get around Hilda's wishes.

'The sooner she comes to accept she can't manage the place any more the better,' said Judy, though a softness in her eyes belied her harsh words. 'And I'm led to believe that my mother thinks you're simply here to do the place up and sell it on.'

'She did give the impression that she didn't fully trust me, though I've no idea why.'

Judy let out a sardonic laugh. 'You'll learn soon enough that in Lobster Bay rumours spread like wildfire, whether they're based in truth or not.'

Emma nodded diligently, taking Judy's statement with a pinch of salt.

'Time will sort that,' said Judy, not unkindly, glancing at her watch. 'Well, I can't stop, I'd better be off.'

Waving Judy goodbye, Emma picked up her painting things and took them to the back of the house, wondering how she might ever gain Hilda's trust and make her intentions clear. *Maybe time will take care of that too*, she mused absently, wishing there was a quicker way.

In the back passage Emma found Wilbur lying in his bed, no doubt sulking after being route-marched home prematurely from his morning walk. He looked up at Emma with mournful eyes and released a canine sigh.

'You don't like your new room?' asked Emma unsympathetically, who couldn't imagine that dogs had much interest in where they slept so long as their basic needs were met – warmth, water, food.

Wilbur followed Emma's every move, from replacing the paint pot on the shelf to sloshing the dirty paint brush around in white spirit.

'Listen, dog,' she said, drying her hands on some blue roll and looking down at Wilbur. 'If something's not right you have to figure out how to show me.'

At that Wilbur got up, used his head to open the door to the laundry room and pushed his way through.

'Hey!' shouted Emma, who was determined the dog should remain in the back of the house and the garden, particularly after his walk shenanigans. No way was she having dog-stink, hair, drool and dirt all over her brand-new guest house, and definitely not on freshly laundered guest towels.

Emma stared incredulously as Wilbur looked into the back corridor, cocking his head between Emma and his bed.

'Not on your nelly, mate!' she said and then, as if the animal had understood and was purposefully defying her, it took a corner of the bed in its mouth and started dragging it through the doorway and into the laundry room.

'You're having a laugh,' muttered Emma, watching Wilbur nudge his bed up against the warmth of the hot water pipes then position himself purposefully onto the mattress. The job complete, he looked up at Emma defiantly before placing his head on his paws and sighing heavily once more.

Emma signed too. Despite all that she found revolting about the animal, she couldn't help but sense it was miserable. Whether he was pining for Hilda or just affection in general she had no idea, but Emma felt a tiny twinge of responsibility.

'Here, have a bone,' she said, returning from the cupboard in the back corridor where she'd gingerly unwrapped the cellophane wrapping. She handled it by the tips of her thumb and index finger, as if it were contaminated, and plopped it down in front of him.

'Well, go on then.' Emma watched the dog over her shoulder as she scrubbed her hands clean at the laundry room sink. The dog sniffed at it disinterestedly and left it lying an inch from his nose.

'I'm not buying you steak as a treat, if that's what you're after,' she said looking down at him, her hands on her hips.

Wilbur looked up at Emma then down, then curled his head into a hind leg.

'Suit yourself,' she said, taking her ringing phone out of her pocket, the screen flashing *Pamela Brydon*.

'Hi, Pamela, how are you?'

'I have good news.'

'You do?'

Wilbur raised his brow, his deep brown eyes fixed on Emma. Feeling a smidge guilty she crept into the kitchen.

'My colleague believes that rehoming falls into "care and responsibility" of the animal.'

'Well, that's great,' said Emma, looking over to where Wilbur lay, wondering why she had a nagging sense of doubt in her stomach.

'As far as we're concerned, you're free to search for a new home for the dog. Good luck!'

Emma clicked off her phone and crouched down next to Wilbur, who avoided her eye.

'So, that's it decided. We can find you a new home with someone who'll give you lots of attention and exercise and treats and, who knows, they might even let you sleep in their bed. How does that sound?'

Wilbur buried his snout deeper into his hind legs and closed his eyes.

'It's for the best, I promise,' she said, giving him a tentative ruffle on his neck and wishing the niggle of doubt that still tugged in her stomach would disappear.

Chapter 8

How am I going to rehome Wilbur without Hilda knowing? Emma thought to herself, on her way to buy meat for the practice breakfast she was planning on trying that afternoon. *Hilda will kill me if she finds out, and something tells me life wouldn't be worth living in Lobster Bay on the wrong side of Hilda Wyatt*, she thought, though she had no real idea of how Hilda's wrath might manifest itself given she was safely ensconced at Seaview.

Passing the butcher-shop window Emma's eye was caught by a smattering of handwritten adverts in the window: *Cleaner needed for holiday cottage. Cat sitter required. Mother's help needed ASAP.* It occurred to Emma that this might be as good as any a place to start looking for a new owner for Wilbur, even if it was on full public view, meaning there was a chance that Hilda might be told about it.

'Hi, Emma,' said Phil, beaming as she entered. 'How are you getting on?'

'Not bad, thanks. I thought I might try a trial breakfast – see how I get on doing cooked breakfasts en masse.'

'Good idea. It's difficult getting all those items perfectly cooked at the same time.'

'Right,' said Emma, worrying that she hadn't given it enough thought. Chris had always been the one to cook the Sunday fry-ups, boring Emma with which bacon was best, which sausage the tastiest, and the benefit of adding thyme to the mushrooms. Now Emma regretted not listening. She wished she'd paid a bit less attention to her weekend papers, and a little more attention to Chris.

'And everyone knows breakfast is the thing that makes or breaks a guesthouse.'

'Do you think?'

For Emma a good guesthouse had to have the correct weight of duvets and high thread count in the linen, quality biscuits, fine tea and a choice of water in glass bottles in the bedrooms, plus a generous sitting room with tasteful decor and an elegant outlook. As far as she was concerned the breakfast was of least importance – she'd be perfectly happy with a continental breakfast rather than a cooked one.

'Round here guesthouses are 10 a penny. The ones that do well are the ones that provide the best scran in the morning, especially if you want to attract the younger market – you gotta have a full belly before hitting the waves.'

'Then I'd better get practising,' said Emma, mentally adding *cookery course* to her never-ending to do list.

'Anything else for you today?' asked Phil once he'd taken Emma's order and bagged it up.

'Would it be possible to place an ad in your window?'

'Sure thing,' said Phil enthusiastically. He removed the pen from behind his ear and took out a small piece of card, poised to write. Emma found herself wondering if there was anything you could ask of this man that would curb his enthusiasm. 'What would you like it to say?'

Emma thought for a moment, thinking how best to word it.

'New owner sought for Newfoundland dog.'

'Ah,' said Phil, stepping away from the note. 'So, the rumour's true?'

'What rumour?'

'That Hilda left Wilbur for you.'

'If the rumour is that she included him in the sale without me knowing then, yes, the rumour is true but, as it happens, I'm free to rehome him,' she said, her stomach tightening again.

Phil scratched the back of his head. 'Have you owned a dog before?'

'Never, hence why I'd like to rehome him.'

He let out a little whistle. 'He's no small undertaking.'

'No,' said Emma, wondering if he'd heard what she'd said. 'And I've my hands full enough what with my first guests arriving in a month and an entire house to do up before then, so—'

'It's just . . .' Phil's forehead creased in thought.

'What?'

'I've known that dog a long time, and with all the change it might be that what he needs is to stay where he feels safe. A new owner *and* a new home might not be good for the dog.'

There was something about Phil's kind, easy manner that stopped Emma from telling him that she had little interest in a dog she'd been lumbered with who moped about the place, had no discipline, didn't know his own strength, slobbered, smelt, and, not least, dumped a load of poop twice a day so large it required a small shovel and carrier bag to dispose of it.

'I can't manage him on my own. *He* took *me* for a walk this morning. I couldn't live with myself if he barrelled someone over and injured them.'

Phil thought before he spoke. 'How about, instead of you putting the ad in the window, I take you and Wilbur out – give you the confidence to see that you can manage him on your own?'

Emma looked heavenward and let out a little laugh. There was something about Phil, his boundless optimism and enthusiasm, that was impossible to say no to and, despite all Wilbur's bad points she wasn't completely oblivious to his large teddy bear appeal. *Besides*, she thought, *perhaps a notice in the window wasn't the best idea. Hilda would be bound to find out eventually and goodness knows how she'd react.*

'Shall we say tomorrow?' asked Phil, his eyes twinkling with delight.

'Why not,' said Emma, mystified by how Phil had managed to change her mind so easily.

*

'Not placing the rehoming advert was not my decision,' Emma said to Wilbur sternly, while turning on the oven. 'You've got Phil the butcher to thank, not me.'

Wilbur, who Emma had allowed into the kitchen, looked up with what she thought was newfound interest in her, until she realised that his curiosity was solely in the large bag of breakfast goods she'd deposited on the kitchen work surface.

'No way – José,' she said, pushing the meat further back so that Wilbur couldn't reach it. She grimaced at the white, bubbly saliva that formed in the corners of his mouth.

The previous evening Emma had spent a little time before bed researching how best to cook the perfect fry-up. Having seen that 'preparation is key', something she remembered Chris used to say too, she gathered all of her ingredients and laid them out on the counter.

'Sausages, bacon, black pudding, egg, tomatoes, mushrooms, bread,' she said, counting that she had all seven ingredients ready.

'Cook the sausages for 15 to 20 minutes,' she said, reading the instructions she had written the night before. Carefully, she positioned them on a tray and placed them in the oven, setting the timer accordingly. She then ran her finger over point two of her notes.

'Snip the bacon fat and grill for two to four minutes each side.'

Emma did as instructed and slid the tray under the grill.

'What's so hard about this?' she asked, opening the window. Wilbur hunkered down on the other side of the kitchen keeping an eye on proceedings. 'Prep the mushrooms and cook for four to six minutes.' Emma brushed, trimmed and seasoned before drizzling them with olive oil and adding them to the grill pan.

'Then cut the tomatoes, season and drizzle. Cook for four to five minutes, turn once. Lastly, remove the skin from the black pudding and grill for two minutes each side.

'All seems straightforward enough,' she said, turning the mushrooms. The scent of the sausages in the oven began to fill the room and Wilbur got up, pining and barking in excitement. His bark, loud and low, reverberated around the room and out the window to the garden.

With everything underway Emma reached for a frying pan from the bottom cupboard, turned on the gas and covered the base with oil. 'Cook bread for two to three minutes each side. Add a knob of butter for a richer flavour.'

That done Emma turned the bacon and black pudding and finally added an egg to the frying pan, which hissed and spat at her. Wilbur continued to bark.

'Wilbur!' she reprimanded, but to no avail. 'I'll tell Phil to put the advert in the window if you don't put a sock in it.' The more she talked the louder the barking became.

'There, job done,' she said, taking a plate, which she'd remembered to place in the warmer. 'That wasn't so hard.'

Sensing food was almost ready, Wilbur sat on his haunches, strings of saliva hanging from his mouth, his eyes squarely on the cooker.

'Delightful.' The sight of his saliva was enough to put her off her food.

It was only when Emma began plating the ingredients that she realised: her sausages were charred; her bacon wasn't crispy; the mushrooms were wet and tomatoes still hard; the bread and black pudding were burnt; the only thing that was remotely edible was the egg, but even that had a split yoke and the white was speckled with dirt from the pan.

'Hmm,' said Emma, picking at the food then pushing it away. 'Looks like it's back to the drawing board.'

Emma was making amendments to her notes when the doorbell rang. Opening the door she was startled to discover Aidan, standing moodily in the vestibule.

'Hi,' she said, suddenly aware of how flustered and pink she felt after the heat of the kitchen, and of how Aidan looked the epitome of masculine composure.

'I heard Wilbur barking, everything alright?'

'Absolutely,' she replied, surprised that he should care. 'I was practising cooking breakfast – I think the smells got him a bit excited.'

'How did it go?'

'Couldn't have been better,' she said, hoping he wouldn't detect the lie, or the smell of charred sausage from the kitchen.

'Are you sure?'

'Why wouldn't I be?' she said irritably.

He indicated to something behind her.

'What?' she asked, curtly. She turned grudgingly to be met with the sight of Wilbur parading through the hall, most of a full Scottish breakfast in his mouth, which he deposited at Aidan's steel-capped boots.

They both looked at the chewed breakfast on the floor.

'If the dog won't eat it, I'm not sure the guests will,' said Aidan, with a smug smile and a wink.

'They bloody well will,' said Emma, slamming the door, annoyed that Aidan had got the better of her again, and mad as hell that she found him infuriatingly good-looking.

Chapter 9

'The place looks amazing,' said Rhona, plumping a cushion and placing it on the sleigh bed in the largest bedroom in the house.

'Even I didn't imagine it would turn out this good,' said Emma, smoothing out the bedspread, embroidered with rosehips, and admiring the freshly painted rich cream walls. 'Have we really done all of this in the space of a month?'

'It's amazing what can be done when you set your mind to it.'

'And when there's help from someone like you,' said Emma, who couldn't be more grateful for the extra hours Rhona had put in, even if it did mean eating into her savings. Between them they'd decorated three bedrooms, the hall, dining room and guest sitting room.

'It's been my pleasure,' said Rhona, tidying the natural linen drapes so that they hung evenly. The early summer sun was bursting through the glass, showing off Rhona's perfectly cleaned windows, and the sea beyond was mirror-glaze still.

'Have we remembered to put soap in all the bathrooms?' asked Emma, whose stomach had been doing somersaults all morning at the prospect of her first guests arriving later that day.

'All done.'

The two of them had spent hours poring over locally sourced soap samples, everything from rose to sandalwood. In the end they'd opted for sea kelp which they both felt was gender-neutral and invigorating.

'And teas and biscuits?'

'Fully stocked.'

Individually wrapped biscuits no longer seemed like such a treat to Emma, not now that she had had to try pretty much every variety out there, considering not only its packaging and flavour but also its price. There was nothing like a trip to the cash and carry to put you off biscuits for life.

'Loo roll?'

'One on the holder and a spare.'

Emma nibbled her lip. 'Anything else I might have forgotten?'

'I doubt it,' said Rhona. 'I've never met anyone with such an eye for detail.'

'Time will tell,' said Emma, taking one last look around the elegant room, hoping everything was perfect for her guests' arrival, and heading out to the hall.

The hallway had taken far longer than Emma had imagined. Under the woodchip wallpaper Emma had discovered ageing plaster that was crumbly and pockmarked and not in any condition for painting. In the end she had had to call a plasterer to skim the entire hall, a job that had cost her far more than she had budgeted for. But Emma knew the hall was one of the first things that her guests would see, so it was important to make it as impressive as possible.

And impressive it is, thought Emma, running her hand down the polished handrail and admiring the seagrass runner, and the set of pictures of coastal fauna framed in black against the brilliant white of the walls. It was clean, crisp and elegant, more than Emma had imagined was possible when she'd first set eyes on the place, and it smelt good too, the smell of dog replaced by just a hint of jasmine.

"Are the table runners ironed?" called Rhona, from the dining room, which was unrecognisable. The large room at the front of the house which had felt oppressive was now airy and fresh while still retaining a grandeur befitting the house. Gone were the patterned carpets and curtains, and instead there were elegant runner blinds and sanded boards.

'All done,' answered Emma, who'd spent the night before ironing linen in front of the telly. She fetched the basket of runners from the laundry room and placed one on each of the tables, admiring the warmth and grain of the old wood, which had come up so beautifully after being sanded. The mess from the sawdust had made Emma cry at one point but now, seeing how fantastic they looked, she figured it had been worth the tears.

'These chairs turned out really well in the end,' said Rhona, positioning the teal-painted chairs with millimetre precision then plumping their coastal-striped cushions.

'You did a lovely job on them,' said Emma, turning the *No Vacancies* sign to *Vacancies*, and recalling how patient Rhona had been painting 10 chairs even if she hadn't been convinced that teal-painted chairs were the way to go.

'I'll get us a drink.'

'Good idea,' said Emma, squaring up an old picture of the house. Jennifer had dropped off the photos she'd found in the museum and Emma had had great fun in having them resized and mounted in matching frames. Her favourite was a photo taken outside the house that showed children in long dresses and frilly aprons playing with an iron hoop and a passing milk cart pulled by horses. She loved the idea that her guests would admire the photos at breakfast and maybe chat to one another about the history of the place. Jennifer hadn't been able to find out much, but she knew it was built almost 150 years ago and had been a hotel or guesthouse since at least the 1920s. One of the items, now framed on the wall, was an advert from a newspaper dated 1923, advertising 'afternoon tea' at the local 'hostelry'.

The dining room complete, Emma wandered through to the living room, thinking about how she might reinstate afternoon tea to welcome her guests on arrival, and slumped down on the newly upholstered sofas. Even after a decade of working as an interior designer it still amazed Emma what a lick of paint, a sanded floor and some new upholstering could do for a room. Emma stared up at the mantelpiece and the picture of Wilbur and Hilda in the garden. She'd been so busy over the last month that the rehoming of Wilbur had taken a back seat. The two of them had settled into a routine of mostly ignoring each other, like two flatmates who had no real issue with one another and no real interest in each other either but who somehow managed to successfully inhabit the same space with only the odd irritation and the occasional moment of unexpected enjoyment too.

'How are you feeling?' asked Rhona, returning with tea.

'Nervous.'

'If Hilda could run this place successfully then you can do it standing on your head, I promise.'

'Thanks, Rhona,' said Emma, taking her tea. 'I worry that people won't like me, or the house, or my cooking!' Since the disastrous trial breakfast Emma had had little opportunity to practise and while she was fairly confident that people would like the house, she had a lot less faith in her cooking.

'I'll be here to help,' said Rhona, taking a seat on an armchair rather than her usual spot on the fireside fender. It occurred to Emma that for once Rhona looked a little tired.

'Have I been working you too hard?' she asked.

'No!' Rhona protested. 'What made you say that?'

'I've never seen you sit on an actual chair before.'

Rhona laughed. 'Ella was up all night with bad dreams, none of us slept that well.'

'Was she okay this morning?'

'She's fine. It's just me that's knackered.'

'I'll bet.' Emma had no idea where Rhona got her stamina from. Not only had she been helping out Emma six hours a day, she'd also been full-time single mum to her four kids, all with conflicting needs and schedules. It wore Emma out just watching her do everything.

'Mum's helping out with the kids this afternoon, so I'll be fine.'

Over the last month Emma had learnt all about Rhona's mum and all she did for Rhona. The way Rhona spoke about her, it sounded to Emma as if they were more like best friends than mother and daughter; though Emma didn't like the feeling, a small piece of her felt a little envious about their relationship.

'You know you can take time off if you need to. I'll get by here by myself.'

'Are you joking?' said Rhona, with a laugh. 'You've got three rooms booked in tonight and it's like that for most of the month. You can't manage on your own.'

'Sure, I can.'

'Emma, trust me,' said Rhona, her tone much more serious. 'It's more work than you think.'

*

The sound of the doorbell just after four o'clock caused Emma to almost jump out of her skin.

'You'll be fine,' said Rhona, who'd stayed a little longer to offer moral support.

'Then why do I feel like I might throw up?' said Emma as she walked to the front door.

'The house is beautiful, you're fantastic, there's nothing to worry about,' called Rhona.

'Here goes nothing,' said Emma, who opened the front door to find a couple in their twenties standing in the vestibule clutching their holdalls.

'Hi,' said Emma brightly, registering that they looked more nervous than she did. 'Are you Mel and Neil?'

'We are,' answered Mel. 'Are we too early?'

'Not at all. Come in!'

Emma immediately felt her nausea subside as she welcomed the pair into the hallway.

'Your home is amazing,' said Mel, gazing up at the chandelier.

'Thank you,' said Emma, who could have hugged Mel. For the first time since moving in she felt a sense of ownership for the old place and that gave her a sense of calm and pride. 'Let me take you up to your room.'

As Emma was climbing the stairs the doorbell rang again. She stalled for a moment, figuring out what to do: leave a guest waiting outside or delay showing Mel and Neil to their room?

'I'll get it,' called Rhona, appearing in the hallway.

'Thank you,' sang Emma. She continued upstairs, enquiring after Neil and Mel's journey while keeping one ear on Rhona and the other arrival too, a man named Finn McCarthy who had travelled in from Ireland but was only staying one night.

'This is your room.' Emma opened the door of the smaller double on the middle floor, aware of Rhona and Finn laughing as they came up the stairs.

'Oh Neil,' said Mel, sitting on the Egyptian cotton bedding and stroking a sheepskin cushion. 'Isn't it gorgeous?'

'Sure is,' said Neil, admiringly.

'Thank you,' said Emma, who was thrilled with how the bedroom had turned out. A room that had previously been stark and cold was now full of texture, warmth and light. It was the perfect romantic retreat.

'These are your keys.' Emma showed them the key for the front door and the one for their room. 'And your WIFI code and breakfast times are in the little frame by the snack tray. If you need anything then please just let me know.'

'Thank you, we will,' said Mel, who Emma heard squeal in delight after she'd closed the door.

'You look like the world's been lifted off your shoulders,' said Rhona, once she'd closed the door of the room at the opposite side of the landing.

'I feel that way,' said Emma, who thought she might cry in relief. 'What's the other guest like?'

Rhona's eyes widened mischievously.

'Rhona?' asked Emma, her eyes widening too.

'Let's just say Finn was a pleasant surprise,' she whispered, heading downstairs.

'A pleasant surprise?'

'Very easy on the eye, an accent to die for, *and* he's a golf course designer.'

'He sounds yummy,' said Emma, delighted that some-one had caught Rhona's attention.

'No doubt he has someone back home in Ireland – no one that fine could be single,' said Rhona, going through to fetch her coat with even more of a spring in her step than usual. 'Can I leave you to manage the other arrival on your own?'

'I've got it covered.'

'Good, then I'll see you in the morning, bright and early.'

'And Finn too!' said Emma, with a wink and a smile.

*

'What are they like, love?' asked Liz, later that evening.

'Everyone's really nice, Mum. There's a young couple, and a single guy. I'm just waiting for the final pair; I've got a feeling they're not going to show,' said Emma, whose earlier sense of calm had been replaced by another bout of anxiety.

'They'll turn up, love,' said Liz, as Emma paced the kitchen floor, watching the clock on the cooker tick by.

'Check-in is between four and seven, it's already almost eight.'

'They've been delayed, love . . . where are they coming from?'

'Australia.'

'Well, there you go. You can't expect people to travel from the other side of the planet and arrive at an allotted time.'

'You're right, I know you're right,' said Emma, chewing the inside of her cheek. The fact that her mother was right did nothing to settle her stomach. 'Tell me something about your day.'

'Gary's not been keeping well so I've been running after him. Not much time to do anything else really.'

'What's the matter?' she asked, wanting to add 'this time' but stopping herself. Emma didn't like to say, but given the amount of time Gary was laid low, she couldn't help wonder if most of his ailments were purely psychosomatic.

'Just general aches and pains, fatigue, you know . . .'

'You should give him one of Jane's "cure all" smoothies,' said Emma, thinking about the hideous-looking concoctions Jane forced her children to drink, and which Emma went out of her way to avoid whenever she was staying.

'You should put those on your breakfast menu,' said Liz, with a laugh.

Emma laughed too. 'If ever I'm looking for ways to get rid of guests that's exactly what I'll do!'

Just then the doorbell rang causing Emma's heart to leap into her mouth and Wilbur to start barking in the laundry.

'Good luck, love!'

'I'll need it,' said Emma, walking to the front door, wondering if she'd ever be able to open the door again without feeling sick.

Emma opened the door, slightly surprised to discover two stout 60-something women in anoraks, backpacks and walking boots.

'G'day, you Emma?' asked the slightly younger looking of the two. Her dark hair was cropped short and she sported at least eight metal studs round the top of her ear.

'I am,' said Emma, feeling a little formal and prim. 'You must be Judith and Robyn.'

'That's right. I'm Judith, and this is Robyn.'

Judith indicated behind her to where Robyn stood folding a map.

'Please, come in,' said Emma, hoping their boots were clean and reminding herself to order a heavy-duty mat for the entrance. 'Did you find the house okay?'

'Robyn took us round the block a couple of times, didn't you, love?'

'Sure did,' said Robyn, neither one of them seemingly bothered by their detour.

'Let me show you to your room.'

Emma led the two women upstairs to their room, hoping they weren't aware of Wilbur, who was still barking at the back of the house.

'This is fancy!' said Judith, gawping as she entered the room.

Emma released a giggle and relaxed once more, consoled by the thought that it wouldn't be long until showing strangers into her home would be second nature. 'I'm glad you like it,' she said, going on to tell them about keys, WIFI and breakfast.

'No worries, thanks then,' said Judith, who was sitting on the bed, kicking off her walking boots. Emma made a mental note to provide boot trays.

'I'll see you in the morning,' said Emma, who felt ready to collapse into bed.

Emma sat bolt upright in bed, a penetrating alarm shattering her sleep. She covered her ears to block out the noise and felt the heavy thud of her heartbeat banging against her ribcage. A bead of sweat tricked down her forehead, and an image of Dawn's bloodied hand in hers leapt into her mind, and then the recurring feeling of guilt, wishing she could have done more.

'What's going on,' she said, her voice croaky and tight, trying desperately to push the vision away.

Scrambling out of bed she reached for her robe and mobile phone. She opened the bedroom door and was immediately hit by the stench of acrid smoke which threw her straight back to Christmas Eve, and the feeling of her nostrils and lungs stinging as everything around her burned.

Unable to see, Emma turned on the lights to the stairwell and fled down the stairs to the middle floor where she banged on the doors of her guests, shouting, 'Fire! Wake up! Fire!'

'You right?' asked Judith, opening her door in a pair of boxer shorts and T-shirt. She scratched her bed hair which stood on end and rubbed her bleary eyes. Other than the fire alarm sounding in the hall, no other evidence of the fire had reached the first floor.

'There's a fire upstairs,' said Emma, dialling 999 as she spoke. 'We need to get out.'

'Right-o,' said Judith sleepily, calling on Robyn to wake up.

As Emma banged on the other two doors, she spoke to the emergency operator.

'A crew is on their way to you. Can you contain the fire?'

'I don't know,' said Emma, feeling scared and alone.

'Make sure all doors are closed, but only if you can reach them safely, and then leave the building.'

Having given instructions to Mel and Neil, who were scantily dressed and wearing bashful expressions, and to Finn, looking sleepy in pyjama bottoms and a sloppy sweater, Emma darted upstairs to close all of the doors then tore downstairs to her guests, now congregated outside on the pavement.

'Is everyone out?' asked Finn, calm as you like. His kind eyes, behind his tortoiseshell glasses, were fixed on Emma's.

Emma did a head count. 'Six in total. Everyone's out.'

'What about the dog, love?' asked Judith, who'd managed to put on a pair of sweatpants and a hoodie.

'Shit,' said Emma, thankful that Judith and Robyn had heard Wilbur after all. She knew there was nothing for it but to go back into the house to get him out of the laundry room.

Running as fast as she could, Emma ran inside, the sound of the alarm still whomping round the house causing the sounds from Christmas Eve – sirens, screams and unanswered phones – to bombard her head.

Opening the laundry room door she found Wilbur cowering in the corner, trembling from the noise that bounced off the walls of the small space.

'Come on, boy,' she said, as gently as the situation would enable. She attached his lead to his collar and tried dragging him to his feet. 'Come on,' she said again, this time more forcibly. When he wasn't forthcoming, Emma pulled and strained and coaxed, but in the end, it was clear that she had no way of moving a 10-stone dog that didn't want to be moved.

Remembering the emergency operator's advice, she closed the door and left him, hoping he'd be fine until the fire crew arrived.

Heading back outside, Emma found Aidan outside the gate talking to Finn. She smiled weakly at him, somewhat comforted by a familiar, if not friendly, face.

'Are you okay?' he asked, his eyes soft with concern, which caught Emma off guard.

'I can't get Wilbur out,' she said, wrapping her arms around herself to stave off the cold night air, not in any mood to find a retort to whatever barbed remark he no doubt had lined up for her.

Aidan pulled off his sweater, exposing a six-pack, and handed it to Emma, who diverted her eyes from his stomach.

'Where is he?'

'The laundry room,' she answered, putting on the sweater, which was warm from Aidan's body and smelt salty and fresh.

'I'll get him.'

Before Emma could protest, Aidan shot into the house.

'Nice to have good neighbours,' said Judith, putting a supportive arm around Emma.

'Yes,' said Emma, who said nothing of how unneighbourly their relationship had been over the last month. Their relationship amounted to the odd nod, grunt and snide comment from Aidan, and Emma overhearing heated discussions through the walls. Other than that, they'd barely spoken.

It felt to Emma as if a whole hour passed rather than the minute it took for Aidan to return, carrying Wilbur with one arm flexed under his chest and another under his hind legs. Wilbur made no attempt to struggle.

'Holy Dooley, that's a big dog,' said Judith, slapping Aidan on the back and applauding his efforts, Finn and the others joining her.

'Couldn't leave the big guy in there, could we, boy?' said Aidan, setting Wilbur down and keeping a reassuring hand against him.

'Thanks, Aidan,' said Emma, meeting his eyes. She held his gaze for a moment then looked away, struggling to understand why she felt so much emotion over a dog and a man she cared nothing about.

Chapter 10

'Geez, Emma,' said Rhona, the two of them standing across the street looking up at the roof.

'It could have been a lot worse,' said Emma, thankful that the fire brigade had arrived when they had and worked so quickly to get the fire under control. In the end the damage had been limited to one corner of the loft and the ceiling below in a top-floor bedroom, which Emma had been using as a furniture store. 'At least the guest rooms weren't damaged.'

'Still, it's a hell of a repair job.'

'I'm more concerned about how to get rid of the stench of smoke.' Emma worried that the smell would linger, that it would be the first thing her guests would smell on arrival. It hardly evoked the calm, tranquil atmosphere she'd spent so much time creating over the last month. She also worried that it would be a constant reminder of Christmas

Eve; up to this point loud noises triggered flashbacks but, on the basis of last night, Emma now worried that smells might too.

'I can help with that,' said Rhona buoyantly. 'A good airing and a deep clean and it'll be as good as new.'

'You don't think we'll have to repaint?'

'Maybe upstairs but the guest rooms should be fine. Try not to fret too much.'

Emma sat down on the wall of the old library and closed her eyes for a moment. The back of her eyelids was a slide show of flashing images from Christmas Eve – smoke, dust, blood – merging with those from the night before.

'You okay in there?' Rhona's voice broke the flash-backs and Emma opened her eyes to the dazzling blue sky above her.

'I feel bad for my guests.'

'It was nice of Ian and Anne to take them in,' said Rhona, who'd discovered, on the school run, about the fire and the guests being put up for the night at the little pub with rooms on the corner of the road to the shops. Emma was learning that news travels fast in Lobster Bay. From what Rhona knew it seemed that the whole village was already talking about what happened.

'They came out within minutes with blankets and flasks of tea, and sandwiches,' said Emma, who couldn't get over their generosity. 'All the guests were so understanding, especially Finn, who was concerned for everyone.'

Rhona's eyes sparkled at the mention of Finn's name. Emma felt a touch sorry that she hadn't had the opportunity to serve him breakfast.

'I see what you mean about him being easy on the eye; he looked particularly hot in his P.J. bottoms,' teased Emma. Despite all that was going on, Emma had still managed to clock Finn's quality pyjamas and cashmere sweater, and the fact that his slightly greying, short back and sides didn't have a hair out of place.

'Told you,' said Rhona, flashing her eyes as if to say *phwoar*, which Emma returned.

'Ian and Anne offered straightaway to put everyone up. It hadn't even occurred to me when they asked that I'd need to find somewhere else for my guests.'

'Did you stay in the house?'

'I had to; I couldn't leave Wilbur on his own.'

'Excuse me?' said Rhona, doing a double take. 'Is this the woman who wanted nothing to do with Hilda Wyatt's dog?'

'I couldn't exactly ask Ian and Anne to put him up, could I?'

'Couldn't he have gone with Aidan?' Wilbur's rescue was almost the first thing Rhona asked about that morning after checking Emma was okay; it seemed Aidan's heroics were the talk of the village.

'I didn't like to ask . . . not after what he'd already done. And besides, you told me he won't settle anywhere else. I didn't want to distress him any more than he already was.'

'Sounds to me like someone might be softening,' ribbed Rhona.

Emma gave her a playful thump on the arm. 'Hardly! I let him sleep in the kitchen, while I tossed and turned on the sofa.'

'Sounds like the start of a beautiful romance!'

'Hah!' Emma laughed, thinking Rhona must have lost her mind.

'At least your guests will never forget their stay.'

'That's for sure!' she said, heading back inside.

As Emma and Rhona went into the kitchen, the doorbell rang. Not expecting anyone, Emma went to answer it wondering who it could be, she hadn't seen anyone walking along the street.

'Aidan!' she said on opening the door, more than surprised to see him there.

'Thought I'd come check on Wilbur; is he okay?'

'He's a bit out of sorts; you can go see him, he's in the kitchen.'

Emma waved him through, unsurprised that he'd think to ask after the dog's welfare and not hers. True to form, it seemed any concern he'd had for her last night had now deserted him.

Wilbur got up as soon as Aidan entered the room, wagging his tail slowly and wandering over to him.

'That's the first time I've seen him move since he was placed there last night,' said Emma, recalling how one of the firemen had lifted Wilbur back inside after Emma's coaxing had failed.

'Hi, Aidan,' said Rhona, putting her Marigolds on. Aidan crouched down beside Wilbur and ruffled his mane. 'I heard you were quite the hero last night.'

'Hardly,' he said, faux-wrestling the dog, Wilbur enjoying the play. 'I'd do anything for this dog.'

'So it would seem,' said Rhona. 'I wouldn't have run into a burning building for him.'

'It was just the roof that was on fire,' said Emma quickly, with an unintentional sneer. 'Not that I mean to belittle your efforts,' she backtracked. 'I'm grateful, of course, it's just . . .' she tailed off. After a month of him being a first-prize moron, she found it hard to give him the praise he was due. She felt bad for thinking it, but still found herself wondering if Aidan was secretly enjoying his newfound role as village hero, a title she wasn't entirely sure he'd earned.

'Have you contacted your insurance company?' asked Aidan, standing up.

'An assessor is coming out later today.'

'And you know you'll need a surveyor and electrician to declare the building safe before you can have guests again?'

'It's all in hand.' Emma sounded shorter than she intended; it was reassuring to have someone check up on her – if her Dad had been alive he would have been the one offering advice – even if it was just Aidan.

Just then her phone rang. 'Hello?' she answered, not recognising the number.

'Emma, it's Wendy, from the care home. Would you mind popping over? Hilda's heard the news about the house . . .'

'Of course,' said Emma, unsurprised that the news had spread so quickly, feeling as if she'd been delivered a crash course in the perils of living in a small community that Rhona had warned her about.

*

After the events of last night it was pretty much the last thing Emma needed but, knowing Hilda was due an explanation, and feeling the need to get out of the house for a while, Emma put on her cardigan and walked the mile or so to Seaview along the coast.

'Good morning, Wendy,' she said, entering the home, her spirit lighter after the bracing walk along the poppy-lined coastal path.

'Hi, Emma, are you okay?' asked Wendy, her brow furrowed with concern.

'I'm okay, thanks.' As Emma signed the log book she noticed that again, Hilda had only one other visitor that day. *Why hasn't Judy been to visit?* she wondered. *Surely the fall-out over the house couldn't be that bad.*

'How's the house?'

'There's not too much damage, thankfully,' said Emma, touched by Wendy's concern. 'Is she in the day room?'

'She's been pacing the corridor all morning, chewing the ear off anyone who passes. I've never seen her so wound up.'

In the central corridor, Emma found Hilda battling off one of the carers who kept trying to support Hilda by taking hold of her elbow. It amused Emma that Judy didn't think her mother could cope any longer; from what Emma could see it seemed Hilda was perfectly capable of looking after herself.

'Hilda, it's Emma,' she said gently, not wanting to give the old woman a start.

'What took you so long?" snapped Hilda, jabbing her walking stick at the floor, only narrowly missing Emma's toes.

Emma exchanged a 'watch out, Hilda's about' look with the carer whose eyes twinkled mischievously before she scuttled away, no doubt delighted that Emma was there to take over.

'How's Wilbur? Did anything happen to him?' Hilda asked urgently.

'Wilbur's fine,' said Emma calmly. 'Why don't we find a place to sit and chat about what happened?'

'I don't want to sit. I want to know what happened to Wilbur,' said Hilda with a petulance that put Emma in mind of a small child.

Emma composed herself with a breath in and slow exhale. 'Nothing happened to him. The alarm gave him a fright, but he was rescued.'

She took out her phone and brought up some pictures of Wilbur with Aidan that she'd taken before leaving for Seaview. 'Look – he's absolutely fine.'

'Let me look at that,' said Hilda, snatching the phone. She scrutinised the images until she was happy that nothing was wrong. 'And what's that imbecile doing in the house?'

'You mean Aidan?' asked Emma, amused by Hilda's description.

'Whatever the beggar's name is, he's a piece of work, that one.'

Emma was keen to know what Hilda meant but, to her surprise, she found herself sticking up for him. 'Aidan's the one who rescued Wilbur last night; he wouldn't budge for me.'

Hilda harrumphed and began walking towards the day room. They passed a poster for the summer fete, which reminded Emma she hadn't had a chance to ask Hilda about it last time she was here.

'How are preparations going for the fete?' she asked, as they walked together at a snail's pace.

'How should I know!' barked Hilda.

'Wendy's keen for you to bake some of your famous shortbread,' said Emma, refusing to kowtow.

'I want nothing to do with the damn thing,' said Hilda, slowly lowering herself into her seat by the windows looking out to sea.

'It could be a nice, fun activity,' said Emma, though she had an idea that Hilda wasn't one for 'activities', particularly those that meant having to integrate with her fellow residents.

Hilda rolled her eyes at the idea. 'How did the fire start?'

The segue caused Emma to take a sharp intake of breath and she felt her body stiffen. 'The fire crew think it was an electrical fault but we're not sure yet. Someone's coming later today to do an assessment.'

'You promised you'd take good care of the place,' said Hilda, sounding less angry now and more saddened.

'I know, and I meant it,' replied Emma, who felt a great sense of sadness and regret about the fire too. The last thing she wanted was for Hilda to feel even worse about losing her home, and nor did she want all of her own hard work undone. She'd spent the few hours of sleep she'd had in the early hours tossing and turning, trying to figure out if there was anything she could have done to prevent it, but she'd come up with nothing. 'I promise, as far as I know, this isn't my fault.'

'No, I suspect it isn't,' mumbled Hilda. 'It must have given you a dreadful fright. I trust you're okay?' Hilda's cloudy eyes scrutinised Emma, who was battling the sudden sound of sirens and alarms in her head.

'I'll be okay,' replied Emma, though she was aware of a jittery sensation in her stomach that she couldn't shift, and her hands were shaking, something that didn't go unnoticed by Hilda's keen gaze.

'I suppose some things are out of our control, we can't blame ourselves, my husband would have reminded me of that,' said Hilda, not exactly gently but with enough understanding that it almost amounted to sympathy.

'Sounds like good advice.'

'You might do well to remember that yourself,' said Hilda, offering Emma a knowing look.

'Yes,' said Emma, wondering how it was possible that an old woman, whom she'd only met twice, gave the impression of understanding more about Emma than Emma understood about herself.

Chapter 11

Emma clenched her hands tightly as she waited for Aidan to answer his doorbell, reeling from what the fire assessor had just told her.

'Do you know how the fire started?' Emma had asked him eagerly, before he had even reached the bottom of the Ramsay Ladder.

'Looks like an electrical fault on your neighbour's side,' he said, scribbling notes on his clipboard. 'No fault of yours.'

'Are you serious?'

'Absolutely.' He pointed with his pencil up through the loft hatch. 'There's a gap in the wall between the two lofts – you can see the wiring next door, despite the damage. Looks as if it's been there for 50 or 60 years.'

'How can you tell?' Emma asked, keen to have as many facts as possible before confronting Aidan.

'I can make out remnants of the old cloth covering. It should have been replaced years ago.'

'Will my insurance cover the repairs?'

'I'd say it's your neighbour's responsibility to claim on their policy,' he said, bringing their meeting to a close.

Emma sucked in her cheeks and stared at the foot of the tatty black front door, rehearsing in her head exactly what she wanted to say to Aidan. *This is entirely your fault . . . if you kept better care of the place this would never have happened . . . I won't rest until your insurance, not mine, pays out. Understood?*

As the door opened, her glare fixed low, Emma felt her fingers tighten.

'I hope you've got insurance,' she began, her jaw steely tight.

'Are you Emma?' asked a woman's voice.

Emma looked up to be met not by Aidan but by the reticent woman from the greengrocer, who was standing with her phone to her ear.

'Sorry,' said Emma, with a slight shake of her head as if she'd just come out of a daydream. 'I'm looking for Aidan.'

'He's in the shower.' The woman indicated over her shoulder with her thumb. 'Do you want to come in? I'm Eve. We met a while back.'

'Right, I remember.' *Though you weren't so talkative then.*

146

Eve led Emma into the house, which was a mirror image of her own, but much darker and definitely messier – there were clothes and what Emma imagined must be boat parts scattered everywhere.

'Grab a seat in the back room, he won't be long.'

'Thanks,' said Emma, taking a seat on a squashy brown sofa in the living room, which had the same commanding view of the sea as hers, though this view was disrupted by a graveyard of boat parts in the garden. She listened as Eve hollered upstairs to Aidan and then headed to the kitchen where she chattered at a mile a minute to a friend on the phone.

It hadn't occurred to Emma that Aidan might actually *live* with someone. She figured there was a girlfriend, all the arguments she'd heard through the wall pointed to that, but when Rhona had said *I don't think anyone depends on Aidan for anything* Emma had assumed she meant he didn't do long-term commitment. And yet here he was, living with the woman from the greengrocer. Emma realised it was ridiculous but, for reasons she couldn't quite fathom, she felt a tiny bit jealous of the woman with the blue hair and big glasses. She knew, no matter how hard she tried, she never had and never would be cool enough to pull off such a style statement, but Emma knew that wasn't the crux of it. The fact was, as much as Emma tried not to, she couldn't help fancying Aidan and, maybe, just maybe, a small part of her wanted him to fancy her and not Eve.

After at least 10 minutes of occupying herself by reading the book spines in the alcove shelves and studying every abandoned mug, sock and Coke can, Emma was at the point of leaving when she heard footprints tumbling down the stairs and Aidan calling, 'Eve, did you shout for me?'

'You've a visitor,' Eve called from the kitchen

'What?'

'Visitor, living room,' she yelled.

A moment later Aidan walked into the living room in only a pair of jeans with a towel around his neck. Emma felt heat rise to her cheeks and prayed they hadn't reddened.

'Emma!' said Aidan, sounding as surprised to see her as she was to see him in only his jeans. 'What's up?'

'I've just had the insurance assessor round,' said Emma, trying desperately not to give any indication of how hard she was fighting to avoid looking at his powerful torso.

'What did he say?' He rubbed his ears dry with the towel, showing no sign of any inhibitions at being semi-naked. Emma couldn't decide if he was oblivious to her awkwardness or purposefully flaunting himself to increase her unease.

'He said the fault was on your side so it's your responsibility to pay for the repairs.'

Aidan sat on the arm of the opposite sofa, his stomach creasing only slightly. If Emma had done the same a roll of flesh would have formed. 'I'll dig out the paperwork tonight.'

'Thanks,' said Emma, parking her well-rehearsed spiel, surprised that Aidan had taken the news so well.

'Shall we go up and take a look?'

'We probably should.'

Emma followed Aidan upstairs, trying not to ogle his broad shoulders and sun-soaked back, which she guessed was as muscular and tanned as it was from working on boats all day. He stopped momentarily on the landing to grab a T-shirt from the radiator, and put it on as he walked up the second flight of stairs. Emma wondered how it was that someone could look even sexier *in* a T-shirt than out of it.

'Ladies first,' he said, allowing Emma to climb the ladder ahead of him. She worried how her bum looked from below and how it compared to Eve's, whose backside was definitely younger and most likely smaller and firmer than Emma's.

'He said it was fabric-coated wiring,' said Emma, as Aidan joined her in the loft space. Compared to Emma's attic, Aidan's loft was remarkably unscathed, though the smell of smoke and charred wood hung heavy. 'There's a hole between the roof spaces over there, which caused the fire to spread to mine.'

Aidan directed the light on his phone to the front corner of the attic where Emma was pointing.

'Jesus. What a mess.'

'It certainly is,' said Emma quietly, feeling the darkness of the attic smother her and the smell of smoke cling to her nasal passages to the point that she could taste it at the back of her throat. She felt herself turn pale and dizzy, and a light sweat broke out on her upper lip.

Aidan shone the torch on her. 'Shall we go back down?'

Emma nodded and attempted to steady her breathing, fighting the sensation to vomit. She was used to the occasional flashback, but two vivid ones in the space of 48 hours was new, and her muscles ached, as well as her mind.

Taking the lead, Aidan descended the ladder first, remaining a few steps below Emma to guide her down as she clung tightly to the rungs with her hands, and struggled to find them beneath her feet.

'Are you okay?' he asked, once her feet were safely on the floor, his blue eyes warm with concern.

Emma shook away the sound of sirens and alarms that were buzzing through her mind, unable to distinguish which were from last night and which from Christmas Eve.

'It's given me a bit of a jolt, that's all,' she said, surprised and gladdened by Aidan's observance.

'You and me both,' he said, pushing the ladder up and away. 'Why don't we take Wilbur out for a walk, get some fresh air, take our mind off things for a while?'

Emma thought for a moment, unsure if his co-operation and attentiveness really wiped out a month of being a total arse but, intrigued by this softer side of his character, she found herself agreeing.

'Sure, why not,' she said, hoping the fresh air might clear some of her troubles, even if it did mean having to take Wilbur with them.

*

'How is it that Wilbur obeys your every instruction when he doesn't listen to a word I say?' Emma asked Aidan after he'd instructed Wilbur to sit at the kerb, and Wilbur obliged.

'Dogs look for leadership; he knows I'm not afraid of him,' said Aidan as they waited for an elderly lady to pass. 'Plus, though it kills me to say it, Hilda did do a good job of training him.'

A wry smile spread across Emma's face as she imagined Hilda scaring the poor dog into submission. Aidan gave a quiet command to Wilbur and the three of them carried on, in the direction of the harbour.

'Do you and Hilda not get on?' asked Emma, recalling how Hilda had referred to Aidan as *a piece of work.*

151

'Does anyone really get on with Hilda?' asked Aidan, raising his eyebrow.

Emma shrugged. 'I can see she's stubborn and quarrelsome but, I don't know, there's something I quite like about her – she's spunky.'

'You can say that again!' said Aidan, jerking Wilbur's lead to stop him sniffing a litter bin. 'But spunky isn't necessarily what you want in a neighbour.'

'Were there issues between you?'

'She wanted her house to look a certain way for her guests and, because our properties connect, she felt our house should look the same way. She was always on at me about keeping spare parts out of the front garden and making sure the back garden wasn't a "blight" for her guests.'

'Sounds a bit annoying.'

'More than annoying. She used to come into the garden and remove things. Once she put five engines into her car and took them to the dump. Do you know how much an engine costs?'

'I'm guessing more than the cost of an ice cream,' said Emma, who was slightly regretting bringing up the subject; she'd clearly touched a nerve. Although the image of tiny little Hilda shifting five boat engines into a skip was worth listening to the rant.

'Thank God the bloke at the dump allowed me to fish them out again. The woman's mad. If I hadn't got them back I would have taken a massive hit that month, and God knows I can't afford setbacks.'

'Is boat-building seasonal?'

'October through April I'm always busy with repairs when the boats are out of the water. Winter and spring, I tend to work on a single commission build, alongside smaller repairs.'

'Feast or famine,' said Emma, who figured she would have to learn to budget the money she made in the summer with a lower income in the winter.

'It's difficult to keep on top of everything when it's busy, and then when it's quieter there isn't always the money to do the jobs that are needed.'

'Like the roof?' asked Emma as they rounded the ancient castle wall that led to the harbour, though she was also thinking about the state of the gardens, the front door, the windows, and now she'd seen the inside she realised that was in dire need of a makeover too.

'Exactly,' said Aidan, stuffing his hands into his body-warmer pockets.

'Well, I'll try not to pester you the way Hilda did,' she said, sensing Aidan didn't respond well to antagonisation.

'*You* can pester me all you like,' said Aidan, with a smile and a glint that Emma might have interpreted as flirtatious if it weren't for the fact that he'd been so cold towards her over the last month, *and* that he was with Eve.

After a moment's lull in the conversation, when Emma was convinced Aidan must be able to hear the loud debate in her head about what his coy comment had meant, Aidan suggested Emma take Wilbur.

'No thanks,' she replied.

'Go on. You're used to each other now.'

'I suppose,' said Emma, who still wasn't confident in walking him. She'd tried everything over the last few weeks: walking him at different times of the day; trying new paths; and switching to a collar instead of the harness; but his behaviour remained erratic and her confidence low.

'Here, just be firm,' he said, handing her the lead.

The two of them meandered down the steep narrow road, past the old stone cottages with their rust-coloured stone and pantile roofs and on to the harbour. Wilbur kept a loose lead and Emma relaxed a little.

'Do you have a boat of your own?' she asked at the harbour edge.

Aidan pointed to a beautiful, old-fashioned wooden skiff with a tall mast.

'You made that?' said Emma, admiringly.

'With my bare hands.'

'It's stunning, like a piece of art.' Just thinking about the imagination, knowledge and skill it took to create something so magnificent made Emma marvel. 'It must have taken you years to master all these skills.'

154

'It's something that you're born into,' he said, deflecting Emma's praise. 'A city girl like you couldn't manage it!'

Emma clocked the cheeky glint in Aidan's eye, knowing he was referencing their first meeting, and was about to find a retort when Wilbur suddenly lurched and let out an enormous bark.

'Let me handle him,' said Aidan, taking the lead from Emma, his hand momentarily touching hers causing a tingle to spread up Emma's arm and through her body which caught her off guard.

'What's up with him?' asked Emma. She watched Aidan's forearms ripple as he used all his strength to hold Wilbur under control.

'He sees Elsie.'

'Who's Elsie?' Emma looked in the direction in which Wilbur was trying to pull.

'The butcher's dog.'

It didn't take long for Emma to spot Phil, hauling a canoe up the beach, with his small white dog, who was pretty much the exact opposite of Wilbur – compact, short-haired and nippy. Aidan released Wilbur and within seconds Elsie was under his feet, running in circles and yapping playfully.

'What a bundle of energy!' said Emma when she reached Phil. Aidan wandered down to the lapping waves and kicked aimlessly at large stones stuck fast in the sand.

'She certainly is,' he said, laughing at Elsie as she continued to bark at Wilbur, hopeful that he might play. 'I was sorry to hear about the fire. Are you okay?'

'I'm fine. Thanks, Phil.'

'And Wilbur's alright?'

'Seems to be,' she said, watching him stand dolefully next to Elsie, seemingly mesmerised by her enthusiasm. Given that the guys hadn't acknowledged each other, Emma sensed it best not to regale Phil with the details of how Aidan had rescued him. *And besides*, she thought, *he's probably heard on the grapevine anyway.*

'Like I said before, if you need any help with him—'

'Of course, thank you,' said Emma, feeling dreadful that she hadn't yet taken him up on his kind offer. Phil's eyes were a bit less sparkly in the early evening light and Emma found herself feeling a smidge awkward that she was out walking Wilbur with Aidan instead of him.

'Or if ever you fancy taking to the water.' He indicated to his canoe. 'Wilbur could swim alongside us.'

'Wow, what an offer!' said Emma, trying not to convey just how out of character it would be for her to accept; neither sea nor wet dog held any appeal. 'I'll get back to you on that – okay?'

'Sure thing,' he said, his usual enthusiasm missing.

'See you around then,' said Emma, lingering a little as she left him to his canoe and returned to Aidan. As she wandered to the other side of the beach, she tried to imagine what could possibly have happened between them to cause them to stop talking.

Christmas Day

'Emma!' said Jane, finding her sister on the doorstep with a holdall. 'What are you doing here? I thought you were going to Chris's parents.'

'We broke up.'

'Shit, Em, on Christmas Day?'

'Long story,' she said, though it wasn't really. Emma had told Chris to go to his mum's without her, to give her some thinking time. After he'd gone, she packed up her stuff and travelled the 40 miles to her sister's. 'Mind if I come in?'

'Of course not.' Jane opened the door fully. 'No offence, Em, but you look like crap. Are you okay?'

'I'm just a bit tired.'

'I'll be in the kitchen if you want to talk about it,' said Jane. 'Make yourself at home.'

In the living room Emma found Gary and her mum, a Christmas tiara perched on her short spiky hair, on the pristine grey sofa with the kids, who were sitting on the floor round the massive telly.

'Emma!' she said, an almost empty glass of prosecco in her hand. Given she didn't question why her daughter was there, Emma surmised her mother had probably drunk several glasses already.

'Auntie Emma, look!' said Jake, bursting with excitement, pointing at the telly. 'A bomb went off in London. A bomb! Can you believe it?'

'Wow! That's exciting,' said Emma, mustering an animated expression. She removed her coat and perched on the edge of the sofa, all the time staring at the screen. The rolling banner declared nine dead and 56 injured.

'Suicide bomber,' her mother mouthed. 'Shocking.'

'Isn't it,' said Emma, her voice trailing off.

The scene, in broad daylight, bore no resemblance to what Emma remembered witnessing the evening before. It was as if she was looking at something else entirely.

'You work near there, don't you?' asked Gary.

'Closer to Oxford Circus,' said Emma, transfixed by the images, scanning them for something, anything that looked as it had last night.

'You were lucky not to get caught up in it, love,' said Liz.

'Really lucky,' said Emma, who knew from the images that this was her memory, which couldn't be shared, no matter how hard she tried. This was something she would have to shoulder alone.

159

Chapter 12

'Mother will be furious when she finds out that it's next door's fault,' said Judy, standing at the top of the steps to the attic and surveying the damage. Emma couldn't help but find the image comical – Judy, up a ladder, in her tweed skirt and court shoes. For a moment it took the sting out of the fire.

'I don't think it's anyone's fault exactly,' replied Emma. Since their walk yesterday, when Aidan had been less guarded, she harboured less ill will towards him. She'd been left with a sense that Aidan had troubles of his own, and that his glib, dismissive attitude might be masking something deeper, though what that was she had no idea.

'I hope they appreciate your good grace.'

'I'm sure they do,' said Emma, putting out a protective hand just in case Judy should trip on a rung. 'Aidan's taking care of the insurance.'

Judy, safely back on the ground, wiped the dust sharply off her skirt. 'All the same, Mother will have a fit.'

'Aidan did mention that the two of them had their differences,' said Emma, leading Judy back downstairs.

'"Differences" is putting it mildly,' said Judy with a tight laugh. 'And, of course, in later years it was me who had to mediate the whole debacle.'

'Did it go on for a while?' asked Emma, offering Judy a seat in the living room.

'Ever since his parents died and he let the house fall into disrepair.'

A pang of sympathy shot through Emma's heart. She knew what it was to lose her father, she could only imagine what it must feel like to lose both your parents.

'I feel for the chap,' continued Judy. 'He hasn't always been the easiest character, but he certainly didn't deserve what happened.'

Emma had to bite her tongue to stop herself asking what had happened exactly.

'Would you like some tea?' she offered.

'Yes, please,' said Judy, admiring the newly decorated living room.

As Emma made tea in the kitchen she heard Judy chuckling in the next room. When she returned she found her standing by the mantelpiece holding the colour photo of Hilda and her family.

'Is that you in the picture?' Emma asked, putting down the tray on the large studded footstool.

'I must have been around 14 years old and my brother, Archie, about 12.'

'Had you just moved in?' Emma had been wondering what the occasion had been to warrant a family photo at the front door.

'I suppose we had,' said Judy, giving it some thought. 'We moved from barracks after my father left the army. It was the first real home we'd had, even though it was also a business.'

'Your father was in the army?'

Judy's forehead creased 'Mmm . . . he never fully left it behind,' she said, a faraway look in her eyes.

'What made them buy a guesthouse?' asked Emma, wanting to ask Judy what she'd meant by the comment but sensing from her distant expression it wasn't something she wanted to discuss.

Judy put the photograph back above the fireplace. 'It was something my mother always wanted to do. I never thought her personality was particularly well-suited to it, but there you are . . . I suppose it did suit their circumstances.'

'I expect she did it very well,' said Emma, pouring the tea.

'My mother did everything well.' She paused for a moment before saying quietly, 'Some might say to the detriment of the family.'

'When did your father pass away?' asked Emma, handing Judy her tea, itching to find out more.

'Just a few years after we moved here.'

'That must have been hard,' said Emma, beginning to join the dots. *Hilda lost her husband more than 40 years ago, no wonder there was no sign of him in the house.*

'Mother coped. That's what army wives do. I went off to university soon after. It was probably hardest on Archie.'

'Where is he now?'

'Malaysia. He's a diplomat,' said Judy, stirring her tea. Emma thought she detected a hint of resentment.

'And you?'

'I was a housemistress at a boarding school,' she said, placing her spoon on her saucer. 'Or at least I was until four years ago when Mother began to need help.'

'You gave up your career to care for her?'

'My career, my home, my relationship.' Judy paused, momentarily lost in thought. It made sense now to Emma why Judy had come to live in Lobster Bay, and she felt a growing sense of empathy towards her. 'Of course, my brother did nothing.'

'Hilda must be grateful to you,' said Emma, offering a sympathetic smile.

Judy let out a bitter laugh. 'Mother is *never* grateful. She *expected* me to help care for her *and* run the business. In the end I had to say, no. I couldn't do it all, something she didn't understand, having done everything for everyone all her life.

'When I told her we needed to sell the house to pay for her long-term care, she not only refused to believe she couldn't cope any longer, but she also resented me selling the house to pay for her care. It was as if her expectation was that I would either look after her myself or pay for it out of my own pocket.'

Emma sat quietly, now understanding why Judy found it so difficult to cut her mother some slack.

'Thankfully my brother managed to persuade her to give us power of attorney, which meant we were able to put the house on the market, but she went out of her way to made it almost impossible for us to sell it.'

'What did she do?' asked Emma, who remembered Hilda's mention of her 'best efforts' to prevent the sale of the house.

'She tried every trick in the book to put people off . . . pointing out old woodworm and saying it was active; leaving the heating off for weeks on end so it smelt fusty and felt like a fridge; at one point she even pulled strips of wallpaper off the walls and told viewers it was due to the rising damp.'

'Wow!' said Emma, impressed by Hilda's devious antics, but also disappointed that she hadn't had the opportunity to witness the old lady in action. 'I wonder what she would have done if I'd viewed it in person?'

'She'd have come up with something, probably something about the ancient phone system and how it's not compatible with the internet. She had a knack for knowing what would put off different viewers,' said Judy with a light laugh, able to see the funny side. It made Emma think of the phone engineer who'd scratched his head for hours over the archaic system. In the end he'd left the analogue connection at the top of the house, calling it 'a piece of history' and installed a brand-new system downstairs for the broadband. 'My mother has a stubborn streak a mile wide, she always finds a way of getting what she wants.'

'But in the end, you did sell.'

'Only because Doreen talked me into lowering the price.'

'I'm glad she did,' said Emma.

'When she called to say you'd made an offer I thought you must be heaven-sent,' said Judy, which Emma thought was an odd thing to say given a closing date had been set; Judy gabbled on before Emma had the opportunity to ask what she meant. 'After three years of not working, running my mother's business, caring for her and living with her, finally there were sufficient funds to pay for her care, and she *had* to accept that it was time to move on.'

'And she went without a fight?'

'Hardly! There was still the issue of the dog, but when we found out you'd agreed to keep him she eventually gave in.'

It was on the tip of Emma's tongue to tell Judy she hadn't known about Wilbur but, not wishing to burden Judy with anything more, Emma decided to keep it to herself.

'Honestly Emma, you've no idea how, towards the end, every time the phone rang, my heart would leap into my throat and I'd wonder if she'd fallen down the stairs or set fire to the place.'

Emma laughed at the irony.

'Oh, sorry,' stammered Judy, flustered by her fire faux pas. 'I didn't mean—'

'Don't worry about it,' said Emma with a laugh, and Judy joined her, her stiff posture relaxing. She placed her cup of tea on the side table and let out a titter causing Emma to chuckle. In the end the two of them giggled together like schoolgirls.

'It's been such a long time since I've laughed,' said Judy, wiping away a tear.

'I think it's time we rectified that, don't you?'

'I've thought of every possible way to make my mother see things from my point of view but until she admits she could no longer cope, and that we had to sell the house to pay for her care, I don't see how we can put an end to the upset.'

'Let me think about it,' said Emma, determined to help the two women come to a truce, and to enable

Judy, clearly worn down by years of drudgery, to enjoy life once more.

*

'Good afternoon, The Guesthouse at Lobster Bay,' sang Emma, picking up the landline from the desk in the living room.

'Hello, Emma? This is Finn McCarthy—'

'Hi, Finn,' Emma said brightly, immediately recognising his Irish accent. 'How are you?'

'Sure, not bad at all, thanks. I was calling to see if I could make another reservation with you.'

'Of course. When for?' she asked, sitting down at the desk, bursting to tell Rhona the good news.

'Next month. The club wants me to come back and present my designs.'

'That's fine,' said Emma, pulling up the bookings calendar on the computer and entering further details of his reservation. 'I'm glad the fire didn't put you off!'

'Not at all. The wee pub was grand like but nowhere as nice as yours.'

'Pleased to hear it,' said Emma, sitting back, delighted by the compliment. 'We'll look forward to seeing you next month,' she said, keen to stress that Rhona would be here too.

Emma had only just put the phone down from talking to Finn when her mobile rang.

'Hi, Mum,' she said, recognising the number. In the background, Emma heard the television being turned down, no doubt after her mother gestured a 'shooshing' motion at Gary.

'You sound tense, is everything okay?'

Emma rolled her eyes, amused by her mother's ability to sniff out trouble even at 400 miles away.

'Mum, I'm fine.' She tapped her pencil on her notepad trying to decide whether to tell her mother about the fire.

'What's happened? Did one of your guests complain? Was there a problem with breakfast?'

Liz's expectant silence made it clear to Emma that she wasn't going to get away without telling her. 'We had a small fire, that's all. Nothing major. It's all under control.'

'What?' said Liz, her voice shrill.

'It was in the loft, some old wiring, it's not a big deal. The assessor has been and the electrician too. It was the wiring in next door's house, not mine.'

'I'll come, you can't manage this on your own,' said Liz, the background noises all but gone. Emma imagined her mother pacing in the kitchen.

'Mum, I can manage,' said Emma, getting up and going to the bay window to look out to sea. 'Everything's fine, I promise you. There's no structural damage and all of the electrics here are sound. Rhona and I just need to do a thorough clean and then guests can return.'

'But what about the damage in the loft. Who's going to repair it?'

'That's the next thing I have to sort out. I've cancelled bookings for the next week and now I need to start calling roofers. It's all in hand.'

'Are you sure?' asked Liz.

'One hundred per cent.'

'Well, okay then,' said Liz, backing down. Emma heard the scrape of her mother pulling a kitchen chair back on the lino. 'Gary's health isn't great, so he'd probably prefer I stay here anyway.'

'Sounds like a good reason to stay put,' said Emma, hoping her voice didn't give away her irritation about Gary.

'The reason I was calling was to tell you I bumped into Sandra.'

'How is she?' asked Emma, who hadn't seen Sandra, Chris's mum, since before the break-up. For a moment she worried that Chris might have told his mum about Christmas Eve and that Sandra had subsequently told Liz.

'She's fine, still working at the health club. She told me Chris's still struggling without you . . .'

'That's not great . . .' Emma tailed off, not certain what to say; she felt awful that Chris was hurting but she also knew getting in touch and giving him false hope was not the solution.

'She said Chris still hasn't told her why you broke up. I think she was looking for me to explain but, well, given I don't know . . .'

A wave of relief flowed through Emma's body, Chris obviously hadn't mentioned Christmas Eve after all. 'Mum, I've told you a million times, he just wasn't the one for me. I know it's disappointing but that's just how it is,' she said, feeling a niggle of guilt for not being able to tell her the full story, that the events of Christmas Eve had given her all the clarity she needed, that she had to move on; that there was no way their relationship could survive what Emma had been through.

'But it came so out of the blue.'

'Maybe to you.'

The memory of the moment when Emma had realised she didn't love Chris came flooding back to her. It was over a year ago now, at his brother's wedding. Sandra had ushered Emma into the photographs of the immediate family, telling her, 'You're part of the family too'. Emma had recoiled, projecting into the future when she knew she wouldn't be part of Chris's life and they'd be left with framed pictures of Simon on his wedding day with Chris's ex in them. 'It should just be the five of you,' Emma had said, and they'd all laughed and dragged her in. The image of Chris's family standing there proudly and Emma, a forced smile on her face, keeping a 'croppable' distance from Chris, still made her wince.

'I don't know, love, I've just always had a feeling that you've left something unsaid, that he did something, or you did something. It feels as if something's unresolved—'

'Mum. There's nothing.'

Emma loathed the fact her mother knew she was withholding information. She wanted to tell her about Christmas Eve, but she clung to the idea that there was no point in telling her, or anyone, if they stood no chance of understanding, and besides, she reasoned, she couldn't live with herself if the burden placed on her mother might cause her anxiety to spiral again.

'Okay, love, if you say so, but you know, if you ever want to talk—'

'I know, Mum.'

The guilt of not sharing everything with her mum the way she knew Rhona did with hers tugged at her heart. She was considering what to do when she heard a whomping sound coming from the next room. Looking into the kitchen she saw Wilbur, his body wrenching, throwing up on the floor.

'Oh my God,' said Emma, fighting not to be sick at the sight of it.

'What is it, love?'

'The dog's just thrown up on the kitchen floor.'

'Is he okay?'

'I guess not,' said Emma, approaching him. As she got closer his back legs buckled beneath him.

'Do you know what to do, love?'

'I probably need to get him to a vet,' said Emma, not knowing if there was a vet nearby, and wondering how she would ever get him up from the floor to take him there.

'I'll leave you to it,' said Liz. 'Let me know how you get on.'

'Will do,' said Emma, ending the call and immediately googling 'vet near me'.

Having found the local vet, she called for an appointment and fetched Wilbur's lead, then coaxed him to his feet and slowly led him to the car.

'Everything okay?' asked Aidan, who was loading tools into his van.

'I'm taking Wilbur to the vet, he's off colour,' replied Emma, opening the boot. Wilbur stood with his head hung low and made no effort to leap in.

Aidan approached and kneeled down next to Wilbur. 'What's up, boy?'

Wilbur didn't look up.

'Do you see what I mean?' asked Emma, who knew something must be wrong if Wilbur wasn't acknowledging Aidan.

Placing a reassuring hand on Wilbur's back, Aidan asked if Emma knew where she was going.

'I've got sat nav. I'll find it,' she said though she didn't feel all that confident about driving somewhere new with a sick dog in the boot.

'Let me come with you,' he said, placing his forearms underneath Wilbur and gently lifting him into the back of the car. He stroked Wilbur softly on his belly before quietly closing the boot.

'I can manage,' said Emma, questioning why she was quibbling with him.

Aidan opened the passenger door. 'You'll never get him out at the other end.'

'Are you sure we're not holding you up? Eve won't mind you nipping out?'

'She's at work, it's fine. Come on.'

Aidan's size meant that Emma's bare arm brushed against his as she plugged in her seatbelt, causing a flutter in her tummy and her brain to momentarily disconnect.

'Key in the ignition,' said Aidan as Emma floundered.

'Sorry,' she said, with an embarrassed laugh. 'This doggy emergency has left me all in a flap.' She put the car into gear, praying that Aidan hadn't picked up on the real reason for her fluster.

'Mind the pedestrian!' Aidan shouted as Emma hit the gas and almost ploughed straight into a woman crossing the street. It was the same woman who'd crossed the road to avoid Emma that first morning when she'd taken Wilbur out for a walk on her own.

Emma stamped on the brakes and the woman continued across as if nothing had happened, which Emma thought a little odd given that she'd almost been hit by a car.

'Who is that?' asked Emma, making out that she'd been in complete control of the situation even though she clearly hadn't.

'Doreen Reid.'

'Doreen?' muttered Emma, who knew the name from somewhere.

'The local estate agent.'

'Huh,' said Emma, who thought it strange that a woman who'd been so friendly towards her on the phone had now, on two occasions, seemingly blanked her.

'Carry on through the next two villages and then I'll direct you from there,' said Aidan once they were onto the main road and Emma had regained her sense of composure.

'Sure,' said Emma, thankful to have him riding shotgun. 'Any news from your insurance company?'

'Not yet, but I've been thinking . . . it could take a while for you to find a roofer, and who knows when the insurance will pay out. What do you think about me doing the work for you?'

'I don't know,' said Emma, surprised by the suggestion, but mulling it over. 'Do you know how to repair roofs?'

'I'm a boatbuilder,' he said, with a laugh. 'Making things weathertight is what I do.'

'Then sure,' she shrugged. 'If I don't have to find someone and you don't have to worry about paying them then I guess it makes sense.'

'Great,' said Aidan, resting his elbow on the window ledge. 'I'll get started tomorrow.'

'Perfect,' replied Emma, thinking it might be nice to have him about the place. *If nothing else*, she thought, *he'll be something pretty to look at while I'll do the laundry.*

Outside the vet, Aidan opened the boot of the car and carefully lifted Wilbur out, who made no effort to struggle.

'I don't know how you manage to carry him,' said Emma, admiring not only Aidan's strength but the gentleness with which he held him too. 'I'd need a forklift truck to do the same.'

'It isn't easy,' he said, concentrating on the task, his arm and neck muscles straining. Emma ran ahead to open the double doors to the surgery.

'Hi, I'm—' said Emma, going over to the semi-circular reception desk.

'You must be Emma,' said the receptionist, immediately coming out from behind the desk and going to Wilbur, who Aidan placed on the floor.

'Right . . .' said Emma, perplexed as to how the vet's receptionist knew her.

'Hilda told us you'd be looking after Wilbur.' She crouched down beside Wilbur and put her face close to his. 'What's the matter, big fella? You not feeling so well?' she said, in a coochy-coo sort of voice, as if talking to a baby. Aidan flashed a look at Emma that said 'this woman is bananas', making her snigger.

'He's been vomiting and then his back legs went from under him.'

'Poor guy,' said the receptionist, stroking his ears. 'We'd better have Cameron take a look at you.'

The receptionist disappeared through a door to the back of the surgery and moments later a burly man in scrubs appeared and approached Emma.

'I'm Cameron,' he said, in a voice that was both assertive and reassuring. He shook both Emma's and Aidan's hands. 'I'll be looking after Wilbur today. How's he doing?'

'Not great, he seems really weak,' said Emma, surprised by just how worried she felt.

Cameron knelt down next to Wilbur and put his stethoscope to the dog's chest.

'How long's he been like this?'

'I only noticed him vomit for the first time about half an hour ago, but he may have been sick in the garden too.'

'Has he eaten anything that he shouldn't have?'

'I don't think so,' said Emma, watching the vet check his eyes, nose and mouth.

'He might have picked something up at the beach last night,' said Aidan. 'We weren't watching him all the time.'

'Like what?' Emma asked, feeling an immediate sense of blame.

'Dead fish, parasitic saltwater, palm oil, to name but a few,' said Cameron, who was now feeling Wilbur's stomach.

'I had no idea a trip to the beach could be so hazardous,' said Emma, hoping the vet wouldn't think her negligent.

'It's not your fault,' he said, standing up. 'We can't be watching them every hour of the day, and Wilbur has a history of eating things he's not supposed to.'

'Will he be okay?' asked Emma, pleased to know that this had happened on Hilda's watch too, and praying that Cameron would say yes. The prospect of having to tell Hilda that she'd killed her precious dog was more than Emma could bear.

'Everything points to dehydration, but I'll keep him in overnight for observations, just to be sure.'

'Thank you,' said Emma, her shoulders dropping by about a foot. Aidan reached out and gave her a supportive rub on her back, and she fought the unexpected desire to lean her head on his shoulder.

'Can I reach you both at home?' asked Cameron.

'Oh . . . no . . . we don't live together, we're not . . .' said Emma, her cheeks flushing pink.

'We're neighbours,' Aidan explained, laughing the matter off.

'Sorry, my mistake, I thought you were a couple. Who should I contact in case of an emergency?'

'Just me, on my mobile,' said Emma, her embarrassment being replaced by a slight sense of sadness. For a while 'just me' had suited Emma well, but now, now that Aidan was in her life, suddenly 'just me' didn't feel quite enough.

Chapter 13

'It's a big job,' said Rhona, wiping her sleeve on her forehead, leaving a smudge of ash behind.

'It's a horrid job,' said Emma, who was sweeping charred remains from the corner of the attic that had taken the worst of the fire damage.

'At least the smell is beginning to go.'

'That makes a big difference,' said Emma, who was no longer bombarded with flashbacks brought on by the stench. 'I'm just thankful it hasn't rained. Hopefully Aidan can make a start on the repairs later before the weather turns.'

'I can't believe he's offered to do the job.'

'There's nothing like a healthy dose of guilt to kickstart a man into action,' said Emma, not really meaning it. She was grateful that Aidan had offered, and thankful that she didn't have to call tradesmen, wait for quotes and place her trust in a total stranger. She just hoped it wouldn't be awkward having him about the house.

'And nice that he helped you out with Wilbur yesterday too.'

'I know, there's no way I could have got him out of the car on my own.'

'You have to be so careful with dogs on the beach. There's no telling what they can pick up.'

'Right, it's a lesson learnt,' said Emma, quickly checking her phone to see if she had a missed call with news of how Wilbur was doing. She'd had a fitful night's sleep with both thoughts of Wilbur and Aidan occupying her mind.

'It certainly is,' said Rhona, bagging up a pile of ash.

'Hey, do you know what the deal is between Aidan and Phil?' asked Emma, trying to sound casual. She'd been wondering about it on and off after they ignored one another on the beach.

'Phil Hughes?'

'Yeah, the butcher.'

Rhona sucked air through her teeth. 'Where do I begin?'

'Sounds intriguing.' Emma absently brushed up more fire damage.

'They've vied with each other since they were wee kids. In primary school they always wanted to be the one who scored the most goals, in secondary it was about scoring women and, after school, about whose business was the most successful. When they were little it was the odd bump or cruel word, as they got older they'd fight, and when they grew up, if you can call it that, they started bad-mouthing each other's businesses. Because Phil's a more laid-back personality he generally came off smelling sweeter, but the truth is they're as bad as each other. It probably doesn't help that Aidan has an explosive temper.'

'But what caused them to stop talking?' asked Emma, unsurprised to learn that Aidan had a tendency to fly off the handle; the arguments she'd heard through the walls were proof of that.

Rhona tied a knot in the bin bag and placed it by the loft hatch. 'Phil took up with Aidan's little sister. Aidan saw red. He thought Phil was using her as a pawn in their game.'

'What happened?' she asked, unaware that Phil had a sister.

'They had a massive brawl one night down at the harbour. They were both badly scraped-up, but Phil came off worse. After that Aidan left town; they never spoke again.'

'Where did he go?' asked Emma, hoping her tone didn't give away the fact that she felt a little sorry for him.

'Nobody knows.'

'Huh,' said Emma, thinking it rather romantic that Aidan had some secrets.

'Anyway, he came back when his parents died. He's been here ever since.'

'Did his sister and Phil stay together?'

'They were only together for a few months, after that she took off to the city. Aidan still gets crazy about it. Nobody mentions it. Everyone knows not to. It's like the town taboo.'

'Huh,' said Emma, who thought it sweet of Aidan to be so protective of his sister.

'So, there you are, the story of Aidan and Phil. For a moment there I forgot you haven't always been in Lobster – it's only when you ask about things that are common knowledge around here that I remember.'

It meant the world to Emma that Rhona already considered her part of the village. She reminded herself that it was only five weeks ago that she'd known no one.

'Here you go,' said Rhona, passing a slightly damaged box to Emma, its lid a little loose.

As Emma placed the box on the other side of the loft, the top slid off exposing its contents: what looked like old filing. Emma was about to put the lid back on again when she noticed a corner of a familiar-looking envelope.

Gently gripping the corner, so as not to disturb anything of Hilda's, Emma tugged it slightly to slowly reveal the letter she'd written to Hilda when she made the offer on the house.

'Please let the letter be inside . . .' said Emma, opening the envelope to reveal the letter still in place.

'What is it?'

Emma held the letter to her chest. 'Something, I hope, that might help me make some headway with Hilda.'

The doorbell rang not long after Emma found the note and she and Rhona headed downstairs for a break.

'Jennifer,' sang Emma, delighted to see her, and loving her ochre, drop-waist dress.

'I found some old floor plans for the house in the archives,' said Jennifer, showing Emma a tattered Manila envelope. 'Is now a good time to show you?'

'Of course, come in,' said Emma and she called Rhona through from the kitchen.

'They're a little tired,' said Jennifer, laying the plans out on one of the dining room tables. 'But I think that adds to their charm.'

Emma bent over the old plans and traced her finger over lines of walls that no longer existed. 'Wouldn't it be amazing to transform it back to how it was when it was first built?'

'I'm not sure 10 guests would want to share one bathroom,' said Rhona, setting down a tray of tea and biscuits then greeting her cousin with a squeeze round the shoulder.

'Four less loos to clean!' said Emma.

Rhona laughed. 'That I wouldn't complain about.'

'How's the big clean-up going upstairs?' asked Jennifer.

'Not bad,' replied Emma. 'It won't be long until we're finished in the attic and can start work on the last two guest rooms. After that I can look into all the little luxuries that will make the house really stand out from the crowd.'

'What have you in mind?' asked Jennifer.

'I'd love to welcome my guests with afternoon tea and provide in-room treatments, and perhaps in time offer tiny wedding packages. Wouldn't it be amazing to get ready in one of the big bedrooms, be married on the beach, photographed at the harbour and then come back to the house for a sumptuous dinner with your closest family and friends?'

'Are you serious?' said Jennifer. 'All of that in Lobster Bay?'

'You guys grew up here so you don't appreciate what you have, but trust me, people would pay through the nose to have a wedding here.'

'Guests always comment on how lucky we are to live here,' said Rhona. 'Emma's right, we do take it for granted.'

'It's a lot of work to do on your own though,' said Jennifer.

'That's why I'd like to take on a full-time member of staff, eventually,' said Emma, watching Rhona from the corner of her eye to try and gauge her reaction, having earmarked her for the role. 'That way I can concentrate on the development of the business while someone else takes care of the day-to-day running of the place.'

'Is that something Rhona could do?' asked Jennifer, taking a seat at the table.

'Are you kidding?' said Rhona. 'There's no way I could run this place on my own.'

'Actually,' replied Emma slowly. 'I kind of had you in mind.'

Rhona's mouth fell open. 'I'm flattered,' she stammered. 'But I couldn't.'

'You're more than capable,' said Emma, reaching for a biscuit.

Rhona shook her head. 'Even if I thought I was able I still wouldn't be able to, not with four kids.'

'They're all at school now,' said Jennifer. 'And your mum would help out.'

'And what happens when one of them is sick and mum has to work?'

'I'd still be here,' said Emma, not wanting to be pushy but not wanting to dissuade her either.

'I wouldn't feel right about it,' said Rhona, joining them in sitting at the table. 'With four kids something always comes up – until they're grown I can't commit to anything full-time.'

'But Craig gets his career,' said Jennifer, an unusual spikiness in her tone.

Rhona hadn't mentioned anything about her children's father, but Emma was certain that's who Craig must be.

'Craig made his decision to leave. His loss is bigger than mine.'

'I just don't think it's fair that your life is on hold and his isn't,' said Jennifer.

'I'd rather be a mother and have a part-time job than have a fancy career and have no access to my children.'

'Fair point,' said Jennifer, backing down.

'It'll be a few years before I can make it happen anyway,' said Emma. 'Maybe by then you'll be more able to consider it, and who knows, maybe Finn will whisk you off your feet before then anyway!'

'That I very much doubt,' said Rhona.

'He's made a reservation for next month,' sang Emma.

'Next month?' said Rhona, sitting up sharply like a meerkat.

'Who's Finn?'

'An Irishman who took a shine to Rhona,' teased Emma.

'Rhona, you minx! Why didn't you say?'

'Because I can't do anything about it. In case you've forgotten, I – have – four – kids.'

'So?'

'So, I can't exactly abandon them while I go off on a mad sex rampage.'

'Sure you can,' said Jennifer. 'What do you think cousins are for?'

'You do have a built-in childminder,' chimed in Emma, pulling out her phone which was ringing in her pocket. She left Rhona to tell Jennifer about Finn, and went through to the sitting room.

'Emma,' said the voice on the line. 'It's Cameron, at the vet's.'

'Hi, Cameron,' said Emma, nibbling a fingernail.

'Wilbur's out of the woods. He's fine. You're free to come collect him.'

'Thank you, I'll come for him immediately,' said Emma, rubbing a hand over her face, surprised at just how much relief she felt that Wilbur was on the mend, and glad that the headway she hoped to make with Hilda with the note wouldn't be hindered by having to tell her that her precious dog had died.

*

'Do you believe me now when I say I bought the house as my forever home?' asked Emma, still uncertain how the note came to be in Hilda's loft.

'How do I know you didn't write this today and post-date it?' asked Hilda, sitting at a table in the small gravel garden of the care home, a blanket wrapped around her legs.

'Because the envelope has a frank mark on it,' said Emma, handing Hilda the evidence.

Hilda pursed her lips. 'Well, aren't you the smart one,' she said, unable to hide a gleam in her eye.

Emma smiled lightly, pleased that she'd won their small battle and that the two of them were now on more of an even keel. 'Did you really think I was just here to do it up and sell it on?'

'It's what Sheena told me.'

'Sheena?'

'Rhona's auntie. She works in the mini-mart.'

'Ah, Sheena,' said Emma, making the connection of how the rumour started. It explained why Judy knew, and why both Rhona and Aidan had known she'd moved up from London. 'I told her the day I moved in that I'd come up from London and had a background in design. She must have put two and two together and come up with five.'

'She also told me about the day Wilbur escaped.'

It took Emma a moment but then she remembered the woman on the opposite side of the road with the small yappy dog. 'Does she have a little dog?'

'A Pomeranian.'

Emma nodded and sipped her tea. 'Well, *that* she got right.'

'How is Wilbur?' asked Hilda, folding the note carefully and putting it back in its envelope before placing it in her cardigan pocket.

'He's okay. He ate something horrid on the beach and had to see the vet but he's back to full health now.'

Hilda snapped a piece of shortbread in half. 'He's always been partial to a rotten seagull or decaying seal,' she said, her eyes twinkling deviously.

Emma choked on her tea in disgust. 'Hilda, that's gross!'

'It sounds to me like you're looking after him. Perhaps you like having him about the place more than you thought you would?'

'I wouldn't go that far, but I will concede I was a bit worried about him last night,' said Emma.

'I wish he could visit but they won't allow it,' said Hilda, a sadness creeping into her eyes.

'Why not?'

'Some health and safety nonsense. They're probably worried he'd bulldoze another resident.'

'They may not be far wrong,' said Emma, who could imagine the scenario well, but then a thought came to her. 'Maybe I could bring him to the summer fete?' she suggested, thinking she could make it her goal to have him fully under control by then and bring him along for Hilda to show off.

Hilda's eyes softened. 'I'd like that.'

'How about I bring him along in exchange for you contributing to the tea stall. You know Wendy's desperate for you to bake the shortbread.'

'I don't usually do deals,' said Hilda, with a primness that reminded Emma of Judy. 'But, in this instance, fine, I'll help out.'

'Brilliant,' said Emma, clapping her hands. 'I'm sure it will be fun and, who knows, you might make some new friends along the way.'

Emma's enthusiasm was dismissed with a shoo of Hilda's hand though Emma was certain she saw Hilda conceal a rogue smile.

'Rumour has it that the fire started next door,' said Hilda, swiftly changing the subject.

'The rumour mill is right,' said Emma, enjoying the feeling of community that was part of being caught in the rumour mill.

'I always told him something bad would come from his lack of care.'

'Don't be too hard on Aidan,' said Emma. She wanted to tell Hilda that Aidan had really stepped up, that he'd helped out with Wilbur and was going to start work on the roof, but Emma had a feeling the news would be met with disapproval, so she decided not to mention it.

'Why not? For years he caused me nothing but trouble, he's always been a bad one. His parents would turn in their graves if they saw the way he neglects that place.'

'Do you know what happened to them?' asked Emma, sensitively, unsure how well Hilda had known them but keen to get to the bottom of what had happened.

The old woman's eyes took on a distant gaze. 'They died at sea. It was an absolute tragedy, the whole village was affected by it. The only good thing their son ever did was come home and keep the family business going.'

Emma gave Hilda a moment or two before carefully asking, 'Do you think it's possible that Aidan hasn't been coping? Maybe that's why the house became a bit unkempt? You know how it is, owning a big house like that – it requires a lot of upkeep. Maybe he hasn't been able to manage it all.'

'He's young and strong, of course he can cope,' said Hilda dismissively. 'You sound just like my daughter – not coping, honestly, people of my generation get on with life, we don't sit around staring at our navels wondering if it's all too much. If it weren't for my daughter and all her agonising about life, I would still be in my home.'

'You don't think it's possible that Judy really couldn't cope either, that maybe running the business and looking after you was too much?'

'You're being ridiculous,' said Hilda, riled by Emma. 'My family is tough, coping is what we do. The only one who didn't cope was my husband . . .'

Hilda stopped abruptly and fiddled with her cup, giving Emma the impression that she regretted being quite so harsh, that perhaps Emma had a point after all.

'What happened to Alfred?' Emma asked carefully.

Hilda sucked in a lungful of air. 'He was injured in the Falklands. A device blew off his leg.'

Emma flinched. 'I'm sorry to hear that,' she whispered, trying to hold back the image of Dawn's leg lying in the middle of the road.

'I was angry for a long time, but Alfred always said there was no point in being angry or dwelling on the past.'

'He survived?' asked Emma, who thought there were many times over the last six months, when she'd battled the anger she felt towards the bomber, that she could have benefited from such advice. She hated that he'd torn Dawn away from her daughters, and damaged so many other people's lives and, at the same time, she wondered what and whom had driven him to such a desperate act. So often she'd half-wished the bomb had taken her, not Dawn.

'He survived the physical injury but not the mental one. A couple of years later he killed himself.'

'I'm so dreadfully sorry,' said Emma, stunned by Hilda's revelation. Judy's comment about her father never fully leaving the army behind suddenly made sense.

'It's not your fault,' said Hilda, surprising Emma by reaching out her hand, her skin paper thin. 'It's nobody's fault. If he'd told me he was suffering I might have been able to help; even if I didn't fully understand I could have shared his burden, but he didn't; he locked it all away. We all have demons to face; better to face them head on than to dwell on them and hide them away from the world.'

'Yes,' said Emma, the word catching in her throat as she thought about her mum and Christmas Eve. *Maybe*, she thought, *it's time I stopped trying to protect Mum, and stopped trying to carry all of this alone. Maybe I should tell her about Christmas Eve. Perhaps, in the end, we might both be lighter for it.*

Chapter 14

'Post checkout coffee?' sang Emma, her head poking through the loft hatch.

'Always,' replied Aidan, who'd become used to Emma bringing him a coffee each morning after the guests had departed. Over the last month they'd fallen into a rhythm of Aidan working on the roof in the morning before he went to work on the boats in the afternoons and evenings, and Emma had managed, for the most part, to keep her crush in check.

'How's it looking?'

Aidan ran his hand over the newly strengthened rafters, which he'd managed to rid of burn stains. It amazed Emma that he'd managed to make a charred, ash-filled corner of an ancient attic look as if it had been built yesterday.

'Bone dry,' he said, knocking on the newly installed plywood. 'Once the slates arrive it'll be as good as new.'

'Do you how much longer they'll be?' asked Emma, handing him his coffee. She worried that until the slates were on there was a risk of water getting in. Aidan had told her about the delay with the order a few weeks ago and, until that was rectified, there was nothing either one of them could do.

'Should be any day; the membrane's keeping it watertight for now,' he said, crouching down on his haunches, giving Emma an eyeful of his crotch.

'Great,' she said, not entirely sure where to look.

'Full house tonight?'

'Three rooms going out, three rooms coming in,' she said quickly, his manhood still in her eyeline.

'You'd better get to it then.'

'Better had.'

Emma descended the ladder, her eyes still out on stalks, and nipped into her private sitting room where she collected a mug from the coffee table that she'd bought for a steal at the local second-hand shop. She plumped a couple of tapestry cushions on the linen sofa and adjusted the seagrass rug before repositioning the heavy cotton curtains the colour of soft clouds.

'There, all in order,' she said, marvelling at the transformation. It was only a few weeks ago that the room had been heavy with the smell of smoke, and Hilda's furniture and decor had sucked all light out of the room. Now, with the help of Aidan and Rhona, it was a beautiful haven for Emma to retreat to at the end of her long days. She often sat at the window of an evening looking out to sea, with a cup of herbal tea, letting the busy day seep away before going to bed.

In her bedroom, also newly decorated, her bed was now positioned so that Emma woke up looking out to sea. She collected her pyjamas from where she'd tossed them on her pale-blue, herringbone bed throw, picked a couple of natural weave cushions off the floor and positioned them neatly on the bed before pulling the simple white blind right to the top to allow the mid-morning light to flood in. She paused for a moment at the window, gazing at the clouds and sea, and thought, just like Hilda, how she could never tire of the view.

With her laundry and washing-up in a small basket Emma descended the stairs to the middle floor where Rhona was busy tossing towels and bedclothes into the landing.

'Today's the day that Finn arrives,' Emma reminded her, not that she needed to.

'I haven't time for a man,' Rhona replied, also in a sing-song voice, which Emma knew was her way of deflecting her nervous excitement.

'I'll bet he's excited to see you,' Emma sang back.

'We'll see-ee,' said Rhona, disappearing into the en-suite of the largest room, where she couldn't hear Emma's chirpings.

Bundling up the laundry, Emma headed downstairs, thinking how easily she and Rhona had slipped into a routine. After the fire, the house had remained closed for seven days but for the last three weeks the house had been operating at full capacity, the warm, dry weather bringing in visitors from near and far. Despite the pain of the early starts, trying to cook six breakfasts at once, the constant clearing and cleaning, laundry and shopping and meeting and greeting, it had been a fun few weeks and together, Emma and Rhona had quickly found a rhythm; it now felt like second nature to Emma to welcome guests, provide them with breakfast, and reset the rooms.

'Even you haven't got in the way too much, have you boy?' she said, entering the kitchen where Wilbur greeted her with a happy wag of his tail. She spoke to him as if he were an infant, just as the vet's receptionist had. '*And* you've given up eating rotten fish on the beach. Who could ask for more?'

In the laundry room Emma put on the first load. She had learned quickly that doing the laundry was a job that required attention every hour and a half, up to six times a day. It wasn't the most exciting of tasks but, as with everything else in the house, it had become part of a routine that now took care of itself.

'Everything's under control,' she said to Wilbur, who followed her back into the kitchen where she began emptying the first dishwasher load of the day.

'That's me off,' said Aidan, entering the kitchen and immediately fussing Wilbur.

'Okay, see you tomorrow,' replied Emma, her heart sinking a little. Over the last month Aidan had become part of the place, a vital cog in the machine. Whenever he left for the day, Emma felt the house was somehow incomplete.

'See you, big guy,' he said to Wilbur, giving him his daily hug goodbye.

'Bye, Aidan,' she said with a laugh, disguising the little bit of envy she felt for the affection Aidan showered on Wilbur so freely, wishing quietly that one day he might hug her goodbye too.

Emma waggled her doughy fingers at Wilbur, uncertain of how to answer her ringing phone with them covered in shortbread mixture. *Mum* flashed on the screen as the telephone vibrated on the flour-covered table. She licked her index finger clean and jabbed the green button.

'Hold on,' she shouted, attempting to put her mother on speakerphone, creating sticky fingerprints on the screen as she did so. Wilbur, lying on the floor next to Emma, watched her with pitying eyes.

'What you doin', love?'

'Baking,' replied Emma. 'Hilda pointed out that it's more cost-effective to bake biscuits for my guests than to buy them. She even gave me her secret recipe and a few tips to achieve the perfect bake.'

'My my, someone must be in favour,' said Liz, with a laugh.

'I wouldn't go that far,' said Emma, though she did feel as if she was beginning to make inroads.

'I've never seen you bake anything, or not since the time you made green fairy cakes for a Brownie afternoon tea!'

Emma laughed at the memory of how nobody had touched her luminous buns.

'You were devastated,' said Liz.

'It put me off baking for life.'

'Until now.'

Liz was right. If someone had told Emma a year ago that she'd be running a guesthouse and baking Scottish shortbread for guests, she'd have thought them crazy, but over the last month she'd really come to enjoy the rhythm of measuring, mixing and cutting. And Emma loved the satisfying feeling of putting the cooled biscuits in individual cellophane bags, personalising the labels and finishing them with an elegant dark green ribbon.

'Strange how things change,' said Emma.

'Sometimes the worst things that happen to us give way to the best.'

Emma wasn't certain if her mother was referring to the loss of her husband or to a hunch about Christmas Eve, or both, but either way she felt confident Liz had hit the nail on the head. Despite the fire, and the flashbacks it had triggered, every day that she was in Lobster Bay seemed to get better and better.

'At the start of the year I could never have imagined owning this house and having such great new friends. Rhona and Aidan have made the transition so much easier,' said Emma, rolling her shortbread mix into a sausage shape.

'How's Aidan getting on with the roof?'

'He's got it weathertight.'

'That's great, love. It can't be easy for him doing the work alongside running his business.'

'It's not. He's been amazing.'

'I'm sure it's nice just having someone about the place.'

'It really is.'

'And particularly someone who's so good-looking!'

'Mother!' exclaimed Emma, wishing she'd never sent pictures of Aidan working on the roof. She'd sent them to abate her mum's worries about the state of the house, and ever since, Liz hadn't missed an opportunity to comment on his looks.

'Well, he is. Don't tell me you haven't noticed.'

Emma felt her cheeks flush and thanked her lucky stars she wasn't on videophone.

'I'd be lying if I said I hadn't, but he's taken so that's that,' said Emma, underplaying the extent of how much she had noticed. With every passing week she found something new to admire: the way his celestial blue eyes were flecked with gold, how his T-shirts clung in all the right places, and the sheer pinch-ability of his solid, muscular bum.

'If I were 30 years younger—'

'Well you're not, and I've no intention of becoming the "other woman".'

'You said yourself, they're always quarrelling.'

'Mother, end of conversation,' said Emma, chopping her shortbread roll into circles, and thinking how odd it was that in all the time they'd spent together this last month, Aidan had never once brought up Eve. She found it particularly strange given the number of arguments that so often drifted through Aidan and Eve's open kitchen window and into Emma's of an evening. It surprised her that he never mentioned the tension and wondered what that said about their friendship. 'Tell me what you and Gary have been up to.'

'Nothing much. He's out at the pub just now.'

'He's feeling better?'

'Seems to be.'

'Did you get to the bottom of what was wrong?'

'Nothing showed up in blood tests the doctor took. Just a bit run-down, maybe.'

'Maybe,' said Emma, placing the biscuits on the baking sheet. 'Why don't you make the most it and come up for a visit? I could look after you for a change. Have a proper break.'

'You know what, love, I think I will. It would be good to have some time alone with you.'

'Agreed,' said Emma, who, since her chat with Hilda, had been wanting to find an opportunity to talk to her mum about Christmas Eve; it was a conversation she could only have in person. 'Why don't you book something for the start of August?'

'I'll have a look at train times tonight.'

The doorbell rang as Emma was washing her hands.

'Better go, Mum, guests arriving. Let me know what you manage to book.'

'Will do, love.'

Hanging up the phone, Emma massaged Wilbur's ears. 'Good boy,' she said, praising him for not barking at the bell; there was nothing less welcoming to Emma than an enormous barking dog.

'Hi,' said Emma, opening the door to a young couple, their arms wrapped around each other. 'You must be Tina and Tom.'

'We sure are!' said Tina, beaming with joy as Emma ushered them in.

Emma had learnt plenty about couples over the last few weeks. For the most part she was now able to deduce on opening the front door which income bracket people fell into, how long they'd been together, and what level of maintenance they'd turn out to be. Emma recognised immediately that: Tina and Tom didn't have much money, their flimsy wheelie-case told her that; they hadn't been together long, the tightness of their hand-holding gave that away; and they were going to be pretty low on the maintenance scale – younger guests rarely wanted anything extra.

'Wow,' squealed Tina. 'Your house is so lovely. We could never afford something like this, could we babe?'

'Nuh-huh,' said Tom, lifting both the bags, his beach-ready body covered in fake tan.

'Let me show you to your room,' said Emma, grabbing their key from the sideboard and leading them upstairs.

'Here we are,' said Emma, leading Tina and Tom into the bedroom that overlooked the village; with its cream wrought-iron bedframe and thick patchwork quilt, Emma thought it the cosiest of the rooms.

'It's beautiful, innit babe?'

Tom looked around, dumbstruck.

'All the information you need is here,' said Emma, pointing to the little frame on the dressing table. 'If there's anything else you need please just ask.'

Emma left, closing the door behind her. As she made her way downstairs she was sure she heard a shriek of pleasure and two bodies flinging themselves onto the bed.

'I think the mattress will be given a good test tonight,' said Emma to Wilbur, whose tail brushed the kitchen floor in excitement as Emma returned. Rhona and Aidan always greeted Wilbur with a chat and a ruffle and, one way or another, their behaviour towards the dog seemed to have worn off on Emma.

'Lucky for some,' she said as an afterthought, washing her hands and then rubbing her trousers down with a lint roller. As much as she was getting used to Wilbur, she still didn't want to answer the door covered in dog hair.

Emma tried to remember the last time she'd been intimate with Chris, but couldn't. Their sex life had dwindled to birthdays, anniversaries and when they'd been drunk, and even then it was boringly routine. Given she'd been sleeping on her mother's couch after leaving Chris, there hadn't been anyone since, and nor was she certain there'd be anybody soon. She'd be lying if she said she hadn't imagined it with Aidan, the two of them pulling urgently at each other's clothes, impulsive and raw, in a way she and Chris had never been. *But Aidan is taken*, she reminded herself, and there wasn't anyone else in Lobster who'd caught her eye, so the chance of anything happening anytime soon was slim.

The doorbell rang again just as Emma was about to unload the dishwasher, and she hurried through to the hall to see who it was.

'Finn!' she said brightly, welcoming him with a kiss on his cheek. 'It's lovely to have you back.'

'Glad to be back,' he said, a mischievous grin forming on his lips.

'Let me take you up,' she said, grabbing his key and starting up the stairs, enquiring about his journey and how he'd been. 'Well, I'll let you settle in,' she said, handing him his key. 'I imagine you're keen to freshen up.'

Returning to the kitchen, Emma smiled as she wiped the cutlery dry, happy for Rhona that Finn had returned. As she sorted the cutlery, sounds of Aidan and Eve arguing from next door came through the window. The kitchens were far enough apart for Emma to rarely hear exactly what was being said but the occasional words would drift across.

'Go screw yourself!' Emma heard Eve scream and then the low, indistinct murmurings of Aidan's reply.

Emma pulled a face at Wilbur. 'Shit, sounds like a bad one.'

Wilbur put a paw over his muzzle, making Emma laugh.

'Oh well, nothing to do with me,' she said, going through to the dining room with the clean cutlery.

Setting the tables Emma heard and felt the shudder of Aidan's front door being slammed shut. Glancing out of the window she saw Eve storm from the house, a small suitcase in hand, and get into her car. Seconds later Aidan appeared in his front garden and threw up his arms in frustration as he watched Eve speed off up the road.

Before Emma could look away Aidan spotted her at the window, walked out of his garden and entered Emma's.

'You okay?' she asked, opening the front door to him before he rang the bell.

'I guess you saw,' said Aidan, looking browbeaten.

'Fancy a beer?' she asked. What she really wanted was to ask if he needed a hug but, despite their growing friendship, she didn't feel quite comfortable in doing so.

Aidan was quick to accept the offer and together they collected drinks from the fridge and headed into the garden, finding a corner still bathed in warm evening sun.

'I wish I lived with you, old buddy, and not Eve,' said Aidan, allowing Wilbur to place his head on his thigh, his big brown eyes looking tenderly up at him. 'Life would be much simpler.'

'But remember, Eve doesn't slobber on the furniture, leave hairballs on the floor or poop in the garden.'

'No, that's more my domain,' said Aidan, and they laughed, causing the tension in Aidan's shoulders to disperse, and he relaxed into his chair.

'A dog and a beer – you're a simple bloke,' said Emma.

'Tell that to Eve!'

'You'll figure things out,' she said, feeling a touch ashamed that a part of her hoped they wouldn't.

Aidan took a long swig of his beer. 'We'll see.'

'Have you really lived in the same house all your life?' asked Emma, hoping to shift the focus away from Eve.

'I was born in the bathroom.'

'You were not!' said Emma, searching his eyes to see if he was joking.

'Was too. My dad was at sea, Mum couldn't drive, and the ambulance didn't make it in time.'

'That's amazing, you live in the same place you were actually born.'

'The old place means a lot to me,' he said, and Emma could tell he was talking about more than his birth.

'It must have been fun growing up in such a big house.'

'Hide-and-seek could take days.'

'I can imagine.'

'I spent hours sliding down the stairs on trays, and shooting soldiers off the banister.'

'And only a hop, skip and a jump away from the beach,' said Emma, wishing her childhood had been so idyllic. To get to a beach from Northampton was a six-hour round trip.

'The beach really came into its own when I was a teenager.'

'Let me guess, cigarettes and alcohol, and girls.'

'I can't pretend there were all that many girls but the fags and booze, maybe . . .'

'Nice,' joked Emma, a smidge envious, not quite able to believe that girls hadn't swarmed around him, especially after what Rhona had said about him and Phil being competitive about women. Emma's own teenage years had mostly been spent in her bedroom, listening to Elbow, Keane and Coldplay. 'And you never moved away?' she asked leadingly, knowing perfectly well that he had, wanting to find out more.

'I did at one point, not that I really wanted to but, you know, I was young . . . I made mistakes.'

'Where did you go?'

'I headed north, where there's more fishing and boats to repair, but I came back when—'

Emma knew how the story ended but, sensing Aidan wasn't ready to talk about it, she redirected the conversation and they chatted idly until there were six empty cans on the garden table and Aidan had forgotten all about his argument with Eve.

'How come you don't have a fella then?' Aidan asked, having had just enough beer to have lost his inhibitions.

'I did,' said Emma, thinking of Chris.

'What happened?'

Emma scrunched up her nose, not having had quite enough to drink to blurt out the events of Christmas Eve. 'He just wasn't the one.' Emma thought for a moment. 'I figure, if my dad were alive he wouldn't have thought him good enough.'

'What happened to your dad?'

'Heart attack,' said Emma, the words catching in her throat.

Aidan reached across and placed his hand over Emma's. It was the only time, other than when he'd rubbed her back at the vets, that he'd purposefully touched her, and the act made her entire body quiver.

'Sounds rough.'

'It was.' An image of her dad in his hospital bed, grey and lifeless even before death, filled her mind. She remembered the flecks of white paint that had speckled his dark hair, face and hands, and she'd known then that he must have been painting a ceiling when it happened. He'd fallen from his ladder and been found by a client, who'd called the ambulance. By the time Liz had got to the hospital and called Emma's school, he was almost gone. He'd left for work that morning feeling fine. Emma still found it hard to fathom.

'I lost both my parents a few years back,' he said quietly, in a way that suggested he might not have vocalised it before.

Emma said nothing, not wanting to say that she'd already heard, and instead allowed a silence that enabled him to talk. She turned her hand so that she was now holding his, and the two of them looked at their interlocked fingers.

'The worst of it is, nobody knows what happened. Just that their boat was found capsized and their bodies washed up.'

Emma inhaled sharply, overwhelmed by the gruesomeness of what Aidan must have gone through. 'I can't imagine.'

He squeezed her hand tight. 'It was shit for a long time. But it gets easier.'

'Yes,' said Emma, who understood that grief did become less consuming over time.

The two of them sat, holding hands, watching the gulls overhead and taking in the gentle sounds of summer – pigeons cooing in the tall sycamore, a lawnmower a few gardens down, and the gentle swell of the sea – when a sound from the house made them turn to each other.

'What was that?' Emma asked.

They listened to see if they could hear it again.

A scream came from inside. It was patently clear that it wasn't a scream of pain but of passion.

Emma and Aidan looked at each other with wide, twinkling eyes.

'Sounds like Tina and Tom are having fun!' said Emma.

Aidan rubbed his thumb gently over Emma's and gazed at her with a look that was both longing and naughty. 'I don't suppose you fancy having some fun of our own, do you?'

Emma scrutinised his eyes, trying to figure out if he was serious or not.

'What about your girlfriend?' she whispered, drawn in by his gaze.

'Haven't got one,' he said, leaning in and kissing her in a way that suggested Eve was a thing of the past.

Chapter 15

Aidan grabbed Emma's hand and together they dashed from the garden and up the two flights of stairs, keeping quiet like secretive children, so as not to disturb the guests. Closing Emma's bedroom door and collapsing on the bed, panting from their exertions, they burst into laughter.

'It is just me or does this feel ridiculously naughty?' asked Emma, her heartbeat racing.

Aidan turned on his side to face her, placing his hand on her waist, his fingers feeling like silk on Emma's goose-pimpled skin. 'It's like being a teenager again and doing it, with your parents in the next room,' he whispered.

Emma laughed, not quite knowing that feeling – she'd left home before she lost her virginity.

'Difference being, now we know what we're doing and exactly what we like,' said Aidan, who unbuttoned Emma's jeans then sat astride her, his weight pinning her to the bed. Emma revelled in the fact that his confidence in no way stalled at the bedroom door.

As Aidan pulled off his T-shirt, Emma inhaled his scent, natural after a hard day's work, her lust rising. She traced her fingers over his powerful chest and stomach, feeling the muscles that lay beneath and the light covering of hair.

'Are you absolutely certain you're single?' asked Emma. For all her excitement she couldn't quite shift the thought of Eve.

'Absolutely,' he said, bending down to kiss her navel, making Emma swell in delight and all her thoughts to evaporate.

Several hours later, having explored every inch of each other's bodies and physically exhausted themselves, Emma lay in Aidan's arms, her lips in a broad lazy smile.

'What are you smiling about?' he asked.

'The unexpectedness of this,' she said, circling his chest hair with her finger.

'You think this is unexpected?'

Emma looked up. 'You don't?'

With a tender kiss to her forehead he told her, '*This* has been on my mind since you let Wilbur escape.'

Emma thought for a moment. 'You mean the day you told me you wouldn't expect a city girl to know how to handle a dog like Wilbur.'

Aidan let out a mischievous laugh. 'Exactly. You didn't feel the same about me?'

Playfully, Emma slapped Aidan on the stomach. 'Are you kidding me? I thought you were a first-class arse.'

'You did not!'

'I did!'

'I guess I can be a bit stand-offish.'

'A bit?!'

'I apologise.'

'You're forgiven. Now I just think you *have* a first-class arse,' she said, reaching under the covers to give it a feel.

'Not so fine as yours,' he said, stretching behind her to give her bum a squeeze, and with that the two of them began kissing again, their lips salty from exertion, and caressing each other once more.

Aidan rolled Emma on top of him and, as he did, a car backfired, causing her to turn in the direction of the noise. Immediately she was hit by a vivid flashback to the white light of the blast and the jolt of being forced off her feet.

'You okay?' he asked, when she froze on top of him.

Emma ruffled her hair with her hands, trying to rid herself of the sensation of dust that seemed to cling to every strand.

'Emma?'

She focused on her breathing, trying to control her light-headedness and racing heart; gradually the sensations eased, and Aidan's voice came into focus.

'What's up?' he asked, his hand on her arm.

Emma, still staring out of the window, tried to shake off the moment. 'Sorry,' she said, attempting to laugh it off. 'I must be going mad.'

Aidan's brow crinkled. 'You'd tell me if something was wrong, right?'

'Of course,' she fibbed, fully focused on Aidan again, not wanting her past to spoil the present.

'You looked the way you did in the attic after the fire.'

She bent down and placed tiny kisses on his collar bones. 'Aidan, I promise, there's nothing to worry about,' she said, even though she knew in her heart that shouldering this alone was no longer a good plan.

Aidan leant up to plant delicate kisses between her breasts. 'If you say so.'

'I say so,' said Emma, returning to what she had started.

*

'Tina and Tom would like bacon and eggs,' said Aidan, the next morning, wrapping his arms around Emma in the kitchen, having just taken the couple's order in the dining room.

'Do they look particularly knackered?'

'By the look of them I reckon they shagged themselves senseless too.'

'Oi!' said Emma, whipping him with a dishcloth. 'Keep your voice down.'

'Sorry, Miss,' he said, playfully stealing the cloth and slapping her with it gently on the bum.

'Make yourself useful and pass me some eggs.'

Aidan handed Emma some eggs which she whisked as he trimmed bacon.

'Better get the toast on,' said Aidan, stealing a little squeeze of Emma's waist as he went to get the bread.

'Thank you,' said Emma, who couldn't believe that in the space of 12 hours they'd gone from being friends to lovers. She felt exhilarated and nauseous both at once.

'Morning,' said Rhona, joining them in the kitchen, catching Aidan nibbling Emma's neck as she fried the bacon.

'Morning, Rhona,' said Emma, batting Aidan away with a slatted utensil. 'I forgot you had a key.'

'So it would seem,' she teased, her eyes twinkling knowingly.

'Finn arrived,' said Emma after Aidan had made himself scarce by taking Tina and Tom's breakfast through to the dining room.

'Is he down for breakfast yet?' Rhona asked, frantically tidying her hair and tucking in her top.

'Not yet,' said Emma, rinsing out the bacon pan. 'But make sure you take his order when he is.'

'I will,' said Rhona, going through to the laundry where she started smoothing and folding towels at a rate that was fast even by her standards.

'Tina and Tom have definitely worked up an appetite,' said Aidan, returning to the kitchen, with a tray laden with empty cereal bowls, fruit skins and yoghurt pots. 'And the Irish bloke has just come down – I told him I'd be back in a minute to take his order.'

'No need,' said Emma, indicating with her eyes to Rhona that she should go through to the dining room. 'Rhona and I can finish breakfast. Why don't you head out and start clearing the shed? I'll join you after checkout.'

'Whatever you want,' he said, watching Rhona scurry through the front before wrapping his arms around Emma and kissing her deeply.

'Go!' she said, prising him off and shooing him away when she heard Rhona coming back through.

Rhona sank back against the counter, placing the order book on the surface. 'God, that guy's gorgeous. And his voice . . .'

'It is pretty special,' replied Emma, trying to make out Rhona's scribble. 'What's his order?'

'Sorry. I had the shakes. Full Scottish with fried eggs.'

'When you take his order through make sure you find out what his plans are for the day,' said Emma, putting a slice of black pudding onto the hot plate and adding butter to the frying pan.

'Why?'

'Because that way, when you go to check everything's okay or collect his plate, you can ask him out.'

'I'm not asking him out!'

'Why not?'

'Do you know when I last asked someone out?'

Emma cast her a blank look.

'Third year of high school! That's when. Over 15 years ago. And if I remember rightly that didn't exactly go well so, no, I'm not asking him out.'

'Suit yourself,' said Emma, circling the mushrooms in the pan. 'But tell me this, if he said "no" what would you have lost? 30 seconds of pride? If he says "yes" what might you gain? Possibly,' said Emma, waggling her bacon flipper at Rhona, 'a lifetime of happiness?'

Rhona let out a disparaging snort.

'I'm just saying,' said Emma. 'It doesn't seem like much of a gamble.'

'Well, maybe not,' said Rhona, after some thought. 'But I'm still not doing it.'

Emma began plating up Finn's breakfast. 'I dare you.'

'I'm not 12, Emma.'

'No, you're not, you're 31 years old and in the prime of your life. Finn would be lucky to have someone like you ask him out. So, go through there and do it, or else I'll do it for you.'

'Just give me his breakfast,' said Rhona, shaking her head.

With Rhona in the dining room, Emma set about cleaning the kitchen down and loading the dishwasher. Rhona returned after a couple of minutes

'Did you ask him?'

'I asked him what type of sauce he would like,' Rhona replied dryly.

'We don't serve the sort of *sauce* he's interested in at breakfast,' said Emma with a smirk.

'I can't ask him out before he has his breakfast.'

'Then make sure you do it after.'

'Fine!' said Rhona, beaten into submission. 'Just give the poor bloke five minutes to eat.'

It felt to Emma like a hundred years waiting for the second hand to move five times round the clock.

'Go, go, go,' she said, when the time had eventually passed. 'And remember, you're a young, hot chick.'

'With four kids.'

'Yeah, yeah,' said Emma, watching Rhona leave.

If five minutes had felt like a hundred then the eight minutes it took for Rhona to return with Finn's breakfast plate felt like an eternity.

'What did he say?' asked Emma, bouncing in excitement.

Rhona eyes were filled with disappointment, and suddenly Emma regretted her eagerness, she'd pushed her friend into an awkward situation, read the signs incorrectly – until Rhona cracked and her face broke into the most enormous smile.

'He said yes!' she said, keeping her voice low and doing tiny rapid claps of her hands.

'Oh my God,' squealed Emma, trying to keep her voice down. She clutched Rhona's hands and jumped on the spot with delight. 'When for?'

'Tonight, so you're on childminding duty if I can't find a sitter.'

'Deal,' said Emma, who'd run to Timbuktu and back in the nude if it meant Rhona could have one nice night with Finn.

After a quick cuppa and a gossip about last night, Rhona headed upstairs and Emma returned to loading the dishwasher with a happy glow. She was only brought out of her reverie when Aidan came back in from outside.

'What's up?' she asked, when she saw his heavy expression.

'I've just been speaking to a former client of mine.'

'Someone you built a boat for?'

'A yacht, to be precise.'

'Fancy!' said Emma, unclear why that had made him so downcast.

Aidan wrapped an arm around Emma. 'The yacht's been hit and the hull's wrecked. He needs me to head down to the south coast to repair it.'

'How long will it take?'

'It's hard to say but, from the pictures, I imagine it'll be around six weeks.'

'And you need the money, right?' she said, looking up at him, gutted that he was going to have to leave.

'It's more than I can make in an entire summer on my own.'

'Then you have to take it,' said Emma, wishing it wasn't the case but knowing he had no choice.

He kissed her lightly on the lips then drank in the scent of her forehead. 'I promise when I'm back we'll start exactly where we left off.'

221

'I'll hold you to that,' said Emma, nestling her head into his chest, hoping the relationship hadn't ended before it had really begun.

Chapter 16

Emma stood over the cooker, whisking eggs, wishing that Aidan was with her. He'd left for the south coast almost a fortnight ago, and now it felt to Emma as if the whole affair had been a very elaborate dream. One way or another all the early starts, cooking and cleaning felt less enjoyable without him about the place.

'Maybe he'll manage to message today,' she said to Wilbur, who was lying next to her, hopeful of a scrap of sausage coming his way. Emma had become far more generous with her titbits, and Wilbur had come to look for them in a way he hadn't done when she first moved in.

'Or maybe he won't,' she continued, wondering why, for the gazillionth time, Aidan hadn't messaged over the last few days. The most she could take from the situation was that she knew he was holed up in a shipyard most of the day with a bunch of beefy blokes and not a woman in sight.

'At least I've no competition,' she said, serving the eggs then carrying them through to the dining room where one of her guests was waiting.

'That looks lovely, thank you, Emma,' said Joan, admiring her full Scottish breakfast. Joan, in her sixties and of ample size, had been staying with Emma for almost a week; she'd ordered the same thing every day.

'No problem,' said Emma, bringing the ketchup she knew Joan liked from its spot on the dresser. 'Would you like your room spruced up today?'

'Yes, please, dear, if it's not too much trouble.'

'No trouble at all,' said Emma, making a note on the little pad she kept in her apron pocket to ask Rhona to give the room a clean.

As Emma was going back to the kitchen, two further guests came down for breakfast.

'Can I take your order straightaway or would you like some time?' asked Emma, hoping that they'd ask to browse the menu so that she could go back to the kitchen to clean some pans.

'I'll take the full Scottish with poached eggs,' said Mark, who was staying for only a night with his friend Andrew. They'd arrived the previous afternoon in their shorts and hiking boots, keen to tell Emma about their walk along all 200 kilometres of the county's coastal path, which they were attempting to walk in just five days.

'And I'll take the same but with scrambled,' said Andrew, helping himself to a large bowl of muesli from the dresser.

'It'll be around 15 minutes,' said Emma, trying not to show how much poached eggs terrified her. A couple of weeks after she first opened she'd spent an evening trying to perfect them with little success. They either came our sloppy and misshapen or a reasonable shape but hard as bullets. Wilbur had eaten more than his fair share of rejects that evening, and Emma had suffered the consequences, having to open the kitchen windows and doors to get rid of his eggy wind. All the tips in the world – vinegar, microwave, clingfilm – failed to help in her quest to perfect them, and guests always had some pointer of their own. The endless commentary on how best to poach an egg drove her potty.

'Right, poached eggs,' she said in the kitchen, having cooked all of the other six ingredients. 'Three-and-a-half minutes and then do the scrambled.'

Emma cracked two eggs into the simmering water and, just as she did, the desk bell rang for checkout.

'Damn it,' she said, quickly setting the timer and hurrying out to the hall.

'Can we check out now?' asked Leah, a young Swedish woman who'd been visiting with her husband for a friend's wedding.

'Of course,' said Emma, grabbing the card machine from its stand. 'How was the wedding?'

Emma regretted the question immediately. Checkout was always the time that her guests wanted to chat and usually it wasn't a problem, when breakfast was over, and the kitchen and dining room had been cleared. Emma was happy to blether for a few minutes about their stay or where they were headed next, but when Emma asked about a wedding she could be standing for the best part of 20 minutes, and this morning Emma didn't have three to spare, let alone 20.

'It was perfect, wasn't it, Lars?'

Lars nodded dutifully, his eyes heavy from the night before.

'The bride looked amazing and you should have seen the page boys – they wore tiny kilts!'

'Cute,' said Emma, punching the amount owed into the machine.

'And the venue is to die for – the views! I can't wait to see the photographs.'

'It certainly is pretty up there,' said Emma, who knew of the old house where the wedding had been held.

'We'll never forget it, will we, Lars?'

Lars shook his head in agreement, but from the state of his pale skin and bloodshot eyes, Emma guessed he'd probably already forgotten quite a lot of it.

'You should have seen the food—'

Emma offered Leah the payment device which she took but did nothing with. Instead she started listing everything they'd eaten the previous day.

'Gorgeous,' said Emma, when Leah eventually stopped talking about the menu. She heard the egg timer ring in the kitchen and began to smell bacon crisping a little too much in the oven. She gently nudged the card machine in Leah's hand.

'The best man's speech was so funny, the groom had everyone in tears. Oh, and then the dancing.'

As Leah launched into a detailed account of the ceilidh, Emma heard the phone ringing. In that moment with breakfast spoiling, the phone going unanswered, guests waiting and Leah chattering on, Emma thought her head might burst.

'Can I ask you to pop in your four-digit code,' she said, and Leah at last entered the numbers and handed the machine back to Emma.

'Thank you,' she said, watching for the device to connect, which always seemed to take far longer when something else needed attending to. 'There we are,' she said, eventually ripping off the receipt and handing it to Leah alongside her card. 'Are you heading straight to the airport?'

'We are,' said Leah, picking up her case.

'Oh well, we all have to get back to the daily grind eventually,' said Emma, ushering them towards the door. 'It's been lovely having you.'

'We'll be back,' said Leah, as Emma reached around her to open the door.

'I'll look forward to it,' she said, all but shooing them out. 'Goodbye now!'

Leah and Lars barely had time to wave before Emma had closed the door and legged it back to the kitchen. She was met by a pan boiling over, with pieces of poached egg pooling on the cooker, and the smell of singed meat wafting from the oven.

Opening the oven door, Emma found the rest of breakfast, which had been perfectly cooked prior to Leah's wedding spiel, not charred exactly but only just on the right side of burnt.

'Bugger,' she said, quickly boiling the kettle again, emptying the pan and refilling it before cracking in two new eggs.

She spent the next couple of minutes scraping black pudding and picking at singed sausages before trying to arrange them on warm plates in a way that showed them to their best and hid most of the cremated bits. After hastily whipping some scrambled eggs together she threw the eggs onto the plates and marched them through to the dining room where she hoped Andrew and Mark wouldn't notice the burnt edges.

'Almost perfect poached eggs,' said Andrew, examining the egg with a knife as if he were a judge on *Masterchef*. 'I find if you—'

'Sorry, I hear the phone ringing,' said Emma, who felt certain if she had to listen to Andrew bleat on about how to poach the perfect egg she would likely grab his plate and whack him over the head.

*

'I'm so sorry to let you down, Emma,' said Rhona, on the other end of the phone.

'It's not your fault that little Ella's sick,' said Emma, trying to figure out how she was going to reschedule an already busy day to include cleaning and resetting three bedrooms on her own.

'I know, but I feel bad to land you in it; hopefully she'll be better in a few days.'

'I promise, it's no problem,' she fibbed; Rhona had done so much extra work for Emma since Aidan left that there was no way she could possibly grumble. 'Any news from Finn?'

'He's busy working on designs. I think he's hoping to be back over in another month or so.'

'That's fantastic,' said Emma, who still got a prickle of delight every time she thought about Rhona and Finn.

She'd been sitting at the dining room window on the evening of their first date and seen them stumble out of the little Italian restaurant across the way, their laughter carrying in the quiet, still night, and she'd watched as Finn placed his hand in the small of Rhona's back as they crossed the road. They agreed to see each other two more times before he returned to Ireland; Rhona had been walking on air ever since, talking to him most days and looking forward to when they could see each other again. 'Let me know how Ella's doing, okay?'

After hanging up, Emma went straight to the bread-bin, took out some waffles and toasted them before coating them in butter.

'Carbs should do the trick,' she said to Wilbur, while mentally rearranging her next few days, wondering if her mother might be able to lend a helping hand when she arrived tomorrow. 'First up, clear the dining room.'

Emma was relieved to find that all of the guests had left, leaving her to rid the tables of dirty dishes in peace rather than having to make small talk or become embroiled in phoning for taxis or giving directions to local places of interest. As she went around the tables she spotted that Andrew and Mark had left about half of their overcooked breakfast, something that rarely happened but which didn't come as much of a surprise on this occasion.

'Lots of scraps for you today,' she said to Wilbur in the kitchen, scraping the remains into a special pot she'd set aside for doggie treats.

Once the dishwasher was on and tablecloths loaded into the washing machine, Emma headed upstairs to start clearing the rooms. As she stripped the bed in the smaller back room, wondering what it was that people did to get their sheets into such a tangle, her phone rang. Her mum's picture, of her and Gary cuddling on the sofa, flashed at her.

'Hi, Mum,' she called through the speakerphone.

'Hiya, love. What you up to?'

'Cleaning rooms,' she said, grabbing the wet towels from the bathroom and throwing them out onto the landing.

'Where's Rhona?'

'She's off for a couple of days; her youngest's not well.'

'Sorry to hear that, love. Can you manage on your own?'

'I might have to rope you in over the next few days,' said Emma, who still wasn't entirely sure how she was going to get through resetting all the rooms, the laundry and ironing, the shopping *and* all the bookings admin before her next lot of guests arrived around 4 p.m. 'Have you packed already?'

'I'm really sorry, love, that's the reason I'm calling – I'm going to have to cancel.'

Emma's heart sank. For all that there were always people in the house, it was rare that she had a chance to have any significant conversation. Until owning a guesthouse, she hadn't realised it was possible to be surrounded by people and feel lonely at the same time.

'Gary's health's gone downhill again, he really needs me to stay here.'

'Fine,' said Emma, emptying the bin next to the toilet.

'You sound upset.'

'I'm not, I'm used to Gary getting his way,' she said, vigorously scouring the loo with a brush, trying to get rid of an obstinate piece of poo.

'That's not fair, love.'

'What about you, Mum? You need a break.'

'I'm fine. I enjoy taking care of him.'

Having finished cleaning the loo, Emma returned the brush to its stand, peeled off her rubber gloves and wiped her beaded brow. 'I guess you must,' she said.

An uncharacteristic silence fell between them as Emma rummaged in the cleaning cupboard for the shower spray.

'Have you heard from Chris?' asked Liz, as Emma rapidly pulled the trigger of the bottle in the shower.

'Mum, why would I have?' she asked, irritated by the question.

'Alright, love, there's no need to sound like that. Honestly, some days I wonder where you get your ability to pigeonhole everything.'

'I haven't time for this right now. I'll call you later,' said Emma, furiously scrubbing the shower door and fighting back tears, hating the fact that her mother had touched a nerve about locking things away. And she hated it even more that she was being prickly towards her, when what she really wanted was to convey disappointment and to talk things through.

It took Emma over two hours to clear, clean and reset the rooms, and by the time she was finished her muscles ached and her head hurt.

'How does Rhona do this every day?' she asked herself, carrying a bin liner of rubbish, a huge pile of towels and a big bag full of bed linen. All she wanted to do was sit down and have a cup of tea but there was the laundry to take out and put on, the dishwasher to empty, and ironing to do before going out for the food shopping.

'Maybe I should have listened to Jane,' she grumbled, dumping the towels and bed linen in the laundry room then taking the tablecloths out of the machine. 'Maybe it was insane of me to think I could ever have managed all of this on my own.'

*

'Hi, Emma, how you doing?' asked Phil, a little later that afternoon.

233

'Not bad,' said Emma, happy to see Phil and his sunny face. Every time she visited his shop she felt terrible for not having had the time to take him up on his kind offer of meeting for a dog walk. She'd put him off so many times that it now felt awkward to mention it.

'What can I get you?'

'Five packs of bacon, 60 sausages and a full black pudding please.'

'Coming right up,' he said, dashing out to the back of the shop to fetch what she needed. Emma had learnt early on after the guesthouse opened that butchers rarely have 60 pork sausages lying in the counter; bulk orders were always handled out back.

As she waited the shop door opened and Judy stepped in, looking neater than ever in a pair of high-waisted trousers with sharp creases down the front, and a pearl-buttoned twinset.

'Hi, Judy, how are you?'

Judy shuddered the way people do when someone walks over their grave. 'I've just had word from Seaview that mother has been "bullying" one of the other residents. Why they think I can do anything about it is anybody's guess.'

'Oh dear,' said Emma, trying unsuccessfully to supress a smile. 'That's the last thing you need. Would you like me to go and see her?'

'Do you think she'll listen to you?'

'She might. We had a bit of a breakthrough last time I visited. I found the note and took it to her, it seemed to thaw the ice,' said Emma, realising she hadn't seen Judy in well over a month.

'I'm glad, where did you find it?'

'In the loft, in a box of paperwork.'

Judy let out a little laugh, mortified by her mistake. 'I was in such a rush towards the end, trying to sort everything out, I must have thrown it in with a pile of other things.'

'All's well that ends well,' said Emma, with a little laugh of her own. 'Let me see what I can do. I'm rushed off my feet this week but if I find a moment I promise I'll visit and see what she's up to.'

'Thank you, Emma, I really do appreciate it.'

'No trouble,' said Emma, mentally adding it to her ever-increasing to-do list.

'Here you go then,' said Phil, returning from out back. 'I'll add it to your account.'

'Thanks, Phil.'

'And remember, just give a holler if I can help with Wilbur.'

'Will do,' she replied, surprised at him mentioning it again.

'How are you getting on with him?' asked Judy.

'Not bad,' said Emma, stopping short of saying how Aidan had been a strong, calming influence on Wilbur, giving Emma the confidence to walk Wilbur when the three of them went out together. With Phil in earshot of their conversation she felt it better not to bring him up. 'Hilda would like me to bring him to the summer fete so that's my big goal, to manage him easily on my own by then; things are much better than they were at the start, although he's been a bit less cooperative in the last few days.'

'I've never had much time for my mother's dogs. There's no way I could have taken him myself.'

Emma laughed. 'I felt pretty much the same way in the beginning.'

'Didn't you have much experience of dogs?'

'None,' said Emma. 'The truth is, I didn't know he was part of the house sale. If I had, I might have thought twice!'

Emma watched the colour drain from Judy's cheeks. 'You didn't know about Wilbur?'

'Biggest surprise of my life!'

'But how is that possible, it was handled by the solicitors?'

'It's okay, it was my mistake,' said Emma, reaching out and offering Judy a reassuring rub on the arm. 'I'd say we're almost friends now, or at least willing housemates.'

'Are you certain?'

'I am, and besides, there's always Phil to help out if Wilbur causes me any trouble.'

'Like I said—' said Phil, as Emma reached for the door.

'I'll let you know, Phil,' she said, saying her goodbyes and thinking, as she left, how comforting it was to know that Phil was just around the corner should she need him.

The light had changed by the time Emma left Phil's shop. Rather than the bright, cheerful afternoon it had been when she entered, the sky was now leaden with rain and there was a distinct chill in the air. As Emma dashed for the house, great heavy drops began splashing the pavements and by the time she reached home a full shower was in place.

After shaking off the rain, Emma sat down at the desk to catch up on some admin. In her inbox she spotted a recent email with the title: *Someone has left you a review*. Always intrigued by her guests' thoughts, Emma opened it to discover it was from Andrew and Mark.

Beautiful property in a charming village. Customer service and breakfast could be improved. 2/5

Ouch, thought Emma, who had to accept that the review was fair. She had been in a hurry and barely civil at breakfast *and* their food was burnt. But, despite the fact she couldn't argue, Emma still felt the urge to cry.

In an effort to cheer herself up and win some brownie points with her guests, Emma decided to bake. She was certain individual bags of home-made Rocky Road, instead of her usual shortbread, would go down a treat in the guest rooms, and a portion or two to herself would be a welcome indulgence after the bad review.

'Delicious,' she said, licking the big chocolatey spoon, not caring that she was smearing mixture all over her face – until the door rang.

'Bugger,' she said, grabbing a moist cloth and rubbing it over her face, resulting in a clammy complexion and damp hairline which gave Emma a sweaty appearance.

'Hi,' she said, opening the door, over-egging the smile to compensate for her soggy look. 'You must be the Bergmanns,' she said to the middle-aged couple who wore formal wool coats and wire-framed glasses. 'I'm Emma. Come in!' Thankfully for Emma her guests had been standing in the rain and hardly seemed to notice that Emma was damp too.

Having shown the quiet German couple to their room, Emma returned to the kitchen to find Wilbur looking sheepish in the corner.

'What's up with you?' she asked, stepping in a puddle and almost instantly releasing a shriek.

'What the hell!' she yelled, her soft pump dripping with dog wee.

'Out!' she shouted at the dog. 'Out, out, out!'

And for the first time in their relationship, Wilbur listened to Emma and skulked off to the back door.

Chapter 17

Having cleaned the kitchen floor to within an inch of its life, finished the day's laundry, set the dining room for breakfast, printed invoices for the next day's departures, and learnt the names of the incoming guests, Emma flumped down at the kitchen table.

'I know you need a walk but I'm exhausted,' she said to Wilbur, her head on her arms, as Wilbur paced up and down the floor. Emma's eyes were about to close when he started to whine.

'Okay, okay,' she said, reaching for her phone and managing to hold her head up for just long enough to type a message to Phil.

I know it's horrid weather, but do you fancy a dog walk? Emma

The prospect of walking Wilbur alone in the rain when she was already worn out was a step too far for Emma and, laying her head back on her arms, she prayed Phil would be able to help. She barely had to wait 30 seconds before he replied.

Absolutely! When? ☺ 🐾 🐶

Despite her exhaustion, Emma let out a little laugh, amused at how Phil's message was just like him – as eager and enthusiastic as a puppy dog.

Are you free now? she replied.

On my way!

Phil was at the front door before Emma had even had time to put Wilbur's harness on.

'Let me get the big fella,' he said, striding through to the back as Emma put on her big yellow cagoule.

'I didn't know you knew the house,' she said, following him through.

'I've been delivering meat to Hilda for the last couple of years. She liked me to put it in the fridge for her, plus I did the odd dog walk for her too.'

'Huh, good service,' said Emma as Wilbur pranced excitedly at Phil's feet.

'Hiya, dude!' said Phil, rough and tumbling Wilbur into a frenzy of delight. 'How you doing?'

Together, he and Wilbur went out to the back corridor where Wilbur traced Phil's every move.

'Ready for a run in the rain?' said Phil, encouraging Wilber to spin by circling his hand around his head. Emma couldn't help laughing at them. At one point, Wilbur jumped up and clamped his jaws around Phil's forearm in excitement.

'Ah-ah-aah,' Phil reprimanded, and Wilbur stopped immediately, sitting down so that Phil could pop on his harness and lead.

'You don't think he'll mind?' asked Emma, who, despite Phil's enthusiasm, still wasn't thrilled about the idea of walking in the rain herself.

'Are you crazy! This dog loves the rain – don't you, dude? Newfies were bred for the water. He'll have a blast.'

'Oh-kaay,' said Emma, still unconvinced, the three of them heading out into the rain.

'Where do you usually take him?'

'Whichever way he leads,' said Emma.

Phil laughed. 'If you want to take him to the fete you need to show him who's boss. Same route, same time every day, until he's used to you.'

'Where did you used to take him?'

'The east beach – there's loads of space for him to run there and take a dip if he fancies,' said Phil, holding Wilbur's lead as they walked in an easterly direction.

'Whatever you think,' said Emma, shielding her face from the rain. She could think of nothing worse than swimming in this weather.

Phil glanced over and laughed. 'You gotta feel the rain, not just get wet.'

'I've never known what that means,' she said, her face screwed up against the elements.

'It means embrace the difficult things; when you do, you experience more.'

'Uh-huh,' she replied, unable to disguise her scepticism.

Phil laughed again and held his chin up, opening his mouth to let the rain fall in.

'Aren't you frozen?' asked Emma, her arms wrapped round her body, wondering how Phil hadn't developed hypothermia in only his shorts, T-shirt and flip-flops.

'This is nothing. You should see what it's like in winter!'

'I don't even want to think about it,' she said, tucking her chin down into the collar of her jacket.

'You'll love it, it's dramatic and wild and it makes you feel alive!'

'I'm happy feeling the central heating and a log fire.'

'A log fire is great, but a campfire is better, especially on the beach with a beer and a burger. You can't beat it.'

'That does sound good,' said Emma as they rounded the corner to the little road that led to the beach, Wilbur sniffing every crook and cranny on the way.

'You sound a bit low. Everything okay?'

'It's just been a bit of a day.'

'Wanna talk about it?'

'It was everything and nothing,' said Emma, gingerly walking down the steep path to the beach, which was slippery from the rain. 'I burnt the breakfast, Rhona couldn't come in, my mum cancelled her trip, *and* we had a row, then I had a bad review and, to top it all off, Wilbur peed on the kitchen floor.'

'Sounds like a bummer,' said Phil, holding out his hand for Emma to enable her to jump safely down onto the beach. 'God knows, Wilbur's bladder isn't small.'

'Right,' said Emma, managing a little laugh, something she hadn't achieved when picking up the cloths sodden with wee and mopping the floor.

'If it makes you feel any better my day was lousy too,' said Phil, releasing Wilbur, who set off along the edge of the dunes, his nose to the ground.

'What happened?'

'My alarm didn't go off, my sausage machine broke, *and* I lacerated my hand.' Phil held up his bad hand for Emma to see. 'All in all, it was a bit of a crap day, until you came in.'

'I blame the weather,' said Emma, not quite certain how to respond to his compliment.

'Why did you argue with your mum?'

Emma shook her head and fought the tears that welled in her eyes. 'I was being needy. I wanted her to come to visit, she prioritised her boyfriend.'

'That's tough. Sometimes we all need our mum.'

'Exactly,' said Emma, enjoying Phil's simplistic analysis. He was right, it wasn't any more complicated than that, Emma just needed her mother.

'Look, let me show you something,' he said, nudging Emma playfully then picking up a handful of stones.

Phil went to the water's edge and began skimming the stones across the sea, which was peppered with rain holes. The stones skipped 10, 11, 12 times on every throw, zipping over the surface like water bugs.

'That's incredible,' said Emma. 'I've never been able to skim stones.'

'Lobster Bay's finest can teach you,' he said, grinning and pointing his thumbs at himself.

'For real?'

'Sure, first you need to find a nice flat stone, triangular is best.' Phil scanned the beach. 'Look, here's a good one,' he said, picking one up and handing it to Emma. It fitted snugly in the palm of her hand.

'Hold it like this,' he said, showing Emma how to grip it.

'Like this?' she asked, not able to copy what he was doing.

'Not quite,' he said, leaning in to reposition her thumb to the top of the stone and index finger to run along one side. Despite the rain his hands felt soft and warm against her frozen fingers.

'Now, stand side-on to the sea, then throw the stone with a slight downward trajectory.'

Emma gave it a try, but the stone landed flat on the water and sank.

'I told you,' she said.

'You can't give up after one try.' Phil handed her a handful of stones and Emma tried again, but on each occasion, she failed. 'You need a bit more wrist-flick and speed, and bring your arm low.'

'Here?' said Emma, not keeping up with all the instructions.

'More like this,' said Phil and he stood behind her, mirroring her position, standing close enough that she could feel him pressed against her. She took a step forward, thinking Aidan wouldn't like it if he saw Phil standing so close. He brought her arm down to the correct position. 'Remember: side-on, low arm, downward trajectory, quick pace, flick of the wrist.'

With all her concentration, Emma gave it a shot. As the stone left her hand she watched it fly out low over the sea and then hit the water with a skip and then another and then one more.

'Oh my God, I did it!' she yelled, raising her hands in the air, a broad smile breaking over her face. 'Can you believe it? I did it!'

'I told you,' said Phil, who mirrored her smile, his eyes sparkling despite the clouds overhead.

'It's fun,' she said, feeling like a small child, and looking for another stone.

'I'll show you what else is fun,' said Phil and he picked up an enormous stick, whistled for Wilbur and threw it far into the water.

On seeing the stick fly through the air Wilbur let out a huge bark of excitement and bounded into the sea.

'Won't he get cold?' asked Emma.

Phil let out a big laugh. 'He's got a double coat of hair and a whole lot of blubber to keep him warm!'

'I've still got a lot to learn.'

'You know *another* thing that's fun?' asked Phil, his eyes wide with mischief.

'What?' asked Emma.

'Joining him!' And with that Phil whipped off his T-shirt and ran in to the water.

'Are you insane?' yelled Emma, gawping at the sight of Phil in only his shorts, swimming out towards Wilbur.

'Come and join us,' he yelled once he'd reached Wilbur and he was treading water beside him.

'Never in a million years!' shouted back Emma, who thought she'd seen everything now.

A few minutes later, Phil walked out of the sea and up the beach, soaked from top to toe. 'You should have come in,' he said. Emma tried hard not to pay too much attention, but she couldn't help noticing his ripped physique and his full arm of tattoos.

'Wasn't it freezing?' asked Emma, half dumbstruck, half admiring.

'It's exhilarating,' said Phil, beaming from ear to ear, and attempting to pull his T-shirt over his wet torso. 'And you loved it, didn't you, old dude?'

Wilbur looked up at Phil, barked satisfactorily and then rolled his head to one side before shaking himself dry from head to tail, soaking an already wet Phil and showering Emma in saltwater.

'Nice,' said Emma, fruitlessly trying to pat herself dry.

'It feels good,' said Phil, shaking his head too, water spraying off his dark locks.

'What a pair,' said Emma, laughing heartily at them both, grateful that Phil was around.

Phil walked Emma and Wilbur home, even popping in to towel down Wilbur so Emma didn't have to. By the time he left she felt ready for bed but not in the way she had before the walk. Being out with Phil in the rain had buoyed her spirits and now she was ready to sleep in the way she imagined people felt after climbing a mountain.

Emma was just about to head up for the evening when Mr Bergmann appeared at the top of the stairs in his pyjamas and dressing gown.

'Is everything okay?' she asked, trying to figure out what would cause this shy man to hurry downstairs in his night-wear.

'There is water in the . . .' he said, pointing to the ceiling, his English failing him.

'What? Are you sure?' said Emma, thinking he must have dreamt it. The room they were in was on the middle floor, nowhere near the roof.

They ran upstairs to the double room at the front of the house where they found Mrs Bergmann, also in her dressing gown, standing in the opposite corner from the leak, which was dripping noisily into the metal bin from the bathroom.

'I'm so sorry,' said Emma, trying to remain composed for her guests even though her hands were full of pins and needles from adrenalin. 'Let me move you to another room.'

Having gone downstairs to fetch the key for the remaining free room on the middle floor, Emma helped the Bergmanns move their things, reassuring them there would be no further trouble, before rushing to the top of the house to find out what was going on.

In the bedroom above, still kitted out in Hilda's decor and furniture, Emma discovered the ceiling had collapsed in one corner and rainwater was pouring through onto exposed floorboards and down into the room below.

'How is this possible?' she asked herself, climbing the loft ladder and shining the torch of her phone into the corner where the fire had happened.

It didn't take long to see what the cause was – Aidan's repair work had come undone. The wind was whipping roofing materials about and the rain was beating through, straight onto the floor joist insulation and through the ceiling.

In that moment all Emma wanted was to call Aidan, to ask him to come over and help her out, but Aidan was away, out of reach and of no help at all. Emma felt suddenly very alone.

The best she could do until morning was to limit the damage. She pulled on her damp cagoule and went out to the shed, Wilbur lumbering out behind her, to find tarpaulins and buckets, anything that might prevent further leakage into the guest room.

'There, that should do it till morning,' she said, sitting on the floor next to the tarps she'd stretched across the floorboards, held in place by bits of furniture. Large buckets peppered the tarps, catching the worst of the rain.

Emma calculated that the buckets would need emptying every couple of hours, and so she went to bed, setting her alarm for two hours' time, ready for a night of hardly any sleep. Closing her eyes all she could hear was her sister saying *just so long as she doesn't find herself in the North Sea without a life jacket.* She hated to admit it, but right now, that was exactly how she felt.

*

'What's the matter with you?' asked Hilda, as soon as Emma sat down. Her eyes wandered over Emma's unwashed hair and heavy eyes.

'I've been up all night emptying buckets.'

Emma had lost count of how many times her alarm had gone off and how many gallons of filthy water she'd sloshed down the toilet. She'd been up as usual at 6 a.m. to prepare breakfast, to let Wilbur out, and clean the laundry room floor after he'd peed in there again. *If there's one thing that's going to finish me off,* thought Emma, trying to keep her eyes open, *it's bloody Wilbur.*

'I thought you had the roof repaired?' said Hilda.

'I did.'

'By whom?'

'Aidan,' said Emma, her tiredness causing the truth to slip off her tongue.

'You had *Aidan* repair the roof? Why?'

'It was the quickest and cheapest solution,' said Emma, anticipating what Hilda would say next.

'He obviously didn't do it very well,' she bristled. 'I told you he's a piece of work.'

Emma didn't want to think badly of Aidan but there was no hiding the fact that his work hadn't held up and now he was nowhere to be seen. She tried desperately to think of something positive to say to counter Hilda's pessimism.

'There's no use in pointing fingers, Hilda. I need practical advice, not needling. If this rain keeps up, I'll have to be home in an hour to empty more buckets.'

'Running a big house isn't so easy after all, is it?' said Hilda, sounding a lot like Jane.

Emma chose to ignore Hilda's snide remark. 'Who did you use for roof maintenance?'

'My roofer has retired. I don't know any of the younger tradesman. Why not ask Phil, he should know of someone?'

'I'll do that,' said Emma, resisting the urge to smile at the memory of Phil and Wilbur swimming in the rain. 'I bumped into Judy last time I was at Phil's shop. She said something about you pestering another resident.'

Hilda did a pretend shiver and grimaced. 'Enid.'

'What's wrong with Enid,' said Emma, unable to contain a giggle at Hilda's schoolgirl gesture. She wondered if being in a care home was a bit like being at boarding school, just with fewer hormones and more incontinence pads.

'She's a pain. Always snitching on other residents and dictating what should be happening at the fete.'

'Well, she's clearly been upset by something you've said.'

'She doesn't like the fact that I stood up to her, that she's not top dog around here any longer. That's all it is. She's gone snivelling to Wendy about me and others who want the fair to be bigger and better this year. If she had it her way, she'd just sell doilies in the dining room.'

'Just be nice, okay?'

Hilda pulled a face at Emma but her eyes, gentler than usual, told Emma that she'd try. In return Emma cast her a 'you've been warned' look, when actually she was chuffed that Hilda was getting stuck into organising the fete and making friends, even if that was at the expense of Enid's pride.

'How's Wilbur?'

'He's peed twice on the floor in the last 12 hours.'

Hilda stifled a titter.

'I've tried really hard with him, Hilda. When Aidan was here I thought we were getting somewhere but if he keeps this up I won't have time for all his additional needs, and I will have to rehome him,' said Emma, sounding harder that she really felt.

'Have you thought about why he urinated?'

'Because he's a dog,' said Emma, trying desperately not to add, 'duh!' to the end of her sentence.

'Emma, no dog wants to foul where he sleeps. You need to think laterally. Is he unwell and unable to hold until he gets outside? Is he trying to tell you that something's wrong? Is he needing attention?'

'Hilda, I haven't the time for doggie psychology right now. I have the roof to contend with, with a room out I have numbers to re-crunch, plus I've a business still to run. I'm sure the Lobster rumour mill has already informed you – I didn't sign up to Wilbur in the first place.'

Hilda sat back in her chair and released a contemplative sigh. 'The things that shape us are often the things we didn't plan for.'

'Meaning?' asked Emma, who was too tired for riddles.

'I didn't plan for Alfred to die when he did, but it happened and that made me stronger, in the long run. I learnt from what happened.'

'Phil was saying something similar last night,' said Emma, trying to recall exactly what he'd said. '*Embrace the difficult things, experience more.* Something like that that anyway.'

'Phil's looks can be deceptive. Underneath all that loose clothing and facial hair is an admirable young man.'

'Right,' said Emma, surprised by Hilda's observation, uncertain if she agreed with it or not. 'You had no sense of what was going to happen to Alfred?'

'I had glimpses of it – he was easily startled, had flashbacks and sweats – but back then things weren't labelled the way they are now. He had no way of knowing it was PTSD, and that he could seek help. He thought how he was, was how he would be for the rest of his life.'

'But it wasn't,' said Emma, intrigued that some of Albert's symptoms were similar to her own.

Hilda shook her head solemnly. 'It took me a long time to find strength from what happened but, in the end, I did.'

'Are you telling me I'll find strength in having Wilbur about the place?' asked Emma, hoping to lighten the mood.

'He might turn out to be the companion you need, a loyal friend when times are hard.'

'Unlikely,' said Emma, unable to see past the dog's toileting, which was only adding to her ever-increasing workload.

*

Emma trudged home along the soggy coastal path, her wellies caked in mud, and sat down on the doorstep to pull them off. As she was gathering herself to go inside and tackle the chaos, she heard Aidan's front door open. Her heart leapt, thinking that he'd arrived back early, that he was coming to surprise her, to finish the roof. In that split second Emma felt both excitement and relaxation pour through her, until she saw that it wasn't Aidan at all. It was Eve.

Chapter 18

'It's so good of you guys to help out like this,' said Emma, holding two corners of a dust sheet while Rhona and Jennifer held one each. Together they billowed it out and positioned it over the double bed.

'It's no trouble,' said Jennifer, who'd come fully prepared for decorating in her bib-and-brace dungarees with a cute red scarf tied round her short hair.

'Yeah, it's a good excuse to spend the day together,' said Rhona, smoothing out the sheet to make sure the bed was fully protected from paint.

'I really appreciate it.' Emma had found it hard to ask for their help with redecorating the damaged guest room. It would have been tough enough for Emma to ask old friends, but Jennifer and Rhona were so new in her life that she had found it particularly tricky; she'd been over the moon when they'd both agreed.

A week had passed since the night of the torrential rain, but the weather had only dried up in the last few days and not before the smell of water damage had begun to penetrate the whole house. Emma had been forced to close the business. 'Remind me never to trust an amateur roofer ever again,' she had said to herself, turning the *Vacancies* sign to *No vacancies* in the dining room window with a heavy heart.

'Any luck in finding someone to repair the roof and ceiling?' asked Rhona, who was now on her hands and knees, pushing the dust sheet on the floor tight into the corners of the skirting board.

'Not yet.'

Despite a week of almost constant phone calls and leaving messages, Emma had been unable to find anyone to do the repair either to the roof or the collapsed ceiling on the top floor.

'That's "trades fortnight" for you,' said Jennifer, mixing a tin of paint.

'Phil did warn me about it,' said Emma.

The day after the rain, Emma had asked Phil for the number of a local roofer and plasterer. He'd given her a few names but warned her most of them wouldn't reply due to it being 'trades fortnight', when all tradesmen in the area took their holiday.

'Thank goodness the weather's meant to be dry for a while,' said Rhona.

Emma opened the window and let the warm summer breeze carry away the smell of paint. Gazing out over the rooftops, she prayed the weather would hold until someone could come.

'Talking of Phil . . .' said Jennifer, her eyes sparkling with mischief.

'Oh yeah, I completely forgot,' said Rhona, getting up from the floor. 'I heard the two of you went out on a date.'

'It was hardly a date,' protested Emma, turning her gaze back into the room. 'I asked him to help me walk Wilbur; it was completely innocent.'

'Aidan won't be impressed,' sang Rhona.

'The less said about Aidan, the better,' said Emma, placing the stepladder by the window. She'd spent much of the week trying to decipher what she felt about Eve's return. She fluctuated wildly between anger and hurt, feeling foolish and disappointed. So much for the promise of Aidan and her picking up where they left off.

'Are you cross with him?' asked Jennifer, who, like Rhona, seemed unaware of Eve's return. Emma had felt too humiliated to mention it, all they knew was that Aidan hadn't been in touch.

Emma shrugged. 'A bit, I guess,' she said, trying to underplay her emotions. 'Mostly I just feel a bit foolish for trusting him.'

'Don't,' said Rhona, holding the steps for Emma. 'Nobody around here will think badly of you.'

'That's the truth,' said Jennifer, though Emma took little comfort from it.

'But you warned me, Hilda warned me. I feel like an idiot for not listening to you guys.'

'Don't blame yourself, Emma. Aidan starts things all the time that he doesn't finish.'

'Right,' said Emma, who was no longer sure if she was talking about the roof or their relationship.

Emma didn't like to say it but the thing she felt worst about was the fact that Eve clearly had no idea what had happened between Aidan and Emma. Every time Eve saw Emma she smiled broadly and waved; all week Emma had had an unshakeable feeling of shame.

'I just can't believe Phil had the audacity to ask you out when he must have known something was going on between you and Aidan,' said Jennifer, reaching up to take the blind that Emma had just removed.

'While the cat's away . . .' trilled Rhona.

'Guys!' said Emma, descending the ladder, recalling how it had been a little surprising that he'd offered to help with Wilbur again when she'd been in the shop last week. 'He didn't ask me out, I asked him to help me out, and besides, there's not a devious bone in Phil's body.'

'I'll bet there's one devious *bone*,' said Rhona, with a laugh.

'Rhona!' said Emma.

'Don't tell me you haven't thought about it,' said Jennifer, a wicked smile creeping over her face. 'I know I have!'

'Am I missing something here?' asked Emma, pouring the paint into the roller trays.

'He's hot!' said Rhona.

'*Really* hot,' said Jennifer.

Emma scrunched up her nose. 'I don't see it. I mean, maybe in a cute, surf-dude kind of a way but—'

'Oh sure,' said Jennifer. 'Because who can be bothered with "cute".'

Emma shook her head and laughed, testing the paint on the wall. 'You guys can think what you like but I'm telling you, I'm not interested in Phil.'

'You'd be the only woman in the village who isn't,' said Rhona.

'Shame he's so choosey,' said Jennifer, dreamily.

'Hey, what about Finn?' asked Emma, passing over Jennifer's comment.

Rhona pulled out her ringing phone. 'That's different. Finn's relationship material. Phil's more, let's see, "friends with benefits" material.'

'There's not a girl in town who doesn't want to . . .' said Jennifer, her tongue in her cheek.

'Well, this girl doesn't want to,' said Emma, surprised by the hint of doubt in her tone. *Because*, she thought, *we did have a really good time, and there's no doubt that his body is amazing, and those tattoos have to suggest there's something more than cute about him.* Feeling a prickle of heat rising in her cheeks, Emma stashed the thought away, thankful that Rhona's phone call had put an end to the conversation.

'I have to pick up Ethan from school, he's been sick,' said Rhona, shoving her phone back in her pocket.

'I hope he's okay,' said Emma, her own phone ringing, which she answered as she waved Rhona off.

'Emma, it's Wendy.'

'Hi, Wendy,' said Emma, surprised to hear from her. 'Is everything okay?'

'Hilda's a little off colour. I don't suppose you could come by, could you?'

Emma hesitated. 'Shouldn't you be calling Judy.'

'Hilda specifically asked for you,' said Wendy, pausing. 'And Wilbur.'

'Seems as though everyone's under the weather today,' said Emma after letting Wendy know she'd be over as soon as she could then ending the call. 'Hilda wants to see Wilbur, so I need to take him over there.'

'Walk or car?'

'I'd prefer to take the car but he needs a walk so . . .' Emma thought for a moment, not yet feeling up to the challenge of walking him such a distance alone, and definitely not up to the challenge of handling him in a building full of vulnerable OAPs.

'I'd offer to help but I said I'd pop into work for a while this afternoon,' said Jennifer, putting down her tools and taking off her headscarf. 'You should call Phil, I'm sure he'd love to help!' she said, her eyes full of mischief.

'I really appreciate you doing this, Phil,' said Emma, as Phil attached the lead to Wilbur's collar. 'There's no way I could manage on my own.'

'No problem at all,' said Phil, giving Wilbur a bear hug then leading him through the house to help walk him along the coastal path to Hilda's care home. 'Do you want to take him this time?' he asked, offering Emma the lead.

'Not yet,' said Emma, nervous about walking him on the narrow pavements. Though she'd followed Phil's advice of walking Wilbur at the same time and on the same route every day, she still wasn't confident with him, and it didn't help that the peeing incident hadn't been a one-off event.

At least once a day for the last week she'd had to get the bucket and mop out to clean up after him and every time she did the thought of rehoming him grew a little louder in her mind.

'He won't pull, not like Elsie. That's one good thing about big dogs, they're much more laid-back than little dogs.'

'All the same. I'll wait until we're away from cars and people.'

'Okay,' said Phil easily, striding along with Wilbur out front. 'Why's Hilda so keen to see you?'

'I'm not sure. Wendy said she's a little off colour.'

'You'd think they'd call Judy.'

Emma let out a little laugh. 'That's what I said, but they still haven't patched things up.'

'Because of the house?'

'Hilda's still convinced she could manage; she hasn't forgiven Judy for selling it.'

Phil glanced over to Emma, his rich brown eyes bright in the sunlight. 'Does she really believe that?'

'Seems to,' said Emma, noticing for the first time how his eyes went from dark brown in the centre to lighter near the edge and then a final rim of black, and how they soft-ened when he thought of Hilda.

'Towards the end she would phone in orders four or five times a day, having forgotten she'd done it already.'

'I didn't know that,' said Emma, sharing a tender glance with Phil, one that felt to Emma as if it went beyond their feelings for Hilda.

'She was in a real muddle,' said Phil, and Emma broke eye contact, surprised to find herself feeling self-conscious. 'Rhona could never be certain if Wilbur had been fed at all or fed six times in one day. In the end, she would feed him in the morning and then lock the dog cupboard so Hilda didn't overfeed him. Left to Hilda's devices, Wilbur would be twice the weight he is now.'

'Hard to imagine!' said Emma, with a laugh, checking out Wilbur's broad back, relieved to shift the focus onto the dog.

'She's definitely in no shape to manage that house,' said Phil, turning off the main road.

'Everyone seems to realise that but her. I wish I had some way of proving it to her, so that she and Judy can put this feud to bed.'

'You know there is something you could do,' said Phil through a wide, roguish smile, his eyes twinkling mischievously.

'What?' she asked, admiring his thick, dark eyelashes, which she hadn't noticed before.

'Invite her back. Tell her one of Rhona's kids is sick, she can't work, you need someone to help out.'

'That's very sneaky,' said Emma, her eyes glinting at the idea, and again their gaze met, this time in mischief, but still it felt intimate, as if Phil was purposefully reeling her in with his eyes.

'She doesn't know you've closed up for a bit, does she?'

'Nope,' she replied, questioning why she suddenly felt so unsure of herself around Phil.

'So, why not?'

'I'll ask.' As they turned onto the path along the coast, Emma dismissed the chemistry, assuming it was all down to the nonsense Rhona and Jennifer had been spurting back home.

'Now then,' said Phil, handing Wilbur's lead to Emma. 'I think it's about time you conquered your fear . . .'

*

'Are you happy to wait here while I find out where to take Wilbur?' Emma asked Phil, outside the front doors of Seaview.

'Absolutely,' said Phil, parking himself on a bench, Wilbur plonking himself on the ground beside him, tired from his walk.

'Hi, Emma, I'm so glad you could come,' said Wendy, greeting Emma in her usual cheerful manner. 'Hilda's been chewing my ear off for the last few hours about when Emma and Wilbur are coming to visit.'

'It took me by surprise when you said she wanted us both to visit. I didn't think dogs were allowed.'

Wendy's expression changed from one of cheerfulness to alarm.

Emma let out a knowing laugh. 'I take it Hilda didn't tell you that Wilbur is a dog?'

'Oh well,' said Wendy, with a brush of her hand and a wink. 'I'm sure we can sneak the little chap in without anyone noticing, just this once you understand.'

'Mmm,' said Emma, holding a finger to her pursed lips. 'I'm afraid "sneaking" probably isn't going to cut it.'

'We couldn't hide him under a coat?'

Emma laughed and pointed through the glass sliding doors to where Wilbur sat next to Phil. 'Not unless you've got Hagrid's coat!'

'Ah!' said Wendy, her eyes wide. 'Well, now, let's have a think . . .'

Wendy decided that the best solution was for Hilda to be wrapped up warm, put in a wheelchair, and brought outside to Wilbur. Emma couldn't understand why Hilda should suddenly require a wheelchair but when she saw her being wheeled into reception it became clear that Hilda had taken a downward turn. Her eyes appeared cloudier, her frame smaller and more rounded, her spirit reduced.

'Woah, big fella,' said Phil, when Wilbur lunged towards Hilda, pulling Phil up from the bench and requiring both his hands to restrain him.

'I thought you said he wouldn't pull?' said Emma, laughing at Phil's efforts to keep him at bay.

'It's every dog's prerogative to humiliate its handler!' said Hilda, her tired eyes sparkling at the sight of Wilbur forcing his way towards her.

'Wilbur, sit!' said Emma, showing him the palm of her hand. And instantly Wilbur's back end dropped to the floor, his tail swishing the ground in excitement.

'I'm impressed,' said Hilda.

'I'm stunned!' said Emma, rewarding him with a treat.

'I was going to ask how you're getting on with handling him, but I see now you're doing just fine.'

'It's all Phil's doing. On the walk here he gave me a few more tips.'

Feeling encouraged, Emma took Wilbur's lead and, as Phil had advised, she kept it short and Wilbur close. Miraculously, he walked at her side towards Hilda.

'Oh, my boy,' said Hilda, enveloping his head in her arms. He stretched his neck upwards so that Hilda might place her cheek against his without straining herself. 'How I've missed you.'

'Looks like he's missed you too,' said Phil, leaning in to kiss Hilda on the cheek.

Hilda gripped Wilbur's head in her hands and stared at him, the unmistakable look of love shining in her ageing eyes. 'It's been too long,' she said, her voice catching.

'I think Wilbur would agree,' said Emma, watching him lick Hilda's face. Usually Wilbur licking anything caused a sensation of nausea in Emma but now, watching the two of them so tender together, she couldn't help but see the beauty in him.

'He's a dear friend,' said Hilda, who, one way or another, looked softer to Emma in Wilbur's company. It reminded Emma of the first time she saw her sister with her fiancé, when all the years of searching fell away and finally she was able to just be herself.

'We should arrange for you to see each other more often,' said Emma, wondering if she would ever find the same sense of peace in a relationship.

Hilda stroked Wilbur's head rhythmically.

'Why don't we arrange for you to come over to the house?' said Phil, and Emma knew he wasn't suggesting it just so that Hilda could see she could no longer cope but because he, like Emma, could see the power of good Wilbur did her.

'I'd like that,' said Hilda, shivering.

'We'll organise it then,' said Emma, tucking the blanket a little tighter around Hilda, who didn't complain. 'But for now, we should get you inside and warmed up.'

Emma wheeled Hilda back inside and, after settling her back into her room, she arranged with Wendy for Hilda to visit the house the following day. She returned to find Phil chatting away to Wilbur.

'You guys look the picture of happiness,' she said.

'We were having a man chat,' said Phil, smiling fondly at Wilbur and tussling his jowls.

'What about?'

'Matters of the heart.'

'Sounds serious,' said Emma, plonking herself on the bench next to Phil.

'I was telling him about Hilda not being as strong as she used to be and how he has to accept she won't be coming home.'

'Were you indeed,' she said, smiling at Phil's silliness.

'I was also telling him how lucky he is to have you as his new owner,' said Phil, holding Emma's gaze, his tone unmistakably flirtatious.

'Potential owner,' said Emma, slightly schoolmarmish in her delivery. 'The jury's still out on whether he's staying, the final verdict depends on pee-gate.'

'But you're doing so great with him. And you like him, right?' Phil's eyes were now almost as wide and dark as Wilbur's.

'Of course I like him,' said Emma, knowing full well they were no longer talking about the dog.

'So, give him a chance, he deserves it, no?'

'Maybe,' said Emma, twisting her lips then breaking into a smile, because for all she wasn't sure she really fancied Phil, there was no denying he was cute.

Chapter 19

'There's a cobweb up there,' said Hilda in the vestibule, as soon as Emma opened the front door. She pointed one of her walking sticks at the offending item.

'I'll get onto it,' said Emma, thinking if Hilda hadn't owned a guesthouse she might well have made an excellent drill sergeant, even in her reduced capacity she'd be up to the job. She opened the door wide and gestured for Hilda to come in.

'I'll leave you two ladies to it,' said Phil, winking at Emma.

'Thanks for the taxi service,' sang Emma, as she watched him leave. He turned to wave and she returned the gesture with a warm smile.

Hilda stood, her hands trembling on her sticks, surveying the hallway. Emma hoped she wouldn't notice the damp smell, which she'd been trying to conceal all morning by leaving the door wide open and lighting candles. 'It looks as if you've been busy.'

It was difficult for Emma to detect if Hilda approved of the changes or not. 'Just a little freshen up,' she said, wanting to pass over the matter. She wasn't sure what Hilda felt about her old home being changed so dramatically, but Emma suspected it must be hard not to take it personally or to feel, in some way, as if her memories had been painted over.

'Come through to the living room, have a cup of tea.'

Slowly, Hilda made her way through, and positioned herself painfully on the sofa.

'I see you kept the bird feeders,' she said, her chest heaving from her exertions.

'Of course,' said Emma, plumping a pillow to place behind her.

'I do miss watching the birds.'

'You enjoy them while I fetch tea.'

In the kitchen Emma could hear Wilbur scratching at the laundry-room door, desperate to get out.

'Wilbur knows you're here,' said Emma, bringing refreshments. 'I swear he knew you were coming even before you arrived; he's been giddy as a pup all morning.'

Hilda held tightly to her teacup, trying to contain her shaking. 'Dogs' instincts are an incredible thing.'

'I found this photo of you and him in the garden.' Emma fetched the photo and the family picture from the mantelpiece.

Setting her teacup aside Hilda took the photo of Wilbur and held it close, her eyes misting with tears. 'We were joined at the hip, the two of us. We still would be if it weren't for . . . well—'

Emma settled on the opposite sofa, tucking her feet beneath her. 'Judy was only doing what she felt best.'

'Judy was taking care of her own interests,' said Hilda shortly.

'Judy gave up everything to look after you; surely you didn't expect her to do that indefinitely?' said Emma, as sympathetically as possible.

'She didn't have to sell the house,' said Hilda with a scowl.

'Financially, I'm not sure she had much choice,' replied Emma, but realising Hilda wasn't receptive to the conversation, she changed the subject. 'How are preparations for the fete?'

'They'd be better if we could kick Enid off the committee.'

'She's still causing problems?'

'We've taken to ignoring her.'

'We?' asked Emma.

'Sylvie, Rose, Bert.'

'Great,' said Emma, glad to hear that Hilda had found a bit of camaraderie. 'And you're still going to bake the shortbread?'

'If I've the strength; it takes a lot of effort.'

'I can help if you need me to,' said Emma. 'I did, after all, learn from the best!'

'Are you and Phil courting?' Hilda asked out of the blue; Emma almost spat out her tea.

'What made you ask that?' she asked, wiping her mouth with a napkin.

'Well, he's handsome and kind,' she shrugged. 'Why wouldn't you be?'

'We're just friends.'

Hilda scrutinised Emma. 'Do you get this flustered about all your friends?'

Uncertain how to respond, Emma clapped her hands in action and got up. 'I've a room to clean, would you like to come up and help me?'

'Why not? I can see what else you've changed around here,' she said mischievously, her eyes twinkling.

Emma offered a hand to Hilda. 'I can manage,' she said, shooing the offer away and inching herself off the sofa.

'Of course,' said Emma, backing away but keeping a careful eye. 'If you'd like to help strip and make up the bed in the big room that would be a huge help.'

'You can't manage on your own?' said Hilda, making slow progress out of the living room.

'You can show me how it's done properly! I'm still not sure how to get the bedding military sharp.'

'Huh,' said Hilda, taking her first step on the stairs. 'I had Alfred to teach me how to do that.'

'I imagine you were a good team,' said Emma, wishing she had someone with whom she could share the business. Despite all that had happened, she'd enjoyed the month of having Aidan about the place.

'We were,' said Hilda wistfully. 'When we first took on the house, Alfred did all the cooking and shopping, while I did the cleaning and greeting. Together we managed the paperwork. But then—' Hilda paused where she stood on the stairs, struggling for breath.

'Is that when Alfred started to deteriorate?'

'He had dreadful dizziness, his sleep became disturbed and he couldn't concentrate on work. Towards the end the nightmares became so bad that it all grew to be too much.'

'I'm so sorry,' said Emma, moving down a few steps to Hilda, who looked increasingly unsteady. She ushered her carefully to the hall bench. 'The truth is,' she said, sitting next to her, 'I have some experience of suicide myself.'

'I sensed that,' said Hilda, placing her hand over Emma's.

Emma's gaze lingered on their fingers and on Hilda's worn wedding ring. 'It was under very different – far more public – circumstances; I don't pretend to understand anything of your loss.'

'In many ways the loss is the least of it, the most important thing is to draw strength from the love we are shown, and to forgive.'

The image of Dawn's smiling daughters on their mother's phone shot into Emma's mind. She prayed that they were being showered with love.

'A thousand acts of kindness are stronger than one desperate act,' said Hilda, squeezing Emma's hand tightly.

'I hope so,' said Emma, smiling weakly at Hilda's reassuring gaze, and wiping away a tear.

'How about we forget about the room for now?' said Emma a moment later, wanting to break the heavy atmosphere. 'Let's go out to the garden with Wilbur instead.'

'Yes,' said Hilda, allowing Emma to help her up. 'That sounds like a fine plan.'

Emma went to the back of the house and made sure Wilbur was secure before taking Hilda out through the French doors in the living room to a seat in the garden.

'You wait here while I get him,' said Emma, positioning a blanket over Hilda, next to the honeysuckle arch, which was bursting with scent. 'I can't imagine how happy he's going to be to see you.'

Returning to the house, Emma opened the laundry room door to discover Wilbur turning in circles of excitement, desperate to get out to Hilda.

'Okay, boy,' she said, trying to calm him. 'Nice and easy.'

Emma had never seen him behave so boisterously, not even around Aidan or Phil. Worrying that his excitement might prove too much, she attached his lead, held him tight and opened the back door. But as soon as Wilbur caught sight of Hilda he lunged with such force that he broke clean away from Emma, who could only watch as he bolted towards Hilda, her arms outstretched, and barrelled her to the ground.

'Oh my God, Hilda!' yelled Emma, racing down the garden steps to where Hilda was lying on the floor with Wilbur stooped over her, licking her face.

'Hilda, are you okay?'

Emma grabbed Wilbur by the collar and pulled him away with all her strength. 'Hilda?'

'Never better,' said Hilda, who Emma now realised was laughing her head off. 'Let him go.'

Emma thought she must have misheard. 'Excuse me?'

'Let Wilbur go. This is the most fun I've had in ages!'

After several minutes of Hilda lying on the floor with Wilbur nuzzling, pawing and licking her, Wilbur began to settle and eventually lay down by Hilda's side.

'Can I get you up now?' asked Emma, bemused by Hilda's reaction.

'If you must.'

Emma picked up both Hilda and the chair and settled her back onto it, the blanket round her lap.

'Hilda,' she said, pulling up a chair of her own, the pair of them chuckling at the absurdity of the episode, 'surely you have to see now that you can't manage either the house or Wilbur—' Emma held back from telling Hilda that it was also clear that *she* couldn't manage Wilbur either.

'Don't worry,' said Hilda, tears of laughter pouring down her cheeks. 'I do see.'

'And do you promise you'll talk to Judy, let her know she was right after all?'

Hilda screwed up her face playfully. 'I suppose,' she said, reaching out for Wilbur and giving him a squeeze, unaware that Emma now had no choice but to find him a new home.

*

'I'm sorry I missed her,' said Rhona, later that day, helping Emma in the front guest room. Emma had managed to put on a first coat of paint after Hilda left and was now starting on the second. 'How was she?'

'In good spirits,' said Emma, who'd already regaled Rhona with the Wilbur incident though she hadn't quite found the courage to tell her that she'd decided to rehome him. She knew Rhona would be disappointed; she felt rotten enough about the decision without adding Rhona's emotions into the mix. 'She finally conceded that she can no longer manage either the house or the dog.'

'Wow, that's serious progress.'

'I know. I'm made-up. She said she'd speak to Judy later and apologise.'

'Well, look at you, Little Miss Peacemaker.'

Emma giggled at the title. 'What about you? How are things?'

'I've been up all night with Ethan; thankfully Mum's been able to step in for an hour to let me out.'

'Poor you,' said Emma who, now that Rhona mentioned the lack of sleep, did notice the heavy bags beneath her eyes. 'Any news from Finn?'

'We're chatting every day. He needs to come back over at some point but he's not sure when.'

'It can't be easy doing the long-distance thing.'

Rhona shrugged. 'I wouldn't be able to see him much with having the kids anyway. Mum's taken on extra evenings shifts so, you know, life isn't exactly flexible. But it's nice to look forward to a FaceTime call when they're all in bed, it's easier this way.'

'You're so pragmatic,' said Emma admiringly.

'Says she, up a ladder, taking care of things when no one else can. What you're doing's not so different from what I'm doing.'

'Though the house doesn't throw up.'

'But it does leak, as does the dog!'

'Talking of which . . .' said Emma, her tone downcast.

'Emma?'

Emma put down her roller and let out a deep sigh. 'I've decided to rehome Wilbur.'

'What?' said Rhona, her mouth falling open.

'I know, it's a really hard decision but I can't have a dog in the house that I can't control. If he can knock down Hilda, he can knock down a guest.'

'Emma, you can't. You guys have come so far. Give things a bit longer. You'll see, it'll all come good.'

'I'd like to believe it, I really would,' said Emma, shaking her head, descending a rung or two to take a break. 'I could live with the peeing on the floor, but his strength and unpredictability are different matters.'

'You know it's not going to be a popular decision.'

'I'm well aware of that, and if I'm honest I'm not sure I even want to, but I can't let my heart rule my head on this one. I did that with Aidan and the roof, and we both know how that turned out.'

'Has anyone been out to look at it?'

'Someone called back and said they could take a look but not until he's done a million other jobs. Honestly, Rhona, sometimes I think I should just go up there myself and bash a few nails in.'

'Phil can't help out?'

'I'm not sure a butcher has any relevant skills. Boat-builder, yes; butcher, no.'

'And we all know how the boatbuilder turned out.'

'Right,' said Emma who, despite knowing he was back with Eve, hadn't quite given up checking her phone to see if Aidan had been in touch. 'You know Phil made it clear that he wants something more than friendship?'

'He did? What did you say?'

Emma winced and went back to her painting. 'I didn't.'

'Why?'

'Because I'm not sure I'm interested.'

'Why not?'

Emma stretched her brush into the top corner, concentrating on covering the fiddly bits rather than Rhona's question.

'Emma Jenkins, are you ignoring me?'

'No,' replied Emma unconvincingly.

'It's because of Aidan, isn't it?'

'Phil's cute and all,' said Emma, ignoring the comment about Aidan. 'I'm just not sure I fancy him.'

'Yeah, right. Everyone fancies Phil. I think you're hung up on Aidan.'

Emma didn't reply. Even if she were hung up on him, what difference would it make? He and Eve were back living together which told Emma everything she needed to know about where things stood between them.

*

Emma woke with a start, gasping for breath, her heart pounding uncomfortably. She stared into the dark, her head on the pillow, trying to orientate herself, her chest heaving with fear. For a moment it felt as if she was lying on the pavement on Regent Street with everything shrouded in smoke.

Breathe, thought Emma, her bedroom slowly coming into focus. *Deep breaths.* But every time she closed her eyes she felt Dawn's hand in hers, and saw her face, pale and contorted, a trickle of blood dry on the side of her mouth. And then the crushing sensation overwhelmed her – of not having been able to do more to spare her children from their loss.

It was just a nightmare, she reasoned, though her light head and beaded brow convinced her it was real.

283

'Breathe,' she said out loud, her voice unrecognisable with fear, replaying the sequence of events – from the initial force of the blast, to finding her bearings, to witnessing the dead. It was the first time she'd had a dream that replayed the whole experience, and she had to resist the urge to vomit.

'Aidan,' she whispered, wishing desperately that he would materialise, to hold her safe in his arms. But nobody answered.

Loneliness swept through her body like a tidal wave, and uncontrollable sobs burst from her lungs. All the anger and sorrow and confusion cascaded out of her in a waterfall of tears.

Eventually her crying subsided and she lay listening to her heart rate gradually slowing, and as she did she became aware of a soft padding sound.

'Hello?' she said, listening attentively, concern creeping into her that someone was in the house. Harnessing all her courage, she sat up and stared at the bedroom door. As she watched, it nudged open.

Emma started.

Her worry dispersed when she made out the shape of Wilbur, laborious in his movement, padding in.

'Hello, boy,' she said, reaching out a hand to him to let him know that he was welcome.

Quietly he sat down, placing his head on the bed, and let out a tired sigh.

'I know exactly how you feel,' she said, inching down the bed to place her head beside his. As their eyes met in the darkness, Emma felt a final tear trickle down her cheek, and a weak smile form on her lips.

Chapter 20

Emma woke to find Wilbur lying on the floor next to her bed, snoring contentedly.

'Morning,' she said groggily, the events of the previous night trickling back to her like a bad hangover.

Wilbur continued to snore.

'Typical male – you pee on the floor, barrel about the place, and then one kind gesture and you think all is forgiven,' she said gently, not wanting to disturb him.

'Well, you might deserve a lie-in, but you know you can't stay. Caroline will take care of you, she sounded really nice,' said Emma, referring to the Newfie expert she'd spoken to yesterday evening about rehoming Wilbur.

At that an eye opened and looked up to where Emma lay on her side talking to him; a seismic wave of remorse washed over her.

'There's no point looking like that,' she said, wishing that her feeling of nausea would subside. 'You don't know your own strength, do you?'

The eye closed and Wilbur returned to his slumber.

'I'll take that as a no,' said Emma, carefully prising back her duvet and then tiptoeing over Wilbur to the bathroom.

In the shower, Emma went through last night in her mind. She'd grown used to the flashbacks, but the nightmare was new, and she worried that what she thought was reasonably under control had taken a turn for the worse. As the water poured over her, she couldn't help thinking about what Hilda had told her about Alfred – the flashbacks, the nightmares, the sweats, the dizziness, and how they'd grown out of control to the point where he felt unable to cope with them any more. Was it possible, thought Emma, that she had PTSD too?

With her towel wrapped around her, Emma grabbed her phone, ignoring the missed-call notifications, and typed in 'PTSD symptoms'. What she found felt as if it had been written specifically about her:

Symptoms may include but are not limited to flashbacks, nightmares, physical sensations such as sweating and

dizziness, avoidance issues, being easily startled,
sleep problems, work-related issues and
relationship breakdown.

'Fuck,' said Emma, slumping down on her bed, Wilbur glancing up at her. 'Guess it's time I confront my demons.' She rubbed Wilbur's tummy with her bare foot. 'Maybe we should start with taking you for a morning walk to tell Hilda both our bits of news.'

It took Emma the best part of half the walk before she could relax and begin to trust that Wilbur wasn't going to pull her off her feet, lunge at anyone they passed, or take off into the distance but, by the time Seaview came into sight, she was beginning to feel a growing sense of confidence which only made the prospect of telling Hilda about her to decision to rehome him all the harder.

'Good morning, Wendy,' Emma said brightly, after securing Wilbur to the bench outside. She signed the register and grinned at the sight of Judy's name, printed neatly in block capitals, from the evening before and early this morning.

For once Wendy wasn't wearing her usual sunny smile, instead she seemed flustered, almost agitated. 'You haven't received my voicemails, have you?'

Emma scrutinised Wendy's face. Her forehead was furrowed, her eyes soft with concern, her usual broad smile replaced by a sympathetic one.

'What's happened, Wendy?' asked Emma, feeling her heart rate increase.

Wendy came out from behind the reception desk and guided Emma to the little waiting area. She sat her down and took her hand. Emma prepared herself for the worst.

'Hilda passed away,' she said gently.

Swallowing hard, Emma shook her head as if trying to dispel Wendy's words.

'How? I mean, when? What happened?' she asked.

'It was very peaceful, she passed in her sleep. When one of our carers went in to see her this morning she was at rest.'

A veil seemed to descend over Emma.

'Would you like to see her?'

Emma nodded mutely, only managing to say, 'Wilbur.'

Wendy glanced out of the glass doors to where Wilbur was sitting, his head propped up on the arm of the bench, looking as miserable as Emma felt.

'Go on then,' she said, giving Emma's hand a squeeze and a smile that said *rules are made to be broken.*

*

'She'd been very happy last night,' said Wendy, going into Hilda's room and adjusting the blind to allow a little sunlight to creep in. 'Judy had been to see her, and she left in good spirits.'

'Judy,' whispered Emma, from where she still stood in the doorway with Wilbur whimpering on a short lead. 'Does she know?'

'She's already said her goodbyes.' Wendy held out an arm to usher Emma in. 'It's okay. She's at peace.'

Emma took a few steps forward, her heart skipping irregularly, the image of Dawn lying dead on the pavement at the front of her mind, then stopped.

'Emma?'

Shaking away the image Emma inhaled sharply and, rather than avoiding the memory, she told Wendy quietly, 'The only other time I've seen a dead body was under very different circumstances.'

Wendy took Emma's hand and guided her and Wilbur forward. 'Don't be afraid. Other than the paleness of her skin she really does look as if she's sleeping.'

Tentatively, Emma moved forward, Wilbur matching her pace, to the point where she could clearly make out Hilda's face. Wendy was right, other than her pallor, she really did look as if she were asleep.

'Why don't you take a seat?' said Wendy, bringing over a small chair for Emma. 'Spend a while together.'

Emma sat down and as she did, Wilbur pushed through the small gap between Emma and the bed, positioning himself as close to Hilda as he could.

'It's okay, boy,' said Emma, stroking his head as he whimpered. 'It's okay.'

Wendy left the two of them alone with Hilda, closing the door behind her.

'Guess you're staying with me, then,' she said, knowing, despite her better judgement, that there was no way she could rehome Wilbur. She couldn't betray Hilda's wishes, not now. A small laugh floated out of her and she whispered to Wilbur, 'Maybe she sensed my decision and planned the whole thing. I wouldn't put it past her.'

Wilbur rolled his eyes back towards Emma, unprepared to lift his weary head from where it lay beside Hilda's hand.

'You were right,' continued Emma, talking directly to Hilda. 'Wilbur is a loyal companion, the friend I needed – you'd have been proud of him last night. He comforted me when I needed someone most. I won't ever forget that. Thank you.

'And thank you for all you told me about Alfred. Your loss has taught me so much about courage and forgiveness. I guess if we can take anything from death it's to draw inspiration from others, and to live our best possible life in their honour.'

It was only then that Emma noticed something in the top pocket of Hilda's blouse. Looking more closely she saw the two photos that had been on her mantelpiece. The first of Hilda and her family, the second of Hilda and Wilbur.

'I guess you were just waiting until everything was in order,' she said, glad that Judy had been to see her. 'You always knew Wilbur would win me over, that he was exactly what I needed,' she said, reaching out to touch Hilda's hand.

The image of Dawn's dead hand jolted into her head, but in holding Hilda's, the image softened, it became one of dignity and compassion, not of terror.

'Thank you, dear friend,' she said. 'Thank you.'

'It's time we went, old boy,' said Emma, ruffling Wilbur's coat, trying to gee him up, but Wilbur sank deep into his haunches.

'Come on,' she tried again, this time standing up, showing him it was time to go.

Again, he remained resolutely still.

'Wilbur!' she called, this time more sternly, trying to be commanding, but the dog didn't even glance at her.

For once, rather than feeling frustration, Emma understood. He had no desire to leave his beloved mistress, as far he was concerned this was where he was staying.

'Hilda was lucky to have a friend like you,' she said, kneeling down beside him and looking into his soft, dark eyes. He let out a long sombre sigh. 'I guess I am too.'

Chapter 21

After a lot of coaxing, Emma eventually managed to move Wilbur away from Hilda's side and the two of them trudged back along the coastal path.

'Fancy a dip?' she asked, winding her way down to a tiny crescent beach, nestled out of view from the path. Wilbur padded behind her, his shoulders slumped, his head low.

She picked up a stick and threw it into the water, but Wilbur didn't respond.

'You're a sensitive old soul, aren't you?' she said, perching on a rock and gazing out to the grey sea beyond. Wilbur sat down beside her, and she wrapped her arm around him, giving him a squeeze whenever he whined.

The clouds had shifted a distance, and Emma had started to shiver, when a movement brought her out of the trance she'd been in. Looking more closely, she made out a small dog, navigating the jagged rocks that jutted out to sea.

'Elsie,' called a figure, rounding the headland.

Wilbur's ears pricked, and Emma felt his muscles tense into action.

'It's Phil,' said Emma, who hadn't recognised him at first – for once, he was almost clean-shaven. Patting Wilbur on his side she tried to encourage him to play but he remained anchored to the ground.

'This is an unusual sight,' said Phil, as he ambled towards them, Elsie charging up behind him and past towards Wilbur. He ruffled Wilbur's neck as Elsie barked and barked, begging him to play. 'What's wrong with him?'

'We've just come from Hilda's . . .' The words caught in Emma's throat.

'Emma?'

Emma swallowed hard. 'She passed away in the night.'

'Jesus,' said Phil. He sat down beside them on the sand and gave Emma a tight squeeze, staring blankly out to sea. 'She was looking a bit tired, but I didn't think things were that bad.'

'No, but maybe *she* did. Maybe that's why she asked for me to take Wilbur over to see her.'

'Maybe,' he said, throwing a stick for Elise to fetch. 'I take it it's hit the big fella hard.'

'Seems to,' said Emma, watching heavy clouds roll in from the north. 'I had no idea dogs grieved.'

'For sure. When I was a kid my gran had a dog that died of a broken heart.'

'Really?' asked Emma, exploring his face, which looked so different without the facial hair. Now she could make out his full lips and jawline, which was far stronger than she'd realised.

'Yup. She had two sausage dogs, Pinky and Grundy. When Grundy died, Pinky stopped eating; she died two weeks later.'

'I'm not sure anything could stop this guy eating,' said Emma, with a light laugh, pulling Wilbur closer.

'You're probably right, but still, keep an eye on him.'

Emma glanced up at the sky, which had turned ominously dark; specks of rain dappled the rock.

'Looks like the weather forecast was right,' said Phil, holding his palms up to the rain.

'What did it say?' asked Emma, pulling up her collar.

'More heavy rain on the way,' he said, and at that precise moment the clouds opened, and rain came pelting down.

'We should go.'

The four of them hurried along the beach and back onto the path. Elsie led the way, tearing up the steep incline with Wilbur following slowly behind.

'Come on,' Emma encouraged, her heart heavy at the sight of him plodding at the rear, his coat already drenched, and his expression sorrowful.

'Has someone been out to fix your roof yet?' asked Phil, as they reached the little road that led back to the main street.

'Someone's meant to be coming tomorrow. For now, I've got buckets and tarps in place, so I'll just have to get up every few hours to empty them again.'

'I can come help if you like.'

'I can manage, but thanks for the offer,' said Emma, who didn't want to lead him on, even though she would have loved his help. More rain meant more damage, more damage meant being closed for longer, which meant more loss of income. And all because of Aidan.

'Let me know if you change your mind,' he said outside his shop.

Emma secured Wilbur's lead to the lamppost. 'I will. For now, I think I might grab a steak for Wilbur.'

'Woah!' said Phil, doing a goofy stagger of surprise. 'Emma Jenkins buying a steak for a dog?'

'Well, not just any dog . . .'

'Are you softening?'

'I might be,' said Emma, playing it cool even though her gentle eyes told a different story.

'Tell me you're not still thinking about rehoming him.'

'Can't.'

'Emma, come on,' he pleaded.

'I'm not still thinking, I've already made my decision.'

'And?'

'And . . .' Emma paused for dramatic effect. 'I've decided to keep him.'

'Oh my God! For real?' asked Phil, his hands on his head in disbelief.

'For real.'

'Jeez, I'm so happy,' he said, taking both of her hands in his, his eyes shining with delight.

'Good,' said Emma, amused by his emotional reaction.

'Hilda would have been chuffed too,' he said, his tone changing from one of excitement to tenderness.

'I know.'

Phil's eyes scanned Emma's, who felt a shift in the energy between them. 'You won't regret it.'

'I know that too,' she said, wondering if Phil was still talking about Wilbur.

'He's dependable and even-tempered,' he said, his eyes honing in on Emma's lips. 'He's a great guy.'

'Yes,' said Emma and, as she spoke, Phil leaned in and pressed his mouth against hers.

The softness of his weather-beaten lips caught Emma by surprise and she lingered for a moment before pulling sharply away.

'We shouldn't,' she said, shaking off the kiss and trying to focus her thoughts.

'But I thought—' Phil faltered. 'I got the impression that—'

'It's my fault,' said Emma hurriedly. 'I got in a muddle. The girls, they egged me on . . . but then last night I—' The memory of waking from the nightmare and wanting for Aidan was forefront in her mind.

Phil took a step back and shoved his hands into his pockets.

'I'm not making myself clear . . . you're a real catch, an amazing friend – kind, helpful, upbeat – you know, what's not to like—' she said, her body tensing.

'But?'

Emma thought for a moment, looking at his kind, beautiful face, knowing everyone would think her mad for turning him down, but then a moment of clarity washed over her, and all the tension dispersed from her body.

'But we're very different people. You love being out in the rain,' she said, looking up at it still pummelling down. 'I'd rather stay inside. You're adventurous, I'm a home-bird, and then there's—'

Emma stopped herself from continuing.

'Aidan?'

'No,' said Emma, knowing how preposterous it would sound to be hung up on a guy in a relationship. 'It's more the *idea* of someone . . .'

'Like Aidan?'

'I don't know,' said Emma, shaking her head, because if there was one thing she did know it was that she had no idea what she felt about Aidan.

'Well, I'm still here for you, if you need anything. Let me get you that steak,' he said, heading into the shop.

'Phil, you don't have to do that,' she said, lingering outside the entrance, not wanting to follow him in.

'Sure I do,' he said, heading behind the counter and then returning to Emma to give her the steak. 'It's what Hilda would have wanted.'

'Well, when you put it like that, thank you,' she said, wishing she found him as attractive as everyone else did.

'You're welcome.'

'See you soon,' she said, placing a platonic kiss lightly on his cheek.

As Emma turned to untie Wilbur, a van roared past the shop. It was past her before she could make out the writing, but the driver looked big and blonde, and for a split-second, Emma could have sworn it was Aidan.

*

By the time Emma and Wilbur got home, both bedraggled from the rain, the buckets were already full. Having towelled down Wilbur and settled him in the kitchen with his steak, she spent the next half hour schlepping containers up and down the stairs before finally managing to take a warm shower to wash away the bruises of the day.

'Caroline?' asked Emma, when she was out of the shower, her phone wet from her hair.

'Yes,' she answered.

'It's Emma Jenkins. Lobster Bay.'

'Emma, hi. How are you?'

'I'm okay, bit of a tough day, if I'm honest, but it's left me thinking: I'd like to keep Wilbur after all.'

'That's great, Emma. Are you completely sure? He's a big responsibility.'

Emma stared out of her bedroom window to the sea beyond. She remembered the first time she'd seen the view, before she'd discovered Wilbur in the laundry room, before she'd met Rhona, and Aidan and Phil, and the rest of the community to whom she'd grown so attached. The Emma from three months ago would have been incredulous at how much had happened in such a short space of time.

'He is a big responsibility, and his strength and my workload haven't changed, but I've a whole support network here who are willing to help. I know I can make it work.

'And besides, I may have underestimated him,' she went on, recalling how she had laughed at Hilda's idea of Wilbur ever being a loyal friend. When she first moved in, she could never have imagined that a dog could be so capable of such sensitivity and devotion. 'In hindsight I think it might be unkind to rehome him,' she said, feeling it would be cruel for him to have to endure the loss of Hilda and a new home. Compounded with Hilda's wishes, and the friend he'd become, it felt like the only thing to do.

'I'm glad you've come to that conclusion. I had a number of people lined up who would have provided for him, even loved him, but a dog of that age would never have fully settled.'

'I see that now.'

'You let me know if I can be of any further help, don't be afraid to ask.'

'Thanks, Caroline, but I think we're going to be okay.'

Putting on her pyjamas and slippers, Emma went down to the kitchen, where Wilbur greeted her with a slow sweep of his tail on the floor.

'How was your steak?' she asked, sitting down beside him.

He placed his head on his paws, stretched out in front of him, and released a troubled sigh.

Emma sidled a little closer and scrunched his velvety ears. 'Didn't hit the mark today, huh?

'What if I told you I called Caroline, you're definitely staying, would that make you feel any better?'

Wilbur's ears pricked a fraction, and he turned his head to place it on Emma's thigh.

'Go ahead,' she said, feeling the damp of his slobber seep through her pyjama trousers. 'They need washing anyway.'

The two of them sat for a while listening to the rain, the whirr of the fridge-freezer and Wilbur's slow, heavy breathing.

'I know you miss her,' said Emma, a knot of grief tangled in her stomach. 'I do too. But I can't bring her back.'

Wilbur's huge eyes looked up and Emma stared into them. 'The best I can do is promise to look after you the way she did. That's what Hilda would have wanted.'

Slowly, Wilbur got to his feet and repositioned himself so that he was sitting side by side with Emma, before placing his chin on her shoulder.

'Thanks, buddy,' she said, the words catching in her throat, tears forming in her eyes. She rested her head on his.

'Who needs a man when they've got a dog like you,' she said, wrapping her arm around him and drinking in his peaceful aura. Emma couldn't be certain but, in that moment, she thought she felt the dog relax, as if he too had come to find comfort in Emma, just as Emma had come to find comfort in him.

Chapter 22

'I'm going to find someone to fix that bloody roof today, if it's the last thing I do,' said Emma, who, after three nights of getting up every few hours to empty buckets, was at her wits' end.

Wilbur glanced up from where he lay at the bottom of the bed.

'I'm serious,' she said, roughly drying her hair and blasting it with the hairdryer, creating a look that was close to how Wilbur looked after he'd been swimming in the sea and shaken himself dry.

'It'll have to do,' she said, figuring she could wrap a scarf around it or wear a hat when she went out later in the day. For now, all Emma was doing was emptying buckets and making phone calls to roofers; she couldn't care less how her hair looked or how big the bags under her eyes were.

Emma was gathering up her laundry when the doorbell rang.

'Who can that be?' she said, before racing down the two flights of stairs, Wilbur hot on her heels, barking excitedly.

'Who is it, boy?' she asked, happy to see Wilbur looking so animated. It was the first time since Hilda's death that she'd heard him bark or move any faster than a snail's pace.

Unlocking the front door, she had to hold on to his collar to stop him from bolting outside.

'Is it the postman?' she said to him, laughing at the little whimpering noises he was making in his eagerness to get to whoever was behind the door.

'Not the postman,' came a voice which made Emma's heart stop dead for a second and her skin break out in goosebumps.

'Aidan,' she said, fully opening the door, and immediately regretting her hair decision, irritated that it mattered to her how she looked to him. Aidan's hair was shorter than usual, which accented his strong jaw, and somehow he managed to look perfectly groomed, despite standing in the rain.

Wilbur writhed and pulled to get at him. Emma let him go.

'Hiya, big guy,' said Aidan, allowing Wilbur to jump up, his paws almost to his shoulders, and rough-and-tumbling him. 'How are you?'

'He's happy to see you,' said Emma flatly, crossing her arms. For all she was furious with him, and he'd treated her badly, there was still a small part of her that wanted to throw herself at him the way Wilbur was doing.

'How are you?' he asked, once Wilbur had calmed down and was content circling his legs. His tone bordered on defensive.

'Fine,' said Emma, who had no idea why he was the one acting frostily. 'Is there something you want?'

Aidan shrugged. 'I just—'

'Because if there's nothing in particular, I need to get on. I've a roofer to find and if I don't find someone today, I swear, I'll put a match to the place.'

'Why do you need a roofer?'

Emma looked heavenwards. 'The work you did didn't hold out, and I haven't been able to get anyone else to repair it.'

'Couldn't you have asked Phil?'

His tone was so venomous that Emma felt like slamming the door on his face.

'Meaning?'

'Meaning, you guys looked pretty chummy the other day.'

Emma paused for a second, calculating how many days had passed since Phil had kissed her.

'You've been back for three days?' she asked, staring him hard in the eyes, a look that said *and this is the first time you've thought to stop by.*

'I've had some things to sort out,' said Aidan, looking at his boots.

'I'm sure you have,' she said pointedly, too humiliated to mention Eve, but certain that her tone implied she knew they were back together.

'Emma—'

'I'm not interested, Aidan,' she said, cutting him off, wishing it were true, knowing it would be easier if it were.

'I—'

'As far as I'm concerned the whole thing between us never happened,' she said, hating that things had come full circle and they were back to being quarrelsome neighbours. 'I gotta get on. Wilbur. In,' she commanded, and Wilbur obeyed.

'Looks like you've got everyone falling at your feet,' muttered Aidan, turning to leave.

'Asshole,' she muttered back, slamming the door, wishing the hollow feeling in her stomach would disappear.

The blank walls of the GP surgery did nothing to help Emma push Aidan out of her mind. Since he'd left a couple of hours ago, Emma had been a mess, unable to concentrate on the phone calls she needed to make, and going from furious one minute to confused the next. How was it possible that he'd come to her door and accused her of seeing someone else when he was the one who was back with his ex, hadn't been in touch, and had left a trail of destruction in his wake. And, more to the point, how was it possible that she wasn't out and out furious with him? She couldn't make any sense of the feeling of yearning that felt like a hole in the heart.

'Emma Jenkins?' called a female voice, bringing Emma out of her stupor.

Emma followed the small GP, her long curly hair flowing down the back of her loose burgundy blazer, down the corridor and into her room.

'Please, take a seat,' she said, indicating to the blue patient's chair next to her desk. 'I'm Dr Callaghan. How can I help today?'

Emma sat on the edge of the seat, her hands clasped tightly together and took a deep breath. 'I'm wondering if I'm suffering from PTSD.'

She heard herself say the words, felt them tumble off her tongue, but despite that she felt completely disconnected from them, as if they belonged to someone else.

Dr Callaghan shuffled back into her comfy chair and tilted her head to one side. 'Have you experienced a traumatic event recently?'

'At the end of last year,' said Emma, fighting back the images of Christmas Eve. She steadied herself with another deep breath, uncertain of how the doctor would react, uncertain of how she would react herself when she spoke of what she'd witnessed. 'The Christmas terrorist attack in London.'

'That must have been very hard,' said the doctor, her eyes soft with compassion.

'At times it's been overwhelming,' said Emma, relieved by the doctor's kindness.

'Have you had any nightmares or unwanted thoughts about the event?'

'Yes.'

'And do you try hard not to think about it?'

'Definitely.'

Dr Callaghan reached for her notepad on her desk. 'Are you easily startled?'

'Like you wouldn't believe,' said Emma. 'Slamming doors, cars backfiring, it doesn't take much.'

'And do you feel numb or detached from people, events or your surroundings?' asked the doctor, making notes as Emma spoke.

'Not so much now, but I definitely did. I moved away from London and quit my job so that I didn't have to revisit the scene on a daily basis.'

Dr Callaghan looked up from her note-making. 'And any issues surrounding blame?'

Tears pricked Emma's eyes and she felt her chest tighten.

'I suppose I feel guilty for not being able to do more,' said Emma slowly, looking at her knuckles, which were white with tension. 'I wish I'd been able to administer first aid that might have saved the woman who died next to me.'

It was only when the doctor offered her a box of tissues that Emma realised she was crying. Dr Callaghan gave her a moment to dry her eyes.

'Have you talked to anyone about what happened, and how you're feeling?'

Emma shook her head while blowing her nose. 'You're the first. I wanted to tell my mother but, well, she has some troubles of her own and last time we spoke we argued and—' Emma narrowed her lips and bit down hard, fighting off more tears.

'You've done the difficult part now,' said Dr Callaghan, reaching out a hand to Emma. 'It sounds to me as if you do have PTSD, and that a little support to work through it would help. Let me write you a referral letter to see a specialist counsellor and we'll take things from there.'

'Thank you,' said Emma, a wave of relief flowing through her body like the sea lapping the shore.

Outside the surgery, Emma untied Wilbur, who'd strolled faultlessly by her side all the way from home. Together they walked the short distance along the drying pavements to Seaview, where she arrived just in time to hear Wendy, in the garden gazebo, take to the microphone.

'Gather round, everyone,' she said, casting her arms wide and waving her hands encouragingly. 'It gives me great pleasure to welcome you to our annual summer fete.

'Some of you will know that much of today's event was arranged by our dear departed friend, Hilda Wyatt, and so we dedicate today to her. Hilda was a stalwart of this community for many years and she will be sadly missed.' Wendy picked up a glass and held it aloft. 'Please, join me in raising a glass. To Hilda.'

'To Hilda,' everyone chorused. Glen Miller's 'Chattanooga Choo Choo' began playing through the tannoy, and Wilbur barked along in excitement.

'Glenn Miller was her favourite, it filled the house when we were little,' said Judy, who'd appeared at Emma's shoulder as the festivities commenced. The garden was chock-a-block with brightly coloured beach hut stalls selling everything from raffle tickets to ice cream.

'Lively, like her,' said Emma, indicating with a flat palm for Wilbur to sit, and he did. 'It's lovely that the fete is being held to celebrate her.'

'She'd have preferred this to a stuffy old wake, that's for certain.'

Emma took out a tin from her bag and handed it to Judy. 'Some of Hilda's shortbread. I'm sorry I wasn't able to bake enough for the tea stall.'

'That's a lovely gesture, Emma. Thank you.'

'How was the funeral?'

'Peaceful. I had a sense that she's with Dad now, as they should be.'

'I'm glad,' said Emma, who liked that Judy had made the decision for the funeral to be held quickly and attended by close family members only. She had a feeling Hilda wouldn't have wanted a lot of stony-faced people listening to some dreary minister preach on about her life.

'I can't thank you enough for helping us patch up our differences. In the end she seemed to understand that she couldn't manage the house any more, and that I couldn't afford her care without selling it. If you hadn't been so instrumental, well—' Tears teetered at the edge of Judy's eyes.

Emma placed a hand gently on Judy's arm. 'I'm just thankful I had the chance to do something for you. After all Hilda did for me, it's the least I could have done. Without Hilda's persistence I wouldn't have Wilbur in my life, and—'

She was about to tell Judy about her PTSD diagnosis when Sheena, from the mini-mart, came over to join them.

'I owe you an apology,' said Sheena in her thick Scottish accent, after offering her condolences to Judy.

'Not at all,' said Emma, who knew Sheena was referring to the fact she'd told Hilda that Emma was planning on doing up the house and selling it on.

'Hilda was my best friend, I was only trying to protect her.'

'I understand,' said Emma, who held no ill will towards her.

'Can I do anything to make it up to you?'

Emma paused for a moment and thought. 'I don't suppose you know of any roofers?'

'I'll send my nephew round in the morning.'

'Thank you!' said Emma, more grateful than Sheena could know.

With Sheena keen to spend time alone with Judy, Emma and Wilbur set off around the stalls, which were full of local produce. She ran her fingers over beautiful, shiny tiles painted with puffins, lobster and crabs; she tasted tablet flavoured with whisky; admired oil-painted seascapes; and breathed in the warm aroma of freshly baked scones, which made Wilbur drool.

Emma was paying for some handmade cranachan soap when she heard her name being called. She turned to find Rhona striding towards her.

'How are the kids?' asked Emma, delighted to see her friend out of the house.

'Three are vomming!' said Rhona with an exhausted laugh. She reached down to fuss Wilbur. 'They've hit a rhythm of one barfing every hour. I've run out of bedding, towels and sanity.'

'Sounds hideous. The bedding and towels I can help you with. The sanity, I'm not so sure about.'

'Don't worry, Mum's helping – she's on puke supervision for an hour while I get out for some air that doesn't smell of sick.'

'She's incredible, your mum,' said Emma, thinking of her own mother and wishing she could be a better daughter. She'd lost track of how long it had been since they fought, but it felt like an eternity.

'You know she's given up her work so that I can work more?'

'You're kidding,' said Emma, her ears pricking like Wilbur's at the news. 'So you can consider working full-time at the house, once we're open again?'

'It's already considered. If you think you can afford it, I'd love to do more.'

'God, that's amazing,' said Emma, clutching Rhona's arm in excitement. Having Rhona on board full-time meant Emma could develop other facets of the business, and really make it the destination retreat she dreamed of.

'What's amazing?' asked Jennifer, joining them, a large twist of candyfloss in her hand.

Emma shared the news as they wandered together past some more stalls until they were stopped by the smell of the barbeque. A couple of tents along, Emma caught sight of Phil, flipping burgers on a hot plate. Wilbur sniffed the air excitedly.

'I didn't know Phil was going to be here,' said Emma, glad to discover that she felt no regret about her decision to let him down.

'Rumour has it that he kissed you,' sang Rhona, playfully.

'Why doesn't that surprise me?' said Emma, laughing.

'Is it true?' asked Jennifer, a little less animatedly than Rhona.

'He kissed me. I deflected it,' replied Emma, who thought she caught a glimpse of envy in Jennifer's eyes.

'So, you're not together?' asked Jennifer, clarifying the point.

'Jennifer, are you interested in Phil?' asked Rhona.

Jennifer's cheeks flushed pink, and Emma and Rhona shared a look of surprise.

'Why didn't you say before?' said Emma.

'I did!'

'I didn't think you were serious!'

Jennifer shrugged. 'Well, maybe I didn't either, until I heard he'd kissed you.'

Emma took Jennifer's hands in hers. 'Jennifer, I promise you, I'm not interested in Phil. If you want him, he's yours.' And with that, Jennifer wandered off towards him.

'I guess you still have your heart set on someone else, right?' said Rhona, casting a glance behind Emma. Looking over her shoulder, Emma caught sight of Aidan, strolling towards them with Eve. Wilbur barked and pulled towards them.

'That ship's sailed,' she said, restraining Wilbur.

'Are you sure?'

'Certain,' she said, giving Rhona's hand an affectionate squeeze before turning on her heels for home.

Chapter 23

The sun was warm on Emma's back as she and Wilbur walked quickly towards home along the coastal path, which was still muddy and slippy from the days of rain. The heat made her raincoat cling to her and for the first time since moving she found herself uncomfortably warm.

'Bloody thing,' she muttered, when her jacket zip jammed. She tried yanking it up and down as she walked, her determination to get as far away from Aidan as possible preventing her from stopping, but it was stuck fast. Desperate to cool down, she pulled an arm out from the sleeve and, as she pulled out the other, her foot caught on a rock and she tumbled forward. Unable to break her fall, Emma hit the ground with a thump, her knee taking the worst of the impact, then stumbled onto her side, her face taking the final hit.

'Shit,' she said, hauling herself into a sitting position and managing, finally, to pull her jacket over her head. Wilbur nudged her gently with his muzzle, trying to encourage her up.

'Thanks, bud,' she said, and she lay her jacket on the ground to use as a mat. She put her hands on it first and then her good knee so that she could push herself up into a standing position without putting weight on the injured knee. She was on her hands and knee, her mud-caked bum in the air, when she saw, through her legs, a figure rounding the bend on the path behind her.

'You have got to be kidding,' she said, instantly recognising the steel-capped boots.

'Wow, it's not often you see someone fall flat on their face,' said Aidan, after Emma had dragged herself up. Wilbur bounded up to greet him. With her back still towards Aidan she picked up her coat and tied it round her waist, hiding the worst of the dirt on her backside, then brushed the mud from her face, which was already drying in the afternoon heat.

'I could help you,' he said, as Emma attempted to walk away, pain searing through her knee.

'You did that before and look how that turned out,' she said, hopping away from him. She clicked her fingers, indicating to Wilbur that he should follow but instead he bounced back and forth between the two of them.

'You won't get very far on your own.'

'I'll call Rhona then,' she said and took out her mobile only to discover her battery had died. She shoved it back in her pocket.

'Emma, come on, let me help.'

Stopping where she stood, Emma swallowed her pride and hopped round to face him. 'Fine,' she said crossly.

'There's a bench round the next bend. I'll support you till we get to it.'

Grudgingly, Emma put her arm around Aidan's shoulder, and he took her weight as she hopped uncomfortably towards the seat, Wilbur leading the way. She hated having to lean on him, hated that he smelt great and felt strong and familiar, hated that he'd ruined what they'd had.

'Just let it rest for a while,' he said, lowering her onto the bench. Emma sat at one end and Aidan at the other. Wilbur plonked himself on the ground, right in the middle. 'You should keep it raised to prevent further inflammation.'

'There's nothing to raise it on.'

Aidan patted the arm of the bench. 'Stretch it over me and put your heel here,' he said, indicating to the wooden armrest.

Carefully, Emma managed to position her leg across Aidan, which felt uncomfortably intimate.

'Thank you,' she said resentfully, as she felt the pain ease.

'No problem,' he said, and they sank into silence.

'The sky is so dramatic today,' said Emma, when she could no longer stand the quiet.

'Two weather fronts colliding. Sun from the south, rain heading north.'

Emma drank in where dark grey met brilliant blue and where shafts of yellow streaked down to the sea. 'Hilda would have loved it.'

'How are you feeling about her death?' asked Aidan, meeting her gaze. She'd forgotten just how bright his eyes could be and, though she wanted to, she struggled to look away.

'I'm feeling grateful for having known her, even if it was for too short a time,' she replied, a little haughtily, wanting Aidan to feel bad for not having been a better neighbour to Hilda.

'And Wilbur?'

She looked at him lovingly, sitting protectively between them. 'It'll take him a while, but he'll get there.'

'I meant, how are you feeling about Wilbur?'

'Oh,' said Emma, laughing lightly at her mistake, despite herself. 'We're doing great. I've told him he can stay. He'll keep the memory of Hilda alive.'

'Sounds like you've been on a bit of a journey since I left.'

'You could say that,' said Emma, wanting desperately to share her diagnosis with Aidan but fighting the urge. If he hadn't left she would have told him in a heartbeat, but now it made no sense; after how he'd treated her he didn't deserve to know.

Another heavy silence fell between them. Wilbur lay down.

'Why didn't you call?' asked Emma, irritated that Aidan couldn't man up and confess to being back with Eve.

'I did,' he said, looking directly at her.

'Aidan, don't lie, we're past that,' said Emma bitterly.

'Emma, I left endless messages on your landline, explaining that I'd forgotten my mobile and you could reach me at my hotel.'

'I didn't get them,' she said.

'Well, I left them, they're there for you to hear.'

Now that Emma thought about it, she realised the landline hadn't rung since the storm had flooded the top-floor bedroom. 'The rain must have damaged the old phone socket upstairs. Why didn't you use my mobile?'

'I don't know your number. I tried to find you on Facebook; when that failed I googled the number of the guesthouse and called, plus I emailed several times.'

'You must have thought I was ignoring you,' said Emma, aware that his email could be in her bulging junk folder, something she hadn't looked at since she moved in.

'It did cross my mind,' he said, laughing sardonically. 'Then when I saw you kissing Phil, I figured it was game over.'

'But the game was already over,' said Emma, confused by why Aidan would care about the kiss when he was back with Eve.

Aidan shot her a perplexed look.

'You and Eve,' she said, stating the obvious.

'Oh. My. God,' said Aidan slowly, a lightness dawning in his eyes.

'What?'

'Do you think what I think you're thinking?' he said, a smile slowly breaking on his lips.

'I have no idea what you think I'm thinking,' said Emma.

'That Eve is my girlfriend?'

'Well, of course,' said Emma, irritated that she had no idea what Aidan found so amusing. 'You live with the woman. And she's back. I let you allow me to believe that you'd split for good and then suddenly she's back in your life.'

'Emma, Eve is my sister.'

'What?' said Emma, her jaw dropping.

'She's my little sister.'

'I thought she lived in the city?' she said, recalling what Rhona had told her that day in the loft. Emma sat dumbfounded, shaking her head, her brow crinkled in

323

confusion, then tingles of excitement began to pepper her skin.

'She did, until my parents died, then we both moved back.'

'But all the fights—'

'We can't agree on what to do with the house. Mum and Dad left it to us, but it's still got a huge mortgage and it needs loads of work. Eve wants to sell it, I want to keep it – I've too many memories tied up in the place. We always fought a lot, despite being close, but this we fight about *all* the time.'

'Hence why you needed the work so badly down south, to pay for the upkeep.'

'And why I offered to do the work on your roof myself. We'd fallen behind on the insurance payments, and until I caught up on them I knew we couldn't put in a claim. I promise, the work was done in good faith, I never had any intention of leaving you in the lurch.'

Emma felt the tension in her chest and shoulders ease. 'Is that what you had to take care of when you got back, the insurance?'

'That and a whole lot of other payments.'

'Did Hilda know you were finding it a struggle?'

Aidan shook his head. 'She wasn't exactly the kind of woman I or Eve found it easy to confide in,' he said, with a laugh.

'Right,' said Emma, laughing too, remembering how hostile Hilda had been towards her before she'd realised her intentions were sincere. 'Is the house the reason Eve took off for a bit?'

'We needed some space. When she found out I was working away, she came back.'

'Which I misinterpreted as you making up with your girlfriend,' said Emma, her cheeks reddening.

'Which explains why you made no effort to call me. Hole in the roof. Me not calling. Back with my ex. God, Emma, you must have thought me a total bastard.'

'The thought did occur to me,' she said, an eyebrow raised, her eyes smiling.

'No wonder you wound up with Phil.'

'Aidan,' said Emma frustratedly. '*Nothing* happened with me and Phil. He helped me out with Wilbur a couple of times, that's all. He got the wrong end of the stick, I promise, you've nothing to worry about.'

Aidan rubbed Emma's ankle. 'Anything else we need to clear up?'

'There is one thing,' said Emma, and butterflies the size of pigeons rose up in her stomach. 'Something I didn't tell you before.'

'Uh-oh,' said Aidan. He stopped massaging her ankle.

'It's nothing personal. I haven't told anyone, well, one person, the GP—'

'Emma?'

'Last Christmas Eve,' she began slowly, taking the GP's advice to talk about it, and going through the events one step at a time.

'I knew there was something,' said Aidan, holding tightly to Emma's hand. 'You should have told me, I could have helped. I had to work through plenty shit of my own after my parents died. I still struggle with the image of their bloated, battered bodies. I went to the mortuary alone; nobody else knows what I saw. People wonder why I'm distant – if they knew the torment of identifying your dead parents, never knowing what actually happened, they might cut me some slack.'

'I'm so sorry,' said Emma, glad that Aidan had shared, feeling both drained and elated that he understood. 'No more secrets?'

'Let me come closer,' said Aidan, and he carefully sidled along the bench towards her.

'Hopefully talking about it is the start of recovering,' she said, as Aidan wrapped his arm around her and she nestled her head into his shoulder, able at last to fully relax. 'I don't want to forget what happened,' continued Emma, who couldn't bear the idea of losing the defining memory of Dawn. 'But I do want to forget the horror, and try to remember the humanity instead.'

'Love will always win,' he said, nuzzling her hair as the two of them sat in comfortable silence watching a rainbow arch over the sea.

Chapter 24

Emma and Aidan sat on the bench, lost in each other's arms until the sun began to lower and the rainbow faded from view.

'Let's get you home,' he said, helping her up and taking her weight once more.

It was dusk by the time they reached the house and Emma was cold and sore. Wilbur disappeared through the back for water and his bed.

'I don't know how I'm going to get up those stairs,' she said, which seemed to rise in front of her like Mount Everest.

'Don't you worry 'bout a thing,' said Aidan, leading her through to the sitting room and positioning her gently on the couch before raising her leg with some cushions. 'I'll be right back.' He handed her the remote for the telly and placed a throw over her shivering body before disappearing out to the kitchen.

As Emma flicked through the channels she chuckled to herself, listening to Aidan talking nonsense to Wilbur and clattering his bowl in the back passage as he prepared Wilbur's supper. He returned a few minutes later with a tray loaded with tea, biscuits, crisps, and a tumbler of whisky.

'For medicinal use,' he said, his eyes sparkling like crystal, handing the glass to Emma then tucking her blanket tightly round her to stave off any more chills.

'Where are you going now?' she asked as he left the living room again.

'You'll see,' he called, his feet pounding up the stairs.

Emma relaxed into the sofa cushions, sipped her whisky and let out a contented sigh, laughing at herself for having spent the last few weeks thinking the worst of Aidan.

'What are you doing up there?' she called, listening to him beavering about upstairs, unable to figure out what the bumping sounds were that she could hear through the ceiling.

'Patience,' he called back.

A couple of minutes passed before Aidan returned again, this time dragging a king-size mattress, with pillows tucked under his arms and a duvet thrown over his shoulder.

'We can set up camp in here until your knee is better,' he said, parking the mattress and bedding before moving the other sofa out of the way.

'You don't have to do this,' said Emma, thrilled to bits by the gesture.

'No, but I want to.'

She watched as he made the bed then he ran up to the top floor to fetch her bedclothes, toiletries and towels.

'All we need now is some supper,' he said, just as the doorbell rang, which he went to answer immediately.

'Tah-dah!' he sang, returning with a white carrier bag of takeaway.

'Curry?' asked Emma, salivating at the prospect.

'The full works.'

If anyone had told Emma this morning, after she'd slammed the door on Aidan, that this evening she'd be cosied up and camping out with him in her living room, she'd have laughed. She pinched herself in delight as he came back with supper plated up on lap-trays and two glasses of beer.

'If it weren't for the burning pain in my knee I'd think I was imagining all of this,' she said as Aidan sat down beside her; she stared dreamily into his eyes.

'I've imagined nothing but you since I left,' he whispered, gazing tenderly at her, and he leaned in to kiss her.

When his lips touched hers all the pain in Emma's leg seemed to dissipate, and was replaced by a rising desire that tingled all over her body.

'Careful!' she said as their curry and beer slipped about on their trays.

'Suddenly I'm not hungry for food,' said Aidan, placing both his tray and Emma's on the floor before lifting her gently from the sofa and lying her softly on the bed.

'Wow,' said Emma, almost an hour later, after Aidan had re-explored every inch of her body. 'Good stamina!'

'Your knee isn't too sore?'

'I'll probably pay for it in the morning, but for now, it was worth it,' she said with a satisfied grin.

From the back of the house they heard Wilbur bark.

'Poor guy,' said Aidan, getting up from the mattress and wrapping a towel round his waist.

'Let him through,' said Emma, sitting up, her back leaning against the couch.

'Are you sure?' asked Aidan incredulously.

'Wilbur and I have come a long way since you left,' said Emma. 'Sometimes he even sleeps in my room.'

'You're kidding?'

'Nuh-uh,' she said. 'You're not the only guy around here allowed in my bedroom.'

'I'm going to have words with that dog,' he laughed, heading through to the back to get him.

'Aidan, you need to pick up the curry before you—' began Emma, but it was too late. Before she could finish her sentence, Wilbur had barrelled into the living room and headed straight for the food.

'Crap,' said Aidan, coming through to find Wilbur devouring two plates of curry and a glass of beer.

Emma laughed heartily. 'Bagsy you pick up his poo in the morning!'

New Year's Eve

Emma felt her heart rate increase as the bus approached Piccadilly Circus a week later. From where she was sitting, near the front of the upper deck, she could see shop windows boarded up, a scorch mark on the road, and pieces of police tape, flapping in the wind.

She stared straight ahead, in stark contrast to the other passengers, who sat forward, pointing and craning their necks as they passed the scene.

Her head began to swim and for a moment she thought she might faint.

Instinctively she reached for the bell, steadied herself as she negotiated the steps then threw herself out of the open doors, gasping for air.

'You awright, love?' asked a passer-by, stepping out of Emma's path.

Emma held out a hand that told them, yes, thank you, though she couldn't find the accompanying words. She was aware of them watching her as she hurried north, avoiding looking across the road to where she was thrown on Christmas Eve.

Further up the street she stumbled into a coffee shop and sat down, immediately pulling out her phone and typing an email to her boss.

Dear Katherine,

For reasons I am unable to explain, I write to notify you of my resignation with immediate effect.

I am extremely grateful for all you have done for me over the last 10 years but unfortunately my current circumstances do not enable me to continue.

Sincerely,
Emma

Emma was about to hit send but, not wanting to act in haste, she instead took a moment to compose herself. She clicked on a link entitled 20 PLACES TO VISIT IN THE UK IN 2021 and scrolled through the usual suspects: The Slaughters, Cotswolds; St Ives, Cornwall; Keswick, Lake District, but then she happened upon a place she hadn't heard of before – Lobster Bay, Scotland, and, without thinking, she googled it.

Looks pretty, she thought, *admiring the snug little harbour and the pantile cottages. She did a quick Rightmove search and was amazed to discover that property prices were low.*

'This can't be right,' she said, clicking on an imposing, seven-bedroom semi-detached house that was on the market for about the price of a two-bedroom flat in Tooting.

An idea sparked in Emma's memory that she'd long forgotten, one she'd had since she was a little girl: to own a boutique guesthouse.

Is now the time? she wondered, *surprised by the feeling of spontaneity that engulfed her.*

Over the last few days, sitting around at her mum's, Emma had thought a lot about how lucky she'd been, not only to have come out of Christmas Eve unscathed but also to have had this wake-up call. If she'd not decided to walk, and had got on her usual bus home, she wouldn't have had her eyes opened. It felt impossible to keep plodding on as normal, if for no other reason than to honour those who no longer had the choice to live the life they wanted most.

And then, as she was scanning through the photographs of the house, and the stunning sea views, a message arrived from her sister:

Happy New Year, Sis. Happy New You!

Suddenly, as if the stars aligned, Emma knew she had to start afresh, go somewhere where nobody knew her, where nobody would ask her questions. And before she had time to think, she reopened the email to her boss and hit send.

Chapter 25

'You did it, girl,' said Rhona, handing Emma a bottle of beer.

'*We* did it,' said Emma, chinking her bottle against Rhona's.

Rhona sat down on the sand and gazed into the fire that flickered against the dusky sky. 'When do the first guests arrive tomorrow?'

'Some time after four,' said Emma, reflecting on the last couple of weeks and all they'd achieved since Rhona started working full-time, and Aidan had come home. The return of guests to the house felt a bit surreal to Emma, but all of the rooms were ready, and the roof and ceiling were finished, even the kitchen had had a makeover.

'Aidan's done a great job on the roof.'

Emma glanced over to where he was standing, manning the barbeque with Wilbur by his side. Since Aidan's return, Wilbur had stopped peeing on the floor, forcing

Emma to accept that Hilda had been right when she'd told Emma that he was trying to tell her something, namely that he missed Aidan.

'He pulled it off in the end,' she said, catching his gaze and holding it. He raised his bottle of beer to her and smiled endearingly.

'I'd like a man who'd spend two weeks repairing my house,' said Rhona.

'You've got Finn.'

'Sure,' said Rhona distantly, staring into the flames.

'Everything okay with you guys?'

Rhona hugged her knees. 'I'd quite like someone to actually touch, you know? Phones are all well and good, but nothing quite beats a hand on the small of your back or the brush of a cheek.'

'You'll see him before long,' said Emma, leaning in and giving her a supportive nudge.

'I hope so,' she said, catching sight of a couple, holding hands, winding their way on to the beach with a small dog. 'Is that Jennifer and Phil?'

'Yup,' said Emma, watching Elsie bolt straight towards Wilbur.

'Does Aidan know Phil's coming?'

'Yes – I've warned him to be on his best behaviour.' Emma stood up, her knee fully recovered, and wiped the sand from her bum.

'You look so cute together,' said Rhona, cupping her hands in delight at her cousin and her new boyfriend as they joined her at the bonfire.

'You really do,' said Emma, greeting them both with a kiss on the cheek.

'We're just glad you turned Phil down,' said Jennifer, and Emma blushed in good humour, sharing a knowing smile with Phil. Jennifer nodded in Aidan's direction and told Phil, 'You should go make your peace.'

'I'm on it,' he said, kicking off his Vans and strolling across the sand.

'This could be a real car crash,' said Emma, watching Phil head towards Aidan.

Her phone rang just as she was about to sit down with the girls round the fire; she went to answer it a short distance away.

'Who was that?' asked Rhona, when she returned.

'Just a supplier,' said Emma, shaking off the call. She gestured towards the guys. 'How are they doing?'

'Not bad,' said Jennifer. 'They appear to be bonding over burger chat.'

'Whatever does it for them,' said Emma, glancing furtively towards the entrance to the beach.

'What's up with you?' asked Rhona.

'Nothing,' replied Emma, trying to sound nonchalant.

'You're acting very cagey.'

Just then the figure Emma had been waiting for strolled in to view.

'Who is that?' asked Jennifer, watching the person walk towards them, a case of beer under his arm.

Rhona stared into the fading light. 'It's not—' she said.

'What?' asked Emma, playing it coy.

'It can't be—' said Rhona, excitement rising in her voice.

'Can't it?'

'Oh my God!' shrieked Rhona when she could finally make out the details of his face. 'Finn!' she yelled and sprinted towards him, throwing her full weight at him.

'Rhona!' he said, dropping the beer and taking Rhona's full force, turning it into a full-on twirling hug.

'Did you set this up?' Jennifer asked Emma, beaming as Rhona showered Finn with kisses.

Emma didn't reply, but her smile said it all.

The evening passed too quickly, the six of them cosied round the fire, sharing stories, beer and burgers. As Emma gazed through the flames towards Aidan, his face lit up with laughter and she found it hard to believe that only four months ago she'd parked her car in the harbour and watched him through her camera lens as he worked on one of the boats. And now, here they were, the two of them together, surrounded by friends, with Emma about to relaunch the business of her dreams.

'To friendship,' said Emma, raising her bottle, and everyone else did the same.

'And family,' said Aidan.

Emma puzzled over what he meant and why nobody else seemed confused by his toast.

'To family,' said a voice from behind.

The voice was instantly recognisable but, out of context, it took Emma a moment to place it. Turning to face where everyone else was looking, Emma's mouth dropped open.

'Mum!' she said, stunned to see her standing in front of her, as if two worlds had just collided.

'Emma,' she said, holding her arms open.

'I don't understand,' faltered Emma, getting to her feet and hugging her mum.

'You're not the only one who can do surprises,' said Rhona, and she pointed to herself and Aidan.

'You *both* kept this from me?' she asked, dumbstruck.

'I asked them to,' said Liz, and she held out her hand to Emma.

Together they strolled down to the water's edge and followed the lapping tide along the sand.

'How are you?' asked Liz.

'I'm good, Mum,' she said, still reeling from the shock.

'You look happy.'

Emma reflected on the statement before saying with certainty, 'I feel happy.'

341

'And Aidan seems very nice.'

'He is,' she said, glancing back to where he sat, relaxing by the fire. The early moonlight and firelight combined to make him appear even more handsome than usual. 'I know you like Chris, but Chris and I never had what Aidan and I have.'

'Which is?'

Emma felt her body fill with energy and desire at the sight of Aidan, who had no idea he was being watched. The difference between how he looked at the harbour that first day, so angry and tense, and now, a picture of relaxation, was extraordinary.

'He gives me a sense of home, of peace,' she said, liking how it felt to acknowledge that feeling.

Liz nodded contemplatively. 'I can see that.'

'I know you think I was running from Chris,' said Emma, casting her gaze out to sea. 'But I wasn't. In truth, I was running from something else entirely.' Emma took a deep breath and started the story of Christmas Eve from the beginning. 'It was the catalyst I needed to give up Chris and the flat, and work, too.'

Her mother stopped walking and turned to her. 'Why didn't you tell me before?'

'I didn't know how,' she said, scanning her mother's eyes for any hint of what she was feeling. 'I didn't see the sense in telling you something you couldn't possibly understand. I was terrified that if I told you that you'd fall back into a depression; I wanted to protect you from that.'

Liz paused. 'I understand that, love, I do. But, you know, it's my job to protect you, not for you to protect me,' she said, and continued walking.

'Mum, I'm 31, you don't need to protect me,' said Emma, quickening her pace to catch up.

'It's instinct. I do it all the time, for you and your sister.'

'You do? How?' asked Emma.

'Like with Gary. I never tell you how much I love him, how much I enjoy caring for him, even if his ailments are a mystery.' She gave Emma a look that told her she was fully aware of how Emma felt about Gary's health.

'I can't pretend to get it.'

'Your father's death was so sudden, it left me helpless,' Liz explained. 'With Gary I'm able to do something. I like that feeling.'

'That I understand,' said Emma, knowing how much it hurt not to be able to help a total stranger, let alone someone you loved. 'But why wouldn't you have told me that before?'

'Because I thought it might upset you, or diminish the memory of Dad for you.'

'Mum, nothing could ever diminish Dad's memory,' said Emma. 'And particularly not you loving someone else.'

Liz reached out for Emma's hand. 'Thanks, love. I appreciate that, not that it will stop me trying to keep you from harm.'

A stillness fell between them, and peace washed over Emma. Her thoughts turned to Hilda.

'Hilda told me sharing would make me stronger,' said Emma, breaking the silence.

'I think Hilda was right,' said Liz, linking her arm through her daughter's, both of them gazing up to the brightest star in the sky.

Chapter 26

'I'd only viewed the house online when I bought it,' said Emma to Kate, an old school friend of Jennifer's, and freelance travel journalist.

'That was brave,' said Kate, running a hand over the fine blue-and-white-striped linen bed throw that hung with just the right amount of drape. Emma had been worried about her choice of bedding in the newly decorated top-floor guest rooms; there was a fine line between casually understated and boring, but looking around the room now with its fresh white tongue and groove panelling, Emma was confident she'd pulled it off. It was hard to imagine the old carpet, fallen ceiling and battered old furniture that once filled the room.

'Or foolish,' she said, as Kate felt the weight of the natural linen curtains and cast her eye over the street and rooftops beyond.

Kate wandered through to the second room, where Emma had used stripped pine furniture, a whitewashed floor, and blue and grey fabrics to reflect the sky. 'What made you want to open a guesthouse?'

'It's been a dream of mine since I was a little girl,' said Emma, repositioning the wicker tea tray on the chest of drawers.

'But why now?'

'I'd worked for over a decade as an interior designer, so I was considering what my next step might be, but then . . .' Emma paused, wondering if she was ready to open up to a stranger about what had happened, then decided to give it a go. 'I witnessed something life-changing, and that gave me the push I needed.'

'May I ask what that was?'

'The bombing in London, last Christmas Eve,' she said, feeling her palms dampen a little but not experiencing any other symptoms, even her heart rate remained steady. She couldn't remember a time when her anxiety levels had felt so low, even before the bombing, and she was grateful for the counselling sessions she'd had so far. 'It gave me the courage to make changes I previously hadn't thought possible.'

'You gave up your career, your home?'

'And my relationship! I gave it all up.'

'For a house and business you hadn't seen in person?'

'I realise it sounds crazy, but it felt right, almost as if there was no other choice. I had the opportunity to do something with my life. Many people from that day weren't so lucky.'

Kate scribbled some thoughts in her notepad before Emma led her downstairs

'Has it thrown up any unexpected problems?'

'Does a fire in the roof count?'

'You're not serious?' asked Kate, passing on the second staircase the pictures of the previous owners of the guesthouse, which Jennifer had found in the museum vaults.

'On the opening night,' said Emma, who could now laugh at the memory. 'The little pub along the street had to take in my guests.'

'An actual baptism of fire!'

'Exactly,' said Emma, showing Kate the guest rooms on the first floor, delighting in the cohesion she'd created across the floors while maintaining individuality in all the rooms.

'What inspired the design palette?'

'I tried to use colours from the local landscape – blues and greys on the top floor to reflect the sky, pine green with accents of gorse yellow and rose-hip pink in the middle, and a more neutral sand and stone palette downstairs. And I've also tried to use natural and locally sourced furniture and materials throughout.'

'You've really encapsulated the beauty of the area,' said Kate, scribbling furiously.

'Thank you,' said Emma, adjusting a lino print of a puffin that she'd picked up at the village gallery.

'Let me show you the dining room and guest lounge,' she said, and together the two of them headed downstairs to where everyone was gathering for the official relaunch party.

'This is our dining room,' said Emma, delighted to see that while she'd been upstairs, Rhona and Aidan had been busy filling the tables with enough food for an army. Plates were laden with chunky sausage rolls from Phil's, cake stands were layered with smoked salmon sandwiches, heavenly scones, Dundee cake and Black Bun, and small bowls were scattered full of tablet and macaroons and boiled sweets in every colour of the rainbow.

'What a feast,' said Kate, her eyes poring over the banquet. 'How do you find time to do all of this?'

'I have a lot of help. A housekeeper, a handyman, local suppliers – there's a whole team behind me.'

'Heart and community on a plate.'

'Thanks, Kate,' said Emma, thrilled with Kate's appraisal.

'And it feels very warm and inviting; I can really see a national newspaper wanting to run a feature on it, particularly given your backstory – the bad giving way to the good,' said Kate. Emma was tickled pink.

Together they went through to the living room where everyone was beginning to congregate.

'Jennifer!' said Kate, spotting her friend and greeting her with a kiss.

'Jennifer, can I leave you to tell Kate a little about the history of the place?' said Emma, who had noticed the arrival of Doreen, remembering her from the day she'd almost hit her with the car.

'Hi,' said Emma to Doreen. 'I'm so glad you've come. I've been meaning to stop into the office and thank you. If it weren't for you giving me a push I might never have bought the place; you can't know how having this house has transformed my life.'

A look of relief washed over Doreen's face. 'I'm glad to hear that, dear. Because the truth is, I have a confession. I'm afraid I told a slight fib—'

'Let me guess,' said Emma, her eyes sparkling animatedly. 'There was no closing date?'

'How did you know?'

'Just a hunch.'

'I had a feeling that day when you called that the house belonged to you. A premonition, an instinct, I don't know what; before I knew it, I'd told you a little white lie.'

'I couldn't be more pleased that you did,' said Emma. 'Have you had a chance to look around?'

Doreen nodded. 'The old place is unrecognisable. I don't know how you did it in such a short space of time. It's a miracle.'

'I enjoyed it,' said Emma, remembering all the backache and heartache, and the laughter.

'You might also enjoy knowing how much it's now worth,' said Doreen, her eyes shining excitedly.

'You know what, Doreen, I think I'd prefer not to know. The true value is it being home, and a place full of friends.'

'Are you sure?' Doreen pressed, itching to tell Emma the good news.

'Hilda would turn in her grave if she caught so much as a whiff that I was interested in the money.'

'Oh well, if you're sure, but if you change your mind—'

'I know where you are,' sang Emma, relieved that Sheena had arrived and wanted a word with Doreen.

'Looks as if we've added value to the house,' said Emma to Aidan, in the kitchen, where he was preparing vegetable crudities at the new island. She brushed her hand across his back as she went to the fridge to take fresh local raspberry cordial to her guests.

'Not that it matters,' he said, throwing a carrot stick to Wilbur where he lay on the floor, sporting a natty green bow tie.

'That's what I said,' she replied, stopping to steal a kiss. Since his return, Aidan had barely been home, helping

Emma prepare the house for the relaunch. The two of them had spent nearly every night together.

'You know, I've been thinking,' said Emma, when in truth she hadn't really been thinking at all, but a feeling washed over her with such intensity that she couldn't ignore it. 'How would you feel about moving in, running this place with me?'

Aidan stopped chopping. Emma fiddled with her thumbnail, hoping she hadn't overstepped the mark. The silence seemed to go on forever.

'That could work,' said Aidan, returning to his chopping as if he'd just agreed to Chinese for dinner rather than committing to a relationship, home and business in one.

Emma stared at him, waiting for him to say something more. He continued chopping for what felt to Emma like an hour before his lips began to twitch into an uncontrollable smile and his eyes danced with joy.

'Aidan!' she said, whipping him with a tea towel as he moved towards her, putting an arm round her waist and pulling her close.

'I've been hoping you'd ask,' he said, drawing her even closer. 'I can think of nothing I want more.'

They were just about to kiss when Rhona came dashing into the kitchen.

'Guys, it's almost time, should I gather everyone outside?'

'Sure,' said Emma, feeling a flutter of excitement in her tummy.

'Time for what?' asked Aidan.

'To cut the ribbon,' she said, taking his hand and pulling him through to the front of the house where everyone had gathered outside, and Rhona had tied a huge green ribbon in a bow around the front door.

'Speech,' called Finn, his arm wrapped around Rhona's waist.

Emma put her arm around Aidan and looked out to the gaggle of friends and family who had joined her, and Wilbur pushed his way in between them. Front and centre was her mum, all dewy-eyed with pride, Phil and Jennifer stood next to Rhona and Finn, and then there was Kate, Judy, Wendy, Doreen and Sheena, and Ian and Anne from the pub.

'I don't know what to say,' said Emma, overwhelmed by the turnout. 'I couldn't have imagined when I arrived that four months later I'd be surrounded by such love and support. Without you guys there's no way I would have the home and business of my dreams.'

Aidan cleared his throat.

'Not forgetting the man of my dreams too,' she said, and everybody laughed. 'Lobster Bay is everything I hoped for, and more. Thank you!'

'Cut the ribbon,' called Rhona, handing Emma a pair of scissors.

'I declare this guesthouse open!' said Emma, cutting the ribbon in two and stepping over the threshold with Aidan, Wilbur barking animatedly at their side.

'What an incredible few months it's been,' said Emma, squeezing Aidan's hand.

'And only the beginning,' he said, pulling her close.

Wilbur jumped up and barked demanding their attention, and the three of them, Emma, Aidan and Wilbur, embraced, ready to embark on their new life together at The Guesthouse at Lobster Bay.

Acknowledgements

The Guesthouse at Lobster Bay began as a grain of sand in early 2020. To turn it into the shiny pearl that it is today took a massive effort from many people during the stormiest of years. At the helm, as always, was my incredible agent, Juliet Pickering, who secured a three-book deal for me in a year that I thought I might not work at all. Steering the way at Welbeck was the imperturbable Jon Elek, whose enthusiasm and straightforward approach guided me through. And the rest of the crew, Madeleine, Rosa, Annabel and Maddie, to name but a few, who all did their part brilliantly to bring the book home.

In Scotland, a big thank you to: Peter, who juggled reshaping a business during the pandemic with Dada duties so that I could write; the Culpins, who gallantly played for hours downstairs while I typed feverishly upstairs; to my parents, who were on hand just as soon as they were able; the real-life Rhona, who bid at auction to have a character named after her in one of my books, and to all the wonderful people in the real Lobster Bay, who help and inspire me every day.

And lastly to Margo and Jerry (my very own slobbering lump of a dog) who kept me company through hours of writing when really, they'd have preferred to be on the beach.

About the Author

Annie trained in London as a classical musician, then worked as an assistant for an Oscar winner, an acclaimed artist, a PR mogul and a Beatle. After several years of running errands for the rich and famous, she went to medical school where, hiding novels in anatomy textbooks, she discovered her true passion for writing. She went on to complete a Creative Writing MA with distinction.

Annie now lives back home in Scotland, by the sea. When not writing, she enjoys swimming with her son, visiting antiques markets with her husband, eating cake with friends, playing the piano, and walking her basset hounds.

Out October 2021

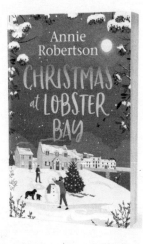

When Emma and Aidan decide to expand *The Guesthouse at Lobster Bay* by merging their two homes, Emma feels certain it's the project she needs to develop her flourishing retreat, and to keep her and Aidan together.

Emma has three months to complete the project before her guests arrive for a sumptuous Christmas in Lobster Bay, but as soon as the work begins, Emma's dream of expansion begins to fall apart . . .

Unforeseen structural problems, the arrival of a long-term guest, plus an errant puppy, determined to chew her way through every piece of pipe and furniture, push Emma and Aidan to their limit, and it's not long before cracks begin to show in their relationship.

Determined not to give up, Emma pushes on. But as the project progresses tensions continue to rise, and when a winter storm blows in, work grinds to a halt, pushing Emma and Aidan to the brink.

As Emma battles to keep her dream alive, will it be at the expense of her relationship? And will she eventually, with the help of some of her friends, pull off her dream of *Christmas at Lobster Bay*?